CURING EMILY

A Novel

Jeremy Hodgson

ISBN: 978-0-6397-1243-7
e-ISBN: 978-0-6397-1244-4

Jeremy William Hodgson
Villa 99, Tamarina Golf Estate
Black River, Mauritius
90922
jwhodgson42@gmail.com

Editing and book production by Liquid Type Publishing Services
Proofreading by Salome Posthumus
Cover design by mr design

For my wife, Michele

1

Monday—February 2023

"That bloody bird!" Dave Tennant mumbled as he struggled out of bed. He stumbled over his shoes before reaching his bedroom window. He yanked back the curtain viciously, and the robin on the windowsill took flight before Dave slammed the window closed. He hardly noticed the sky as he turned back to bed, already regretting he had frightened his friendly robin.

He was about to lie down again when a thought surfaced. He fed the bird some crumbs every morning. "*Is it that late?*"

For close to an hour, he stopped thinking. Functioning on automatic, he followed his morning routine: coffee, shave, shower, dress, muesli. More coffee. Wash the cup and bowl, lock the flat, and walk to the Underground.

After five steps on the pavement, he stopped. "*Shit, I've forgotten my umbrella.*"

The rain would soak him before he got to the station. Every step back to his apartment, up and down the stairs, was an effort that deepened his foul mood.

The weather didn't help. It was below three degrees centigrade, with a miserable rain carried by the wind swirling between buildings. Dave turned the collar of his coat up, holding it closed with one gloved hand, the umbrella in the other, and hunched his shoulders to stop the wind forcing its way down his neck.

On the escalator down to the platform, he didn't notice the people riding the up-escalator. Still, a small part of his mind registered every one of them—survival during his teenage years had developed this basic animal instinct.

He boarded the next district-line train without hearing the voice that said, "Please mind the step."

His mind slowly came alive. "*Oh shit, I forgot to take the sheets off the bed and drop off the laundry.*"

The train started with a jerk that his laundry-occupied mind had not anticipated.

He staggered, his movement cushioned by a stout woman with greying hair and a shopping bag.

Invariably polite, almost to extremes, he apologised. "Sorry, ma'am."

"That's ok, young man, not your fault."

He thought she was "nice", like all the women who called him "young man" were nice. It triggered a stray thought from his waking mind: *sometimes too nice.*

At sixteen, Dave had carried a woman's shopping bags to her home, hoping for a tip. She had asked him to take them up the stairs and then offered him a cup of tea. He had understood what bonus she proposed to give him when she came out of the bathroom wearing a diaphanous gown that revealed her pendulous breasts. So he left in a hurry.

He had seven minutes to his stop. Just enough to examine why he felt so depressed this morning.

Was Uncle Paul the cause? He had been an unexpected addition to Dave's Sunday routine: clean and tidy the flat, a salad lunch, a bus to the hospital to visit his mother. Uncle Paul, his mother's brother, whom he hadn't seen for more than a year, was already beside his mother's bed.

Dave remembered to get off at the third stop, and he reviewed his yesterday as he walked miserably to the lab.

Dave's mother, an advanced cancer case, had been in the hospital for over three months; according to her oncologist, she would never leave except in a hearse.

Every visit Dave made to his mother was depressing enough. Instead of his regular, exhausting run in Ravenscourt Park to relieve the stress after the hospital visit, yesterday he had gone to a pub with Uncle Paul to explain his mother's prognosis without her hearing.

Uncle Paul, a usually cheery smallholder farmer from Derbyshire, had come to London for an agricultural show and extended his stay to see his sister. His sadness was catching as Dave explained her illness.

"Uncle, her cancer is not getting better. They slow the progression and even get a slight reversal after a period of chemotherapy. Then they must stop the treatment, allowing her immune system to recover. Her cancer then increases again, and they try a different chemo cocktail.

"Her oncologist says he doesn't know how long they can continue this process. It may be two or three years. It may be six months. But he offers no hope of remission."

"But she is so cheerful and looks nice. She doesn't look that ill."

"It's one of her better days, Uncle. She has been off chemo for four weeks. That's a wig she's wearing; the hospital got it for her, as she has no hair, and an assistant comes and does her makeup before the visiting period.

"I've seen her when she can hardly speak; she's so tired and sleepy."

"And there's nothing else they can do? What about all these fancy drugs they write about in the newspaper?"

"You know I'm a bioscientist and that I work in a medical lab. You don't know that I've studied cancer every night since my mother got it twenty months ago. I've read hundreds of articles and technical papers about the disease. Most of the progress is due to the work of pharmaceutical labs. Research done by universities helps, but it's very hit-and-miss. The labs produce something that might help, and then they test it. They might try dozens of treatments before finding one that is effective, but it only works for some cancers—for others, it doesn't make a difference. The drugs help, but they make life horrible. Mum is in the middle. Without them, she would die in four months."

Uncle Paul became maudlin. "Such a shame; she was a wonderful girl when we were young. What can I do? I must do something."

"Come to see her every month or six weeks. Please tell me when you do. Talk to her about when you were kids. She likes remembering that period before she married. Bring some photos of the time. And others of Aunt Mavis, the farm, and the animals. Give her something interesting to discuss."

Dave said goodbye when Uncle Paul left for St Pancras to catch his Derby train.

But it was one beer too many; and too late to run.

He went to Marco's.

A week after starting work at BaVir Labs at the beginning of 2020, Dave lost his way going home and found a small, unique takeaway pizza shop by accident.

The alley leading to it had a sign on one wall: "Pizza Out". Further down the white-painted alleyway, an iron gate that looked like it belonged at the entrance to a medieval castle, complete with spikes, lay flat against one wall. On the opposite side, an unknown artist had written and illustrated a tag stating, "Tag here, and Marco busts your balls!!!"

The man behind the counter was a first-name greeter. "Hi, I'm Marco. What can I get you?"

"I'm Dave, Dave Tennant; I'll have a medium *Quattro Stagioni*, please."

"Sure. Do you play chess?"

"An odd question, but yes."

"Then would you like a quick game while you wait? There're tables in the room through that door. I can introduce you to another chess player; anyone who comes for a pizza and wants a game can usually find a partner for a game while they wait. I've got bottled beer and soft drinks if you're thirsty."

Dave felt like Alice falling into Wonderland as he followed Marco into the next-door room and enjoyed a short game with a young, bearded student called Fred.

With no friends nearby, chess became a habit for Dave once or twice a week. He learned Marco's history and recounted part of his.

One day, when Marco asked Dave how he had learned to play chess, Dave answered, "I was thirteen when I started. It sounds like a fairy tale, but the guy who first taught me was a tramp called 'Old Tom', who slept in a doorway."

"How'd you meet him?"

"I couldn't miss him; he installed himself in the same doorway every evening. He had a dozen sheets of cardboard, stashed behind an emergency stairway, that he laid out to sleep on. He carried his blankets and stuff in an old shopping trolley, and his dog slept with him.

"I passed him by many times; his dog just looked at me without barking. Sometimes, he would be playing a board game with another tramp; I thought it was draughts.

"Then one evening, when he was alone, Old Tom said, 'Hey lad, Rufus likes you, come and say hello.'

"I sat down with him on a sheet of cardboard and stroked Rufus, who put his head on my leg, and Old Tom asked, 'You play chess, lad?'

"That's how it started, Marco. I don't know if he was any good, but I beat him a year later, and after he disappeared to London for the winter, I never saw him again. But I continued to play. At first, the kids thought I was nuts, but they all learned to play.

"It's a game that teaches patience and the value of planning, and for a kid who has little to boast about, it gives a feeling of achievement when he wins a game."

Dave liked Marco and in him felt he had a friend he could trust.

When Tansy called Dave only a week after he'd met Marco, he took her to play chess. She protested that she hadn't played for years. He had last seen her when he began studying at Kent University. She had been under sixteen then, and he knew she adored him, but three years is like a hundred at that age. He had brushed it off as a schoolgirl crush.

Tansy at twenty-nine was a different story. She was one metre seventy-four, and her dark hair, in an elfin cut, framed her pixie-like face and large brown eyes. Her body curved everywhere, and her breasts were proud, but her lips ... He had lost the first game thinking only of her lips. To Dave, her smile made her beauty unusual and captivating; her mouth was wide, and her grin spread to her ears.

They had a passionate, three-month-long affair until she found a new boyfriend. Dave didn't mind; Tansy was an electronics enthusiast, and they had only their pasts in common, so it was natural that she be with Greg, a likeminded electronics nut.

Marco was the first person Dave told when his mother got cancer.

Three months ago—after taking his mother to the hospital, feeling depressed because he felt he had passed a milestone into an empty wasteland—Dave had met Valerie.

When he'd entered the pizzeria, his greeting was not his usual cheerful, "Hi", but rather an expressionless, "Hello Marco. How about something different tonight? A Hawaiian?"

Marco knew him too well to ignore his expression. "Problems, Dave?"

"No, just a milestone I wanted to avoid passing. I took my mother into the hospital today."

"Shit, can they do anything?"

"Maybe delay it, but not cure it."

"That's sad news. I suppose you don't feel like playing?"

"Is someone waiting?"

"There's a lady, thirty or so. She comes here occasionally; she told me she's a child psychologist. Always has a Margherita with olives and lots of garlic."

It made Dave smile. "Then a good guess is she's not married?"

Marco nodded. "No ring anyway."

"Ok, I'll play. How good is the lady?"

"I think you could beat her in a straight game, but she's heavy on false moves."

Marco introduced him to a woman dressed in a business suit. "Valerie, this is Dave; he's about your level if you are interested in a game."

She looked up and studied Dave with interest. "Ok, Marco, it's why I came."

She held out her hands clenched in fists. "Choose."

Dave got white, a slight advantage, and made his first move. As the game progressed, he felt her tension, bordering on aggression; some of her moves seemed foolish, but they were all threatening. Because of Marco's warning, every time she moved a piece, Dave considered three possibilities: a direct attack, a defensive move, or neither—a feint made to deflect his attention from an attack through another chess piece. It took half an hour of careful thought, but he finally said, "Checkmate."

He added, "Thanks, Valerie. That was interesting and very educational."

"Dave, I want to play against you again; it might take many games, but I *have* to beat you."

He hadn't thought of meeting her again—the tension he felt was unsettling—but her emphasis on the word "have" surprised him; he thought if he refused, it might hurt. Dave didn't like hurting people, so he offered a solution: "Ok, Valerie, let's exchange cell numbers. If I'm coming here, I'll send you a text checking if you can make it. You do the same."

"Sounds good, Dave."

After exchanging numbers, they fetched their pizzas. Dave trailed behind to look. She had a good figure, a trifle slim, and would be ten centimetres shorter without heels. He liked her swaying walk.

Marco was boxing the pizzas.

Dave thanked Marco and then turned to face Valerie. "Nice meeting you; see you again."

A week later, Dave had nothing to do on the evening Valerie's first SMS came.

"Dave, please play tonight, at seven pm. I need to play."

He remembered how desperate she'd seemed to play him again, and he didn't want to let her down, so he said he'd come.

Marco gave them a corner table. "For you, I'll do pasta. If you want pizza, then ok; you choose. If you like pasta, I'll bring you a bowl. I also have ice-cream. You can eat it here. I'll tell the others you are guests, and you can stay as long as you like."

Dave and Valerie played three games, talking and eating between bouts. Dave thought she concentrated well during the last one.

Each time they met, Dave learned more about her. She was an orphan raised by nuns who ran a convent orphanage. Amongst the children were many traumatised by the death of one or both of their parents. Valerie had managed to get a scholarship to study psychology; she wanted to help children who had the problems she had experienced first-hand.

She told Dave of a girl taken in by an aunt after the girl's parents had died. The girl had repeatedly fallen into a withdrawal trance before being handed over to the nuns.

Then of a boy whose uncle had taken him in but had handed him to the nuns because the boy was violent if told to do something.

And of a girl who at fifteen kept leaving to look for love and finally returned to the convent, pregnant.

Dave had told her about his mother. His job. His studies of cancer.

With his meeting with Uncle Paul still on his mind, Dave wandered into Pizza Out, greeted Marco, then added, "I'll have my usual, but I won't play tonight."

Marco could sense his depression. "Is your mother ok, Dave?"

"No, but it's no more than I've had to endure for months; it slowly wears you down."

9

"Yeah, I know. You want to talk?"

"No, Marco. Forget."

Marco said nothing; he thought he might make things worse.

Dave's mind, tired, decided to wander somewhere else. While waiting for the pizza, he thought of nothing.

Then, with the pizza in hand, he plodded down the alley.

Concerned, Marco watched him go.

2

The tiredness was overwhelming as Dave turned in to the lab building; the front steps felt as if they had grown higher during the weekend. It might have once been an impressive Georgian building with evenly spaced rows of windows facing the street, but the windows were now trompe l'oeil, bricked up and painted to resemble what they once were. The necessities of lab safety and air conditioning ruled. Once with massive wooden doors and monstrous bronze knockers, the porticoed Georgian entrance now sported a revolving glass door.

As Dave went in, he avoided an embarrassing clash with the imposing woman standing inside.

"Dave, you look like you've had a rough night." One of the few at BaVir Labs who knew about his mother, Emma Thompson, the HR Manager, added, "Is your mother ok?"

"Yes, Emma. She's off chemo and having a good period now; she's quite cheerful."

Emma's eyes showed concern as she asked, "Then what's worrying you?"

"Nothing new. My uncle, Mum's brother, came to visit. I explained her treatment and prognosis to him, which wasn't easy.

It made me feel angry that I was so impotent. If only I could do something instead of this endless wait."

When she heard Dave's words, Emma realised that she hadn't thought about the effect having a mother dying of cancer would have on the man she thought of as the most stable and likeable person in the company. Emma had worked fifteen years at BaVir and was highly prized by the Managing Director, for, unlike his previous HR Manager, she cared. She didn't simply view her job as being the person who interviewed new job candidates. Nor as being the disciplinarian who would mete out punishment to employees who did not toe the line and follow company policy. She knew she was the person who kept the complex relationships between all the employees calm and stable. She was a mother to the young recruits taking their first steps after school or a degree; she never advised unless asked or sensed it was necessary.

"Dave, all of us feel that way sometimes. The only thing we can do is grit our teeth and do our best to solve the problem.

"Do you have a comb?"

"No, why?"

Emma swung her bag off her shoulder and extracted from it a small packet. "Here, a traveller's necessity pack. Go into the change room. Wash your face. Use some cologne. Take a few deep breaths, and tell yourself you will find a solution. Comb your hair and force a smile. Your new QA Manager, Meghan, is due at any moment. After I've been through all the safety and security protocols with her, I'll bring Meghan to say good morning to you and your lab staff before the IT department can brainwash her. The way you look now, she might not come back tomorrow."

Dave did as Emma had said. One look in the change-room mirror was enough to realise she was right. He stripped, put on his white lab boxers, and dressed in his lab coat and safety gear; then, with a mask and gloves on, he went through the entrance lock and mumbled a "Good morning" to everyone he passed until he entered his glass office in the far corner. There he could remove his gloves and mask.

The paperwork occupied him fully. Every Monday, he had to complete purchase orders for all the reagents used the previous week and for any glassware breakages. A centrifuge that whined had to go for repair, but only after a temporary replacement was found.

None of it cheered him up, but the routine did take his mind off his problems. There was no further news of the DNA equipment or the new lab contract to lift his spirits.

When Emma knocked on the door, he had begun his daily check of the dual proof analyses.

At his signal, she came in, followed by a slightly shorter and much slimmer young woman with reddish-blonde hair, and Dave remembered green eyes.

"Dave, you will remember Meghan MacDougal from her interview."

"Indeed, yes, welcome to BaVir, Ms MacDougal. I'm glad to have you here, we have a lot for you to do, and I'm sure we will work well together."

"I'm sure we can, Mr Tennant, but please, I dislike 'Ms'; I think it's a gender-neutral excuse. Please use 'Miss'; I consider it far more flattering—or better still, 'Meghan' or 'Meg'."

Her reply shocked him; he had used "Ms" for years when addressing women. He was abrupt, suppressing an impulse to snap his reply. "Certainly, Miss MacDougal."

Meghan said nothing, but Dave's harsh tone bewildered her. She thought: "*What did I do to deserve this?*"

Emma saved any further discussion, sensitive as she was to Dave's mood. "I'm going to take Meghan to meet the lab staff. Then I've arranged for Hermione to take her to lunch and show her the canteen. After that, she has a session with IT on system use. She will be, I hope, up to speed tomorrow morning."

"That's great, Emma." He added, "Miss MacDougal, I'll see you tomorrow then to discuss QA."

Once they were out of earshot, Emma said, "Meghan, Dave had a difficult day yesterday—family problems—but he's usually not so sharp. You'll see."

Meghan didn't reply. She planned to probe Hermione at lunch if she had the chance.

Dave returned to his analyses checks, had lunch late, and was approaching the end of the Monday paperwork load when a call came from Philip Jones, the Operations Director of all three labs in the building, relayed by his secretary.

"Mr Tennant, Mr Jones would like to see you at four-thirty."

It was usual for meetings to be held at that time; it allowed staff to change out of their safety gear into regular clothes and go home after the meeting without needing to change back into lab clothes.

"What's it about, Mrs Peterson? Do I need any documents?"

"I've no idea, Mr Tennant. I don't think you need to bring anything."

The lack of a meeting subject alarmed Dave; it sounded like Philip was preparing a rebuke for something. At once, Dave's mood dropped two notches further down from sombre.

At four-fifteen, Dave left the lab and changed. He then went to the admin wing, where he entered Philip's offices at the far end of the corridor on the fourth floor.

Mrs Peterson said, with a gesture, "Go on through, Mr Tennant."

Philip Jones was a short, pugnacious Welshman, a competent administrator who never played office politics; he had fought his way up the hierarchy through hard work. Dave and all the lab staff—even those who didn't like him—respected Jones. The directors trusted him to do whatever they required without fear or favour.

Dave thought he sounded annoyed when he spoke without as much as a "Hello".

"Dave, I've received a complaint email from a client, Doctor Morrison, concerning an analysis we did. Here, I've printed it; please read it."

Dave read it carefully. Twice.

Dear Philip,

Please refer to all earlier reports. Regrettably, I must question the accuracy of the figures in this report. The patient has cancer. His treatment at Princess Margaret Hospital failed, despite medication and chemotherapy. The patient voluntarily ended his medication nine months ago.

All earlier reports show a progressive increase in cancer, yet the last report shows a trend reversal, indicating remission.

Regards,
W. Morrison
MBBCh

After three years of working with him, Philip trusted Dave implicitly. Dave was meticulous and precise, and his reports were always on time and faultless. He had never received a complaint about Dave's lab, and Dave's staff had never complained, unlike the employees in his other two labs.

"Well?"

Dave refused to offer any excuses. "Sir, I know this case; I've followed it for years. I don't think I've seen the last analysis yet because it is not one of those selected for a proof analysis by the QA system. Therefore, this is new to me. I know we have the sample, so I'll look up the results and re-analyse at once."

"Good, and if you find an error, I think you should personally visit Doctor Morrison and apologise in the name of BaVir."

"I'll do so, sir. However, there may have been a problem before delivery to us. I think we owe it to the doctor to ask for another sample and redo the analysis, error or not."

"Fine. Keep me in the loop."

Dave didn't go home; he returned to the change room, got back into fresh work gear, and re-entered the lab. Some staff had already packed up for the day; others were tidying up. He saw Meghan at her desk, intent on the screen in front of her. He remembered he had been almost rude earlier.

Dave had learned the value of politeness shortly after his twelfth birthday, when his father had abruptly left, leaving him to find his way in the adult world, so he approached Meghan and said, "Miss MacDougal?"

Visibly, he had startled Meghan when he spoke.

"I'm sorry, I didn't mean to surprise you."

She turned to him. "Mr Tennant, I was so focused on the screen I didn't hear you approach. Can I help?"

"I'm afraid I was rude this morning; I came to apologise and ask what you would prefer me to call you."

Meghan wasn't ready to forgive him that easily. "Thank you, Mr Tennant, apology accepted. My friends all call me 'Meg'. I hope we can be friends, but if you don't feel easy with 'Meg', then 'Meghan'. As colleagues, I believe the formal 'Miss' is not conducive to cooperation."

Her attempt at severity delighted Dave; it raised his spirits instantly. He grinned at her and said, "'Meg' sounds nice, and I'm all for cooperation. Call me 'Dave' unless you prefer to continue with 'Mr Tennant'. If you used 'David', I wouldn't know you meant me."

Meghan smiled in return; her first negative impressions washed away by his grin. "Thank you."

"Meg, are you working overtime?"

"No, but I dislike leaving something incomplete; I want to finish reading this QA doc before going."

"Ok, I'll leave you to it."

Dave entered his office, logged on to his terminal, opened the analyses file on Doctor Morrison's patient, noted the sample ID numbers, and then went to the sample-storage room to fetch the offending batch and the one taken before that. He would redo both analyses. The early one would prove the procedure used had not changed.

As he laid the samples on a workbench, Meghan, who had finished reading and logged out of her terminal, asked, "Please, can I ask what you are doing?"

"We have had a complaint from a doctor who thinks an analysis we did is incorrect. We've done analyses for the same patient for years. I'm going to redo the last two to see if we did make a mistake."

"The QA procedures I've read state that we do a random selection of analyses a second time. Is the complaint about one of those?"

"No, it's not; I checked. The app did not select it for a retest."

"Can I help? I'm competent, and this is a QA problem."

"I don't doubt your competence. It will only take me a few hours. I can't ask you to work late on your first day."

"I've nothing planned, and you aren't asking; I'm offering because it interests me."

"Ok, if you do one sample and I do the other, it will be much quicker. Log on to the next work position and load procedures, uh—" Dave looked at his screen, "—4144 to 4157."

As she did so, he passed her a blood sample.

"Dave, there's no process trace sheet; how do we know the reagent batch numbers that the lab staff used in the initial tests?"

"We don't. We give the retest to a different person, so the reagent batch numbers should differ. When I must retest, I look at who did the test and fetch reagents from a different person's workspace."

Meghan frowned. "That's going to change. I want you to log the batch number of every reagent you use, and I'll do the same."

As they began the analyses, Meghan noticed his hands in the transparent gloves through which she could see his skin. And then she watched his hands as he worked. They reminded her of those of a surgeon, gentle but with hidden strength in his fingers, precise and powerful, moving with no hesitation. As he reached over and picked up a reagent bottle, she shivered.

Three hours later, with few words spoken, except those necessary to coordinate their work, Dave and Meghan completed the two analyses.

First, for the older sample, then for the latest one, Meghan read the original analyses line by line, and Dave checked the results they had just obtained.

"Haemoglobin value: thirteen point two."

"Check."

And on down every value. Any discrepancies were so minor that they considered them insignificant.

"Meg, that proves it. The analysis was correct. Thanks for helping."

"What do you do now?"

"Make an appointment to see the client, Doctor Morrison, tell him there was no error, but ask him for another sample for a final check. His patient is a cancer case. If there was some problem before the sample arrived, the doctor might give his patient incorrect information. We don't want that to happen."

"Can I go with you? I need to learn how you manage these problems when they occur."

Dave thought this unusual, but she had been a significant help; he could hardly refuse. "Of course, I'll let you know. Now, let's clean up here, get changed, and go home."

While they put away the chemicals, washed the glassware and loaded it into the steriliser, Dave had a thought. "Meg, where do you live?"

"Since more than a week ago, in Chelsea."

"Do you take the district line?"

"Yes. Although the walks are longer than taking the bus, overall, it's quicker."

"Then I'll walk with you to the station; it's been dark for an hour."

Although the rain had stopped, they walked close to each other, for it was cold. Meghan wondered about him; she thought he was somehow different from the other men in her life. Walking with her to the station, she thought, wasn't just politeness; he cared about her safety.

Then she had a weird feeling: Dave wasn't there; she walked with a ghost. She looked down; his shoes looked like crepe-soled ones for walking. His almost-black trousers and coat blended with the darkness. It took her several seconds to realise that he walked so quietly she couldn't hear anything of it—no shuffle or stamp of the feet, no clink of a disturbed pebble, not even the rhythmic rustle of clothing.

"Dave?"

"Yes, Meg."

"How can you walk so silently?"

"Habit, I suppose; I learned to do so when I was a teenager."

"Where are you from? I thought you were a Londoner, but now I'm not sure."

"From the docklands in Tilbury. The suburb of Medway. I studied at Kent University."

"Why did you study for a bioscientist's degree?"

"Because the natural sciences fascinated me, and Pathology was too expensive, I chose the degree I could afford that was as close to my interests as possible. I love it, for the analyses tell the story of human frailty, and I believe my contribution is valuable.

"Tell me, Meg, what do you do for exercise in Chelsea?"

"I've only been in the flat for a week, so I've not explored all the possibilities. I have a membership at a gym to swim in their pool. On fine days, the common is ok for a walk."

"Do you jog?"

"I used to before moving to Chelsea, but the common is too small and the streets too crowded."

"Well, I have the whole of Ravenscourt Park; it's great on a sunny afternoon or evening. I usually go on Sunday afternoons. Having someone to run with would be great if you are up to it."

"I'll think about it; let me know when you plan on going again."

"Which station are you going to?"

"Because it's late, I'll go to South Kensington; more people are around than at Gloucester Road."

"Would you like me to come with you?"

His question left Meghan in a quandary; one part of her wanted to say yes, but the other said, "*You're a big girl now; you don't need him to walk you home.*"

She solved the problem diplomatically. "I would because I've enjoyed the walk and talking with you, but I'll be safe with the people on the streets. We can talk tomorrow. Good night, Dave."

They left from different platforms. Unlike most men she had met, Dave was a mystery for Meghan to uncover.

Aware of a grumbling stomach, Dave went to buy food before he got home.

Dave bought a takeaway from Pret a Manger. His mind was busy; he didn't dwell on Meghan—instead, he focused on a tiny sliver of hope that changed everything, a cancer case that might be in remission without any medication.

He had searched the world for papers on cancer; he would now do so with a new keyword—'remission'.

3

Meghan only had two stops on the Underground to Chelsea, or three if she continued on from Gloucester Road to South Kensington. After a day indoors at work, the exercise of walking to and from the stations, armed with an umbrella, was stimulating, even if the evening drizzle began, as it had, only moments before, after deciding that Meghan needed a wetting.

"Oh, bloody hell," Meghan grumbled, "that damned key must hate me."

Her key had squirmed its way from the easy-access pocket of her bag to burrow into the depths. Trying to find it while holding her purse and an open umbrella needed three hands. Frustrated by a rivulet of water running down her neck, she pushed the door buzzer, three *bips* and a *beep*, hoping her flatmate, Alice Greenwood, was home.

The front door of number thirty-four unlocked with the unmistakable *zzzuk* sound; Meghan pushed it open and clumped up the stairs to the first floor. On the right of the stair, the door to flat number four was standing open; she pushed through, kicked it closed, rammed the dripping umbrella in its stand, and dumped herself on the couch with a sigh.

"Meghan, is that you? I'm in the kitchen."

"Who else would it be, Ally? Unless you are waiting with trembling thighs for the prince of your dreams to arrive."

Alice was slightly taller than Meghan. She was thinner too—without an ounce of fat—but still curvaceous. She had a bonnet of close-cropped brown hair. To Meghan's disgust, Alice had cut her long hair when the restaurant promoted her to Third Assistant Chef; it had been their only significant disagreement since they'd met. Alice's justification that she had to wear a hair net cut no ice with Meghan.

They had met a year ago in the restaurant where Alice worked. Back then, Alice was waiting on tables, but she was now Third Assistant Chef.

When Meghan had taken the BaVir job, she had known that the commute from her flat would take too long, so she had discussed a move with Alice, and the two had agreed to share an apartment, share the housekeeping, and allow male friends for the night only when the other was away.

Alice came into the lounge from the kitchen—mutually agreed to be her territory. She took one look at Meghan and exclaimed, "You sound edgy and look bedraggled. Give me a minute to turn down the hotplate. Sit; I'll bring you a whisky on the rocks. Actually, I'll get us both one."

Minutes later, Alice plumped down beside her on the couch, a drink in each hand. "Here, take a giant slug; you look like you need it. Was it a bad first day in your new job?"

Meghan took a mouthful of the icy drink, holding it in her mouth to taste it before swallowing. As the fiery mix went down, she relaxed and breathed again. "Ahh, that's good. Nooh, it wasn't a difficult day, just intense."

"Why?"

"Well, to begin with, Emma Thompson, our HR Manager, introduced me to the procedures for getting into the building and the lab. She gave me a key-code locker in the change room and told me about the requirements for wearing lab-safety gear. I got to keep my underwear, with a recommendation to buy a dozen pairs of white cotton panties and bra, and change them every day, even twice a day, if I leave the lab at lunchtime. She said if I mark them with my name, I can have them washed by a free service. It's like being at boarding school. I can't wear anything else except the lab coat and protective gear. There are several types of gloves, bouffant caps, different masks, and face shields—the distinct kinds for entry to other labs. I had to memorise everything so I don't screw up tomorrow."

"You must look like white zombies in the lab. Can you wear anything personal?"

"Only a name tag. Mrs Thompson gave me four. Before pinning them to my lab coat, I must put them into a microwave oven with a UV light.

"Then we went into the lab I'll be working in; she showed me to a desk and gave me the login details to access the lab network and internet—another thing to remember. She showed me how to pull up the file of one of the girls in the lab and then took me around all sixteen of the lab staff, starting with the Lab Manager—a lot more to remember. I spent the rest of the day reading the personnel files on the lab staff—their education, skills, training, and experience—and making a list of who was working at what desk. Of course, I only have access to the files of those working under me, so our Lab Manager, Dave Tennant, is still a mystery.

"You must remember when you started in the kitchen at the restaurant, Ally. I recall you saying it took ages to learn what every pot and plate was for and where they kept it."

"What's he like?"

"Who?"

"Dave."

"Ally, for how many years are you going to ask me about the men I meet?"

"Probably until I die. I'm a woman; men are important until you find the right one, but even then, I'm not sure—so many wives find out their husbands are not the right one."

"Well, I met him at the interview; he's a genuine hunk. He welcomed me but left me with Mrs Thompson. One of the girls later told me he's a thirty-five-year-old bachelor."

"Wow! You've thrown a six!"

"Well, if you think about a metre-eighty-six, fair hair, blue eyes, and a body that looks like he spends hours swimming and exercising in a gym every day, is throwing a six, then yes."

"Double six!"

"But the girl, Hermione, who showed me to the canteen at lunchtime, said he's a nerd and terrified of a sexual-harassment accusation. She said he always uses 'Ms' with the person's surname, never their first name, and none of the girls have had any sign of interest, although they've all tried. Oh, and he has a photo of his mother on his desk."

"I'll take back the dice; maybe the guy's gay."

"I don't think so; the girls would have sensed it by now. He's just avoiding a relationship at work. I only said good morning when Mrs Thompson took me to the lab, and then I upset him. I hate it when anyone calls me 'Ms MacDougal'."

"So what did you say?"

Meghan thought back to her short exchange with Dave. "Well, he said, 'Welcome to BaVir, Ms MacDougal. I'm glad to have you here, we have a lot for you to do, and I'm sure we will work well together.'

"Then I replied, 'I'm sure we can, Mr Tennant, but please, I dislike "Ms"; I think it's a gender-neutral excuse. Please use "Miss";

I consider it far more flattering—or better still, "Meghan" or "Meg"'"

"Wow, that's telling him. I wouldn't dare. How did he react?"

"Abruptly. He answered, 'Certainly, Miss MacDougal.'"

"Meg, when will you learn? You put him down; now you have a hill to climb."

"Not at all; he surprised me just before home time by coming to apologise and ask what I preferred people to call me."

"I hope you didn't say, 'Miss MacDougal'."

"No, I said 'Meg', and then he replied, '"Meg" sounds nice ... Call me "Dave" unless you prefer to continue with "Mr Tennant".'"

"That's a nice guy; I'm impressed."

"So am I; he's not like I thought he was at the interview." Meghan took another big gulp of whisky.

Alice thought about it before answering, "Good thing to get that sorted straight away. Why were you late? Did you go to buy panties?"

"No, I don't know where to get plain ones. Dave had received a complaint about a test; a doctor, one of our clients, claimed it was wrong. Dave was going to do two retests. As errors are one of the things I was employed to eliminate, I volunteered to do one of them.

"When we finished, he almost insisted on walking me to the station because it was dark."

"Ah, that's good; at least he's interested."

"I don't think so, Ally; he's very polite. I felt he was saying thank you for me doing the analysis. Hermione said he always says thank you. But I did learn something about him."

"What?"

"He has nice hands. Dave might look like he could punch his way through a brick wall, but he has gentle hands, the hands of a surgeon."

"Hands are special. Do you ever get a shiver when you look at a man's hands, at the thought of him touching you?"

"Only this once. Is that what the shiver means?"

"For me, yes."

"Where do I buy the underwear?"

"A place called Bits and Pieces. It's in Knightsbridge. That's where I go."

"Do they have anything that's not schoolgirl? Since I left school, I'm not fond of bloomers."

"You're not alone. Ask the saleslady; she's got a vast selection. Some are very sexy, and a few are positively erotic. Let's eat. I must get to work; I'm on the late shift."

When Alice left for work, Meghan cleaned up, collected the laundry from their respective baskets, and walked down Manresa Road to the laundromat next to Lightfoot Hall, thinking of Dave. His being a scientist passionate about his job and confined to a lab or office didn't gel with the fact that he was a superbly fit man who walked silently like a cat. She wondered if he had once had another occupation.

It was only the second time she had visited the laundromat since moving into the flat with Alice. The first time was last Thursday ...

Meghan remembered that several students had taken over all the machines last Thursday and that a babble of discussions filled the room. Meghan had felt out of place, for everyone was much younger. One of the young girls took pity on her and said, "Miss, if you wait a few minutes, my machine will have finished."

"Thank you. Is it always this busy?"

"No, students come on Thursdays, before the weekend festivities. Older residents come on Fridays and Saturdays; other days, it's young working people. Sundays and Mondays, it's quite empty."

A young man offered her his chair, which she accepted with pleasure. He was older than the other students.

"I've not seen you here before," he said. Then he asked, "Have you moved into Chelsea?"

"Yes, a week ago. Is everyone here a student?"

"Most, yes. Next door is Lightfoot Hall, student accommodation; I live there too."

"Are you a student?"

"I'm interning at the Royal Brompton."

Meghan guessed his age at twenty-five or -six. "Specialising?"

"No, that comes next. You seem knowledgeable. Are you a doctor?"

"I'm a microbiologist; I work at BaVir Labs. What speciality do you favour? Heart and Lung?"

"I thought I did, but now I wonder if Pathology might be better."

"I've known several pathologists; they all said they switched to Pathology because of the stress of their patients passing away. But when changing speciality, they also lose the thrill of saving patients. It's a personal choice."

The girl butted in, "Miss, my machine has finished."

Meghan stood up and went with her to a machine. She loaded her clothes, started the washer, and returned to her seat, which the intern had kept for her.

As she sat down, he said, "I'm Barry Dickens. My laundry is dry, so I'll go back to my studies for the internship. It's been nice meeting you."

"Likewise. I'm Meghan MacDougal."

"I had already guessed you were from Scotland from your accent. I hope to see you here another evening."

As she watched him walk away, Meghan wondered if she would ever lose her accent. She had eliminated "och aye" from her speech and tried to say "no" and not "nooh".

As the girl had told Meghan last week, few customers were at the laundromat on a Monday.

While waiting for the washing machine to go through its cycle and then for the dryer to finish, Meghan had time to think.

She would buy the white underwear and a laundry marker tomorrow at lunchtime. Although re-analysing the samples with Dave had already led her to determine the first changes she would make to the lab's QA procedures, she still had to finish reading the documentation about the process. However, she had taken the job because of the promised DNA lab—her area of expertise—and she had seen no sign of it; another thing to investigate.

Barry Dickens interrupted her thoughts. "Hello, Meghan; I didn't expect to see you on a Monday."

She looked up into his smiling face.

He was standing in front of her without a bundle of laundry.

Meghan assumed he inspected the laundromat every evening, hoping to meet a girl. "Hello Barry, I could say the same about you, but where's your laundry?"

"In the machine at the end of the row. I spent the weekend in the country on a friend's farm, and I had nothing but muddy clothes, so I popped them in while I went for a burger. The machine should finish in a minute, and I'll put them in the dryer."

"Well, I decided to avoid the student crush and come today."

Barry excused himself and transferred his clothes from the washer to the dryer. When he came back, he and Meghan struck up a conversation about medical things. Meghan told him that after four years of routine minor analytical work, she had moved labs for a more exciting job. Getting the position had made her investment in two more years of study and night school, learning about DNA and sequencing, followed by a demanding course in QA in medicine, worthwhile.

Barry told her about life as an intern in London, which she

concluded was not much different from her experiences in Edinburgh.

Meghan thought he was attractive but too young for her. He reminded her of a student lover she'd had during her last two university years.

After their breakup, she had come to London from Edinburgh with no interest in men while studying. However, Peter had invited her out several times in the last three months. Barry might be fun for a fling.

Barry's dryer warning light went green. "My clothes are dry; I must get back to the grindstone."

While waiting, Meghan thought of Peter, an accountant at an auditing firm in London.

Meghan had met Philippa, at the time a BCom student, at a horserace at a course near Edinburgh. They were both passionate about watching the races and quickly became friends.

Philippa went on to complete her articles and find work at a chartered accountancy. She installed herself in the bedroom of a young lawyer called Craig. When he had transferred to the London office, she had done the same to avoid losing him.

It was at Philippa's flat-warming party that she had met Peter. Meghan's relationship with him hadn't progressed beyond a good-night peck, for he was either working late on an audit, or out of London, looking at some or other company's books. He had promised to call whenever he could.

He had done, on four occasions in the last three months. They had gone to the same restaurant each time—either he lacked imagination or really liked the place.

Meghan had thought of telling him not to call, but he had a fund of amusing stories about the people he'd met at the various companies he visited. Meghan thought of him as a raconteur, and dinner, when you have nothing else planned, made her accept on each occasion.

She took the dried laundry back to the flat, wondering why she now didn't care if Peter never called.

4

As Dave left his flat for work, with yesterday's blues chased away by hope, he recalled something Old Tom had said on a morning like this, biting-cold but with weak wintry sunshine peeking between the low clouds. Dave had asked, "Tom, how can you stand the cold, sleeping out like this?"

Old Tom had replied, "My tarp, a blanket, and a warm dog at nights, lad, and for the days, I store a little sunshine in my head, so it shines every day."

When Dave got to work, he called Doctor Morrison's receptionist.

"Doctor Morrison's rooms, good morning; how can I help you?"

The voice was low-pitched, throaty, and warm; Dave felt a shiver down his spine—years ago, he had met a girl whose voice had charmed him into her college bed.

"Good morning, Dave Tennant from BaVir Labs here. I want to make an appointment with Doctor Morrison regarding an analysis."

"I'm sorry, but Doctor is out visiting until one-thirty. I'll tell him you called and ask him to give you a ring. Can I have your number, please?"

Dave was about to give her the lab number but decided to provide his mobile one instead. He might be out. He gave her the number and then said, "He can call any time. To whom am I speaking?"

"His receptionist, Monica Beasley."

"Thank you, Monica; I'll wait for Doctor Morrison's call."

Meghan arrived late with a parcel of underwear to leave in her locker. The saleslady had been charming when Meghan explained what she needed. She looked Meghan up and down, then asked, "Bust thirty-six B or C?"

Meghan replied, "Thirty-six B and a bit."

She smiled at the "and a bit", then said, "I think I've your size; low-cut or full?"

"Can I try both?"

"Of course, and I've one with cotton lace. Do you prefer the shoulder or sports type with a single back strap? It'll keep your breasts closer and higher; better support—" she smiled, "—and better cleavage."

"I'll go for the sports type; I wear one when I run."

"Right then, panties. Do you spend a lot of time sitting?"

"Yes."

"Then you need a full cover at the back and a high waist to hold it up. Thirty-six as well?"

"Yes."

"I'll show you full and narrow fronts. Would you like no lace, lace on the front, or lace around the thighs only?"

"Let me see them ... definitely lace."

After trying on the bras, she loved the low-cut fit. She chose the narrow-front panties with lace. Meghan bought a dozen sets and a clothes-marker pen. Although no one except the people who handled the laundry for BaVir would see her bras and panties, they might talk, and it wouldn't be long before the female staff knew she wore sexy underwear, but Meghan knew she would feel good in them.

When she arrived at the lab, Meghan found a thick paper file labelled "DNA LAB" lying on her desk.

The moment she opened it, she realised why it wasn't all in electronic data files—much of it was manufacturers' documentation on the equipment, and a large foldout drawing showed a lab layout. After reading the equipment list, she took the file and went to Dave's office. She knocked and, after Dave looked up and nodded to her, went in and asked, "Dave, did you put this file on my desk?"

"Yes. It's not for immediate attention. Please review it and let me know your opinion of the equipment choice and the layout of the lab. Then we need to collaborate on consumables."

"Ok, but one thing isn't clear. Where is the lab?"

"You're standing in it, Meg."

The bewildered expression on Meghan's face delighted Dave, who laughed, a pleased laugh. "I'm not joking. Contractors are clearing and converting the office next door as we speak. We have taken over the lease. Part of this office will be the airlock from this lab into the addition."

Meghan had recovered her poise. "Ok, that makes sense. Where is your office going?"

"I get a glass box in the DNA lab, but with its door into the existing lab, so I don't need to go through the airlock to get to my office. It will be much bigger, for us both. If you wish, we can put a separation between us. A technician will use your current desk area; the installers will convert it. Our new office will be ready for us in two weeks."

The thought of sharing an office with Dave gave her an odd feeling; she wasn't sure whether she felt good or bad but said nothing about a separation. "I noticed an electron microscope on the list of equipment. How did you manage to get one? I wasn't expecting it."

"Do you know how to use one? I didn't ask at your interview, and I should have."

"My last lab had an electron microscope, the same model as the one on the list. I did the full training course."

"That's marvellous. I think you'll get some practice using it. The budget for the lab was generous, mainly because most of it was a government grant to upgrade DNA sequencing to identify Covid virus mutations. I managed to squeeze the microscope into the budget."

"I see. I'll get back to my QA file now; I may not get to the DNA lab info until tomorrow."

Doctor Morrison called at one-thirty; Dave thought the doctor had yet to see his first patient at the surgery. Dave asked for a meeting to explain the procedure they had followed after the doctor's complaint.

Doctor Morrison was belligerent: "Do we need to meet? I'm too busy to listen to excuses. Can't you tell me on the phone?"

"I think a meeting would be best, Doctor, just a short one—we have no excuses to make; we're hoping for cooperation in finding a reason for the apparent discrepancy."

"Let me check."

Dave could hear a discussion with Monica; her voice was easily recognisable.

"Mr Tennant, can you make it at five-thirty? I can give you thirty minutes."

"Certainly, Doctor, thank you. We will be on time."

As he put down the phone, Doctor Morrison had a moment to wonder why Mr Tennant had insisted on a meeting. It seemed so simple—send a new set of results and an apology: Was there something he had not noticed?

As soon as Dave got off the phone with Doctor Morrison, he told Meghan about the meeting.

"I've an appointment with the client, Doctor Morrison, at five-thirty pm. He's the one who complained. It will take about thirty minutes in a taxi to his surgery, and a cab can take you straight home. Can you come?"

"Yes, no problem, I'll be ready in reception at a quarter to five."

A sign stuck to the surgery's front door read, "Please wear a mask". Dave took two from a box on a stand next to the door and handed one to Meghan. After they put their masks on, they entered the practice.

"Good evening, you must be Monica; I spoke to you earlier. Dave Tennant."

The doctor's receptionist, leaning over her keyboard to peer at her computer screen, looked up. Then hastily sat up straight. She smiled at Dave.

She had dark hair and sparkling brown eyes. She was twenty-five or -six at most, Dave guessed.

"Yes, Mr Tennant, Doctor should be free in five minutes and will see you then."

They sat in comfortable waiting-room chairs. Dave only had time to glance at the cover of a medical magazine before a patient came out of the surgery and the desk phone buzzed. Monica answered: "The people from BaVir Labs to see you, Doctor."

Monica stood and walked to the door; she opened it, looked in, and then turned back. Dave stepped back for Meghan to enter first, and as he went past Monica, she said, "Doctor is sterilising; he will be with you in a sec. Please sit down."

Meghan said nothing, and Dave thought she looked as rigid as an ice lolly; perhaps she had a horror of surgeries.

The doctor, also wearing a mask, appeared from an alcove that must have had a washbasin, as he was drying his hands. He looked to Dave like the archetypical family doctor. The general practitioners who treat the everyday pains of millions, sometimes with little more than a sympathetic ear and aspirin; a copy of the doctor who had diagnosed his mother's cancer.

"Good evening, Doctor. I'm Dave Tennant, the BaVir Lab Manager, and this is Meghan MacDougal, our QA Manager."

Dave guessed Doctor Morrison to be in his early forties, younger than he had expected; he mentally kicked himself for not looking up the doctor's background before coming.

"Good evening to you both. I didn't expect two visitors from the lab; I usually get a terse email saying the matter is under investigation."

"We take complaints very seriously, Doctor; lives may be at stake, and your complaint is a problem."

"Why?"

"A small confession on my part to begin with: I'm particularly interested, for personal reasons—call it a hobby if you wish—in data on cancer cases and their progress. Your patient, Mr Kravitz, is unique in that we have an unbroken string of analyses over many years—five to be precise—plus two and a half years of three-monthly samples since his cancer developed."

"Are you the person who wrote the comment about possible cancer on the sixth one?"

"I am, Doctor, and since then, I've kept the sample remaining after analysis in cryogenic storage."

Doctor Morrison had mellowed. "Unusual, but I don't object, and I must thank you for that comment; without it, I might not have picked up a problem."

"Sir, I must offer an excuse for not taking notice of the cancer reversal in your patient's last analysis. I knew that he had been at Princess Margaret's for chemotherapy. I didn't realise he had voluntarily terminated treatment, so I naturally assumed the chemo had caused the reduction. I should have seen that the analysis request was from you, not the hospital. I checked and saw the last three samples in the sequence are from you, so I assume these are after he terminated treatment."

"That's correct, and I appreciate you did not know. There had been no improvement after two years of chemotherapy and other drugs. I remember there were short periods when it seemed to stagnate. After two years, the oncologist told him there was nothing further he could do unless Mr Kravitz came into the hospital for continuous monitoring during treatment with a drug protocol still classified as experimental. Boris came to see me and asked for advice. He said he didn't want to spend what could be an active two years in hospital as a guinea pig. He is divorced, what I call a 'Covid divorce', resulting from couples not having enough time apart from one another during the lockdowns. He has no children or relatives in England and said he could continue to work and intended to visit Poland on holiday to find some relatives.

"Of course, I can't advise that, and I thought if I recommended he continue treatment, he would walk out, and I would never see him again. So I said it was a courageous decision but asked him to continue the tests to track the progress of his cancer, and I would advise him accordingly. That's why I continue to send in samples for analysis, and that last one is so unexpected I had to bring it to your attention."

"I'm glad you did, Doctor. After your complaint, I recovered the sample in question, and the one before it, then Meghan and I redid the tests on both, simultaneously, using an identical procedure."

"I understand; I won't try to guess the outcome."

"Both samples gave results identical to the reports sent to you, so there is no doubt of the *indication* that the cancer is in remission. Unless this is true, the only possible explanation is that the blood sample became contaminated or diluted during the process of extracting it from the patient."

Doctor Morrison picked up the inference. "Or there was a mix-up in test tubes and labels. Now I understand why you are here; surprisingly professional and much appreciated. I'm afraid most labs would have said 'No error' and left it there. What do you propose?"

"Can we get a new sample from Mr Kravitz? The lab won't charge for the retesting we have already done or for a new test."

"I'm confident Mr Kravitz won't object, but we may have a delay. He's an aircraft engineer who is frequently out of the country.

"He goes, sometimes for weeks, to those places I and many others like me can only dream about—those with palm trees or elephants—although he has said there are others far less attractive where he's bored stiff.

"So I don't know when he can come to give new samples; I'll email him and find out. There's nothing critical about his condition, so a week or two won't influence the result."

The doctor then asked, "If the result of a new sample test is the same, is Mr Kravitz experiencing a spontaneous remission?"

"Anything is possible; there have been many reported cases. Unfortunately, there seems to be extraordinarily little data on whether or not such cases have later relapsed. I expect it's because the patients move around, and tests by different labs are not correlated."

"Mr Tennant, I know it's a commonly believed fallacy that doctors cure illness. A colleague of mine calls it the arrogance of the medical profession. He insists that we intervene with drugs only to combat the initial onslaught of infection, giving the body the time needed to do the job. He maintains that final cures result from the immune system getting the upper hand. Is it possible that in Mr Kravitz's case, the two years of therapy he followed were enough to allow his body to do the rest?"

"Certainly, Doctor; it would appear too much of a coincidence that he would pick up an agent combating his cancer shortly after terminating treatment."

Meghan butted in, "Dave, there can only be two outcomes to a new test. Either there was an error, and the cancer is unchanged, or there was no error. In that case, the question becomes: What has caused the remission? We might not have any clues from one sample, but can we keep the sample at body temperature from when the doctor takes it? We could then culture anything we find, and Mr Kravitz should continue his tests at the same intervals; we may only learn something with a time series of data."

"That's a great idea, Meg; we have standard warm boxes and chem packs. Doctor, I can send you one if you accept."

"Certainly; we have done so before. What can I tell Mr Kravitz?"

"Whatever you wish, Doctor. He may not know what Meg meant by culture; please don't frighten him. Tell him it's no different from how a botanist might grow plants for study; if the blood has interesting cells, we will keep them in conditions suitable for growth so that we can study them."

"I don't think it's that easy, from what I remember from med school."

"No, growing plants isn't either; you need the right climate, plant foods, soil conditions, and amounts of water."

Dave then said to Doctor Morrison: "Can you let me know when you need the warm box? Here's my card with my email address."

As they stood, Doctor Morrison asked, "Whatever you find out, I assume you will keep me fully in the loop?"

"Of course, Doctor. We have identical aims and will cooperate fully."

As they left the practice, Monica wished them goodbye, smiled at Dave, and added, "I hope to see you again soon."

Once outside, Dave and Meghan called for separate taxis. While waiting, Dave felt Meghan had cooled again as she asked, "Dave, I've not been around you long enough to know you well. Do you always have that effect on young women?"

"What effect?"

"She took one look at you and puffed out her chest, and I swear her nipples had hardened."

"I didn't notice. Are you sure it's not your imagination?"

"And then, she showed us through the door to the surgery. Doctors' receptionists don't do that; the patients must open the doors themselves unless they can't, and you don't look incapable."

"I never thought of that."

"Didn't you notice the slinky-sexy walk and swaying hips?"

Dave thought back to that moment. It hadn't registered then, but picturing Monica, he realised her body had hills, valleys, and distinct twin peaks. The slinky-sexy walk, though, he hadn't picked up. "No, I didn't notice; I was looking at you from behind, and you looked like an ice lolly for a moment."

Meghan laughed. "Dave, you're an innocent, and I'm a sensitive fool. Here's my cab; see you tomorrow."

In the taxi, Meghan silently scolded herself: "*What business is it of yours if a woman is attracted to Dave? Last night, you were contemplating a fling with an intern hardly out of school.*"

Then she thought, "*Oh hell, face it, babe, you fancy him.*"

Dave, in his taxi, thought, "*Why did she say she's a sensitive fool? Does she fancy me?*"

It brought up another question, "*And do I fancy her?*"

After thinking it over until halfway home, he decided, "*Yes, I think she's wonderful, but she works with me, and lab relationships are a no-no. I must be careful."*

5

Dave's mobile phone rang in the taxi before he reached home. The call was from an unknown number.

"Hello?" Dave answered.

"Good evening, is that Mr Tennant?"

"Yes, speaking."

"My name is John Harrups; I represent an American corporation with a hundred and forty-two labs in the USA and one in England. The UK lab needs a Director of Operations, and your name is on our list; we would like to meet with you to discuss an offer."

Dave was sure he was talking to a head-hunter. "I'm always willing to listen, Mr Harrups. Where and when?"

"I'm trying to organise interviews for next week at the Belgravia Hotel. We have a meeting room booked. Would Wednesday the eighth, at six-thirty pm suit you?"

"That would be fine."

"I've marked you in the schedule. Ask for me at reception."

Meghan came into Dave's office with a file in one hand and a pen between the fingers of the other.

"Good morning, Meg," Dave greeted. "Tell me something, do you always have the same hairstyle and the same colour lipstick?"

"You do ask intriguing questions, Dave. I change when I go out in the evening, run, or attend the Highland Games. Why do you ask?"

"Because I just noticed that we all look the same wearing lab gear every day; I must look at a calendar to learn what day it is. I wondered if we could change that; it might liven things up a bit. But what's in your file?"

"I want to show you what I propose doing for the process trace and hear your suggestions. Is this the right time?"

"Pull up that chair so we can look at it together."

When she sat beside him, he pushed his mouse to the far side of the desk to give her the space to put the opened file in front of them. He had to force himself to concentrate, as he could smell her perfume and feel her warmth in the air-conditioned office.

While they were huddled together over the file, Dave managed to block out his senses so that they could work through the proposal. He thought it was the work of an expert, and when they got to the end, he had made only three suggestions; she'd noted these on the document in pen. She sat up and pushed back her chair.

Preparing to rise, Dave reached over for his mouse and inadvertently knocked her pen to the floor.

Without thought, she leaned down, picked it up, and saw him looking down at her while she straightened up. A glance convinced her that her gaping lab coat revealed a generous view of her low-cut bra and cleavage.

She looked at him with a smile. "Peeking, Dave?" He was embarrassed, and that delighted her. "Dave, you can look all you want; women buy pretty underwear to be looked at, but not by men who leer and make bad jokes."

"You have lovely underwear, and what's in it is beautiful."

She felt a gush of something she had never felt before. "Flatterer."

Meghan felt tired but satisfied with her progress by the end of her first week. Alice was home when Meghan arrived, for she had the late shift in the restaurant kitchen on Fridays.

"Meg, are you going out, or do I cook for both of us?"

"I'm staying in. I'm going to wash my hair and have an early night. It's been a busy week. Pete called; he's taking me to dinner tomorrow."

"I don't like him."

"Why not? You only met him once."

"I don't know. I thought about him after you introduced him. There's something that bothers me. He left me totally cold, and I feel at least some sympathy for most men. Then I thought it must be his smile."

"What's wrong with it? He smiles a lot."

"Yes, but it's only around his mouth."

"I don't understand, Ally."

"It doesn't go up to his eyes, which don't crease. They are not smiling eyes."

"Well, I haven't noticed. Now you've said it, I'll have a look myself."

When Peter launched into mostly humorous stories about who he had met since the last time they had dinner, Meghan watched his face intently. He thought he had her enthralled. After a while, she decided Alice might be correct and tried to remember the expressions of her younger brother, Rory, and brother-in-law, Hamish, for comparison. It didn't work because the only face she could picture was Dave's and his laughing eyes when she had tried to be severe after he'd asked how she preferred to be addressed.

When they left, and Peter tried to embrace her, she turned her face to the side, so his kiss landed on her cheek.

"Why can't I kiss you, Meg?"

"I'm not that kind of girl, Pete; I must know you far better before I do.

"Now, I must get home. Good night."

Dave's mother had recovered further since his visit last Sunday. From when he had brought her to the hospital, he had never missed the two-hour visiting period.

Emily Tennant was the daughter of a Tilbury dockworker. She was born in a small house built during the expansion period when shipping preferred to dock before navigating the Thames to London. She grew up in a close-knit dockworker community where the men worked, watched football, and drank in the pub, and the women kept house and children. One of four kids, she had never known luxury.

She made a mistake when—instead of marrying the dockworker her father wanted her to—she allowed a travelling salesman with a flashy car and an expense account to seduce her.

When she became pregnant, her angry father forced her into marriage. He had told her beau that it was either marriage or broken limbs.

Dockers are united in more than a trade union.

She discovered the consequences after the marriage. The wives of the community shunned her; she didn't realise that they did so out of fear and jealousy. With a husband away for a week or two at a time, she was a ripe target for a wandering husband, and the wives classified her in that group of women who had used sex to step up the social ladder. Two of her friends from school days had gotten married to sailors. They introduced her to their circle of sailors' wives—women who had empty beds for weeks and doted on their sons and daughters.

Dave spent his childhood with their children, a gang of little

46

boys and later teenagers, known disparagingly as "the sailors' kids", with no fathers to guide them.

When Dave's father left them and filed for a divorce, the consensus was that Emily deserved it. "That's what comes to those who want to pee in an inside toilet."

Emily concentrated her love even more on Dave. She secretly decided she would make him leave the docker community, so she spent long hours working in a supermarket to put food on the table, dress him in more than rags, and pay for his education. When he graduated from university, she felt her efforts rewarded.

When the doctor diagnosed cancer, she believed it to be a punishment for sex before marriage and thanked God for holding off cancer until Dave was an adult.

"Ma, do you remember the first time I took you skating?" Dave asked.

"I'll never forget it; I was so scared I almost wet my pants. But then, when I saw you gliding around and your graceful moves, I was so proud."

"But you came onto the ice anyway, Ma; I remember thinking it was brave of you."

Emily smiled. "But you held me; I remember thinking how strong you were."

Dave grinned. "Not all the time."

Still smiling, Emily said, "Well, I didn't try to fall on you. It was like collapsing on a cushion.

"Dave, I want to say something to you."

"What, Ma?"

"Before I got this cancer, I thought you would get married; I could tell you were looking for a girl, although I was happy when you let Angela go. I don't know how long I'll be here. It's my destiny, and I will accept whatever happens, but it's not your destiny. You need a wife who loves you, and you have always needed someone to love; I'm grateful you have loved me so much since you were born. You must find a girl, Dave."

"Ma, it's true I once looked at girls with the idea of marriage in my head, but since you got cancer, I haven't had the time to look, what with work, looking after you, and studying the disease. I don't think any woman would marry a man who hasn't got time for her."

"You said you would cure my cancer, but that's in the hands of God. I don't want you growing old and missing marriage and children because of me. I don't want to be the reason for your unhappiness; it would destroy all I have done for you. Before I die, I want to know you have a woman to love, who will love you, and with whom you can have children that will give you the same joy you have given me."

"Ma, I will try, but if I find one, she will be a gift from God."

"Is there not even one?"

"No, Ma. The only one I have met in the last three months that I could love is working at the lab, and the company rules prohibit that."

When Dave left the hospital, he dreaded the thought of Emily's coming chemo treatment.

There were many more people in the park when he went for a run. It should have been pleasant, but he gave the impression to those who looked at him that he was running from something.

Dave used the next three days to complete the monthly stats and accounts reports.

Meghan was busy training the staff to use her process trace sheets, and they hardly spoke. Occupied, he didn't notice the sudden flowering of lipstick shades in the lab.

Dave was on time for the job interview. He learned the lab was in Belgravia, and they needed an operations director because the American pathologist was leaving after his contract ended in three months.

"I hope you know I am not a qualified pathologist?"

Gwen, the American HR woman, replied, "We know, Mr Tennant, but you are a fully qualified member of the American Society for Clinical Pathology; in our view, you're suitably qualified for the job. Many of our labs have members of the Society as directors."

Dave left the interview with an inventory of the equipment in the lab and a promise that they would send a list of the procedures they did. He thought they had another candidate at seven-thirty pm because he saw Harrups glance at his watch at least twice.

Dave felt uneasy and didn't know why. Was it the accent and language? Gwen was antipathetic, and he felt the men were not completely open.

He decided to research the company and its London operations. He had sensed the hire-and-fire culture, especially from Gwen, and found it foreign. He knew, deep down, the time was coming when he would want a change, but as the job was in London, he would still be close to his mother, and it might be a good move.

Dave sat down to review the company while eating his supper. After four hours of gathering information, he concluded the company had made a terrible investment. The pathologist may have resigned, or perhaps they had fired him because the lab was not doing well. Consequently, their looking to hire someone new was an effort to correct the problem.

He slept poorly. Could he make the lab profitable? Should he decline if they offered him the job?

Dave knew who to call for more information about the American company. John Miller was a schoolboy chum of Dave's and the manager of the lab he had worked at before starting at BaVir. Dave called John up and invited him for a chat over a pub lunch.

To Dave, John had gone from a happy-go-lucky teenager, always ready for a lark, to a seriously overweight executive who spent too much time in the office. Dave thought John must know this, for he had opted for a well-cut suit to hide the excess weight rather than spending time exercising. However, Dave said nothing, and they spent two beers comparing notes on their careers since Dave had left for BaVir.

Then John asked, "How is your mother doing?"

"She's in hospital, and the oncologist's prognosis is discouraging."

"I'm sorry; I always thought her a fine woman."

"Thanks, John."

"You mentioned you wanted some information on the Yank lab in Belgravia ..."

"Yes, as I told you, they've expressed some interest in hiring me, but I'm not happy with what they said and what I've learned about them. Most of it, I must admit, is American information."

"I'm glad you are suspicious. I called a couple of contacts. The lab is in serious trouble. You must look at the big picture of how labs operate in England and why the American company doesn't fit in. It has never operated a lab in a country with a national health service. Or with controlled analysis prices; their cost structure is way too high. Furthermore, that lot are not scientists; they do the mass, run-of-the-mill standard procedures that churn a cash flow from turnover, not the more complex work that requires strict guidelines and QA. They have stayed alive until now with the deluge of Covid tests, but now that the pandemic is over, they have a big problem."

"John, you've summed up my conclusions well. Their pathologist is leaving, and they have shown interest in offering me the job of Director of Operations."

"That will make it worse. You have the qualifications, don't doubt it, but a lab in England needs a qualified doctor pathologist. If the lab doesn't have one, the work will go elsewhere; England and the National Health Service think that's the way it should be. Your clients would accept you if it were a research lab, but not one dealing with doctors trying to cure sick people."

"Thanks, John. I'll tell them I'm not interested. I was suspicious from the start because the lab is in one of the most expensive parts of London, and that's no place to run such a business. I would have put it in Whitechapel next to the Royal London."

"True, but satisfy my curiosity; why did you go to the interview?"

Dave was silent for a long moment while John looked at him curiously. "I hate to admit it, but sometimes I wonder what the future will bring after my mother dies. I know I won't want to continue in the same place and the same lab, so I'll need a change of job, town, or country. That's the only reason."

"If that happens, talk to me; my lab chain has operations in Europe and South Africa, and I'm sure we can find you something interesting."

"Thanks again, John. Have you met any of the old gang members recently?"

"I met Graham Tookbridge a couple of months ago. He wore arty, colourful clothes, black trousers, a yellow shirt, and a white tie. He has an art gallery; I can't remember where, but it's near South Kensington. Strangely, he went to business school."

"What, Tooky, at a business school? He could hardly add two and two."

"He must have changed; I think he's doing well. He said he was unmarried."

"I'm not surprised; he never fancied girls, and I thought he might be gay."

"It takes all kinds, Dave. I must go."

Back at the office, Dave opened the email he had received from the American company. It contained the list of procedures they performed, as well as an offer of employment. He clicked "Reply" and explained, tongue-in-cheek, that he had decided not to pursue their *kind* offer of employment.

"Good night, Meghan; see you tomorrow," Dave said.

Meghan smiled as she looked up and waved him goodbye as he left the lab.

The trip home felt longer than usual. When he arrived and went into his flat, it seemed lonely. He could feel his frustration building. No message had come from Doctor Morrison, so he had no idea when Boris Kravitz's new sample would arrive. Had he made the right decision about the job? He couldn't concentrate on his research and thought he needed exercise.

He changed into running gear and went to Ravenscourt Park, ran hard for an hour, and left at seven pm. It didn't help.

As the week ended, Dave had given up hope of a message from Doctor Morrison and faced a Saturday of worry that would destroy his concentration while researching cancer remission.

Meghan came to see him before leaving for the weekend. "Dave, I'll be in the DNA lab a lot next week. I want to store the consumables that have arrived. I must do it myself, else I won't know where things are. Can you manage the retest comparisons for the week?"

"Yes, no problem. If I can, I'll visit you in the lab to see how things are going."

Dave was about to wish her a pleasant weekend when he had

a thought. "Meg, this is a late invitation. Can I offer you a run in Ravenscourt Park tomorrow afternoon? Followed by dinner and a show?"

Meghan was surprised. She immediately regretted having agreed to spend Saturday with Hamish. He was in London for one of his regular political meetings—as a junior member of the Scottish National Party, based in Edinburgh, he came to London to confer with the Westminster MPs—and they were going to Sandown Park to watch the horseracing. Hamish had promised to take her to the Derby if he was in London.

"Sorry, Dave, I would love to, but I've got a date all day tomorrow. I'm going to the horseracing. I used to go regularly in Scotland."

"That's ok, Meg. Next time, I'll try to invite you before you get booked up, then we can plan a horseracing day, and you can introduce me to it; I've never watched a live horse race."

"That would be fun, but don't you have a girlfriend?"

"Not really. A woman I know calls me from time to time when she needs relief from the stress of her job. I never call her. Is your boyfriend a long-term attachment?"

Meghan thought he meant Peter; she didn't realise he had assumed Hamish was her boyfriend.

"No, and like you, he only calls when he's in town; he's an accountant and often works in other towns doing audits."

"So, we are both unattached part-timers. Have a good weekend."

Meghan left with a niggling question in her mind: "*What did he mean by relief?*"

Dave continued with the last items in his inbox. He was about to leave when his mobile phone rang.

"Dave Tennant, good evening," he answered.

"Hello, Dave ..."

"Monica, I would recognise your voice anywhere. How can I help?"

"Well, the first thing is that Doctor Morrison asked me to tell you that Mr Kravitz will be coming to the surgery on Friday the twenty-fourth; Doctor said he's on a training course in Seattle. I was going to send an email, but then I thought I could ask you a favour, so I called."

"That's good news, thank you. You can tell Doctor Morrison we will have a warm box for the samples delivered on time. Please, ask your favour."

"Dave, I was going to a nightclub in Soho tomorrow night—drinks, music, and dancing—but my partner has cancelled. Can you come with me?"

Dave at once thought fate had stepped in. Without asking anything else, he answered, "Of course, Monica, it will be a pleasure; where do we meet and what time?"

"The Bang-Up Club, Frith and Old Compton. I'll meet you outside at ten pm sharp."

Adventure seemed to call. "Ok, Monica, you're on."

"Wear jeans, no jacket or tie, and soft shoes, like trainers."

"I shall do; see you then."

For some unknown reason, he felt he could face Saturday.

6

Dressed as ordered and with a jacket over his shoulder, Dave met Monica as planned. She wore a tight and oh-so-short skirt, an oh-so-tight top, and sneakers—the expensive, fashion kind with spangles—and carried a handbag big enough for grocery shopping.

They passed through what seemed like an airlock but was a sound lock, and the second padded door opened onto ear-bending sound so powerful the bass made the guts wobble.

Monica grabbed his hand and took him to a far corner of the room, opposite the bar that stretched the length of one wall. Dave was grateful that it was as far from the exploding speakers as the room allowed. The flashing lights and mirrors were enough to lose a newcomer in a throbbing roomful of rocking, swaying, and bobbing humanity.

Monica introduced him to a group of friends; it was the kind of introduction that means you don't need to remember the names. "Hi guys, this is Dave." Then, pointing at each one, she gave a quick run-down: "Jenny, Pete, Henry, Margie, Fluffy, and Kurt."

Jenny and Margie appeared to be younger copies of Monica wearing the same clothing. He couldn't see Fluffy clearly, but her dress seemed looser. Nor could he make out her features clearly in the poor light but thought she was older than the others.

Monica dispatched Dave to the bar: "Get me a double Knocker." He ordered himself a G&T.

While he waited for the drinks, he remembered what his old varsity friend Toby had told him about drinking G&Ts.

One day, Dave had run into Toby, and they had caught up on their respective careers. Dave hadn't said much. His job involved repeating the same analyses day after day. However, Toby had an endless fund of stories gathered during his experiences as a salesman. At university, Toby had developed a reputation as a beer drinker; Dave was surprised he was drinking G&T, so he said so.

"Dave, if you had taken as many clients out for an evening as I have, you would too."

"Why?"

"Some are hard drinkers, and you must match them, drink for drink. With a G&T, you can stagger to the gents, feigning drunkenness, hold the ice cubes in the glass with your fingers while you pour half of it away with your piss, and then fill it up with water as you wash your hands.

"You can stay sober, and they don't; amazing what you can learn."

As he paid for the drinks, Dave decided that the travelling salesman gambit seemed a good strategy. He joined Monica and her friends, sipping gingerly at his G&T.

The crowd consumed enough alcohol to become frenzied but sloppy dancers as the night progressed. It was a completely new experience; Dave was learning the jiggly jumpy dancing and had finally concluded that he was not bopping along with Monica but with anyone that looked female, although sometimes he was doubtful about that. Most of the time, he recognised Monica,

Jenny, Margie, or Fluffy as a partner, though they came and went continuously; but he hadn't worked out why he was there.

On his seventh visit to the bar, he had one of those chance encounters. A voice behind him said, "Dave, I didn't expect to see you here."

It was another varsity acquaintance, the Casanova of his class, James.

"Likewise, James."

"I'm a regular, but I've never seen you here before."

"You wouldn't have; it's my first time. A girl I met invited me, and I accepted because I was intrigued. However, I'm still unsure why she invited me; or why I'm here."

"I can explain both. These girls are out for a good time. To them, that means loud music, frenzied dancing, and too much alcohol. They aren't foolish and know they can get into serious trouble drinking too much with strangers, so the girls invite a man they know to come with them. When the club closes or your partner reaches the crawling stage, it's your job to ensure she's not left in the gutter. If she brought a big handbag, it's got her toothbrush and stuff in it, and she expects you to take her home with you.

"I call them 'tarts', but most are savoury tarts—delicious, harmless to your health, and enjoyable in bed.

"As for why she chose you, look in a mirror. You are big, well-built, and reasonable to look at, and she can proudly show you to her friends."

They talked a bit more. Dave asked, "Did you join the army, James? You intended to when we last saw each other."

His reply didn't invite further questions. "Yes, I've been in security since then."

So Dave left him at the bar. "See you, James; I must get these drinks back to the girls."

As the evening progressed, he learned that taking a break from the frenzied dancing was acceptable, so he tried to take as many as possible. Jenny and Margie spent their pauses in a tight cuddle in the corner with Pete and Henry, respectively, but Kurt, like Monica, preferred to exhaust himself in the jumping crowd, so Dave managed to speak to Fluffy. He found he could blank out the blasting sound when face to face; it didn't require shouting, just a louder-than-normal voice. It was like talking to a person as if you were hard of hearing; if you could see the other speaking, it focused the hearing and filtered out the surrounding din.

Dave caught himself from asking the stupid question, "Do you come here often?" Instead, he asked, "Why do you come here?"

"For the music."

"What do you like about it?"

"It's the beat that gets to me; it's transcendental; I forget where and who I am, and problems disappear."

Her reply was beyond his comprehension, so he changed tack. "Do you go to other clubs?"

"I lived in the south; my favourite club is there—breakbeat music—but now I live north, and it's too far to get home late."

"Don't you stay until daylight?"

"Not any more; I go home before the others, while I can still walk. Why did you come, Dave?"

"Because Monica asked. Before tonight, I had never been to a club."

"So you know nothing about techno music?"

"No."

"Then, any time you want a lesson, call me. You can take me to my old club; they play a selection. Have you got your phone?"

Dave produced it, and she added her number.

"Now come on, waste that bottled-up energy; let's dance!"

James had been right; Dave had to take Monica to his flat. She might have collapsed on the doorstep if he had put her in a taxi.

He almost had to carry Monica up the stairs; she made it into the toilet for a pee, then came out, her skirt and G-string dangling from one hand. Then she fell on the bed, half on and half off, and passed out. Dave wondered what to do; he worried she might puke during the night. He fetched the rubber sheet from his mother's bed, lifted Monica's legs and hips onto the bed, removed her top and bra to save them from vomit, and then rolled her onto the rubber sheet with her head sideways. Dave was impressed with what he saw.

He covered her with a sheet, put a bucket on the bedside table, took a blanket, and stretched out on the couch.

Dave was making coffee well after sunrise when Monica awoke and came to the kitchen, bleary-eyed, the sheet wrapped around her.

"Dave, did you undress me?"

"Yes, Monica. I thought you might wake and puke in the night. You passed out. Getting you onto the bed and the rubber sheet was an effort."

"You're a nice guy, Dave; I know you didn't touch me."

"Well, no more than I had to."

She sat on one of the two chairs, letting the sheet drop to her waist. "That's ok. Is that coffee ready yet?"

"In a minute. How do you like it?"

"Black, no sugar."

He gave her a cup, took one himself, and then straddled the other chair, unconsciously putting the chair back between them, while she sipped her coffee. He thought the view was better than a sunrise.

"Dave, I'm sorry I drank too much; I was hoping for a romantic end to the evening."

"So was I, but things don't always go the way you hope."

She finished her coffee in three gulps. "I need a shower; then I must go. Can I have the bathroom?"

"Of course."

She stood up, let the sheet fall to the floor, and then walked away. As she got to the bathroom door, she paused, turned sideways to look at him, and said, "Dave, if you want to call me and take me to dinner or something, I'll drink sparkling water."

Dave felt uncomfortable, thinking that when a beautiful naked woman says that to a man, he should answer, "How about dinner tonight?" But he felt Monica was handing him the lollipop he didn't get yesterday; they would have nothing to talk about at dinner. "I'll think about it, Monica," he said.

She was undoubtedly savoury; unfortunately, it didn't end as James had said.

Dave drank more coffee while she showered. She refused a taxi, so he let her out the front door and got an enthusiastic kiss.

"Thanks, Dave, you're a gem."

Dave went back to bed. He awoke after two hours with the image of a naked Monica still in his mind. It made him think about the girls in his life.

Before his sixteenth birthday, there had been none, his time taken up with study and the housework in the flat while his mother worked long hours. Then one or two kisses and a tentative grope when invited to a party, but he never had enough spare money to invite a girl out.

He had lost his virginity to a barmaid in the storeroom of an off-licence where he worked between school and university. She had cornered him, then taught him a thing or two.

His only durable affair had been with Angela, a veterinary

student. She seemed to think he had already decided to marry her, and she was not the kind of girl to parade naked in front of a man.

It had dragged on because vet students took much longer to qualify, while he had to earn a living, and then it had dwindled once he moved to London and BaVir; he supposed they hadn't been in love. Since then, apart from the brief affair with Tansy before his mother fell ill, he hadn't had a girlfriend.

Valerie was in a different category; she didn't count as a girlfriend. He cared for her but without passion. As he lay in bed, he remembered the first time he had been intimate with her.

The first Saturday after New Year's Day, he had played chess with her for the fifth time. Unlike the earlier games she had played with fury, this time he could sense she wasn't concentrating, and he beat her quickly.

When the game finished, although it wasn't yet eight pm, she said, "Dave, I need comforting. Please, take me home with you."

Dave interpreted comforting as sex, and Valerie was a nicely built woman. But he was wrong.

When they were at his flat, he said, "Val, let me find you a toothbrush."

"Thanks, Dave."

He took a new toothbrush to Valerie and then went into the bathroom. While he was brushing his teeth, Valerie came in and started to brush hers.

He went into the bedroom, stripped, and got into bed.

A few minutes later, a nude Valerie joined him.

He wrapped his arms around her. She snuggled tight, sighed, and then like turning off a switch, went to sleep. It left Dave in limbo, wondering what was wrong with her.

He realised then that nakedness was a way of getting closer, and he couldn't release her; she had her arms around him and was holding tight. He told himself, "*If she needs sleep so much, I can't wake her.*" So he fell asleep himself.

When he awoke, he looked at Valerie, slid off the bed, and went to the bathroom. When he returned, he found her still sleeping, so he slipped under the sheet beside her.

After eleven hours of sleep, she awoke and said, "Wait for me, Dave," and then went to the toilet.

She returned to snuggle in his arms. "Dave, I expect you would like an explanation?"

"Well, it would help me to understand you."

"Close your eyes; it will make it easier to tell you.

"I don't have a disease or anything weird. I went to sleep from exhaustion.

"I told you about the kids I must manage. Some of them are impossible. 'Rude', 'cheeky', 'insulting', and other words don't do them justice. The language they use is crude. They call me things like 'stupid cow'. And that's a polite one. 'Fucking bitch' is more common. It's almost impossible not to hit them, and I'm not allowed to do so. They know it and get pleasure from torturing me to make me strike them. Then they can complain, and I'll lose my job and never get another because a report goes to Social Work England.

"I can ignore the insults, but they say things to denigrate me, to make me feel I'm less than human; I won't repeat some of the things they say. Over days and weeks, I wonder if they aren't right, that I'm abnormal, somehow deformed. I sleep less and less, and then I desperately need someone to assure me I'm normal."

Dave kept his eyes closed. "Don't you have a boyfriend?"

"I've tried, but none of the men I've met want to stay with a mixed-up person like me."

"And why don't you change jobs, Valerie?"

"I'll have to; most child psychologists who deal with these

children can't stand the strain for long. But I have no idea what else I can do. I'm stuck because I don't want to move into a different field within child psychology. I've thought of being a career-guidance counsellor, for example, but I think it won't be long before the same problem happens again."

Dave had listened, not knowing what to say. Was she different today from how she had been at the first chess game? Hadn't they enjoyed their fun and telling each other about their lives? He knew now he had learned less about her than he had imagined. He had thought her his friend. Not more or less.

Dave opened his eyes. Her breast was close, so he leaned forward and ran his tongue around the nipple. She gasped. The response was immediate, so he took her nipple into his mouth. Their coupling took a long time.

Dave hadn't seen Valerie since.

When he saw what time it was, he concluded the evening with Monica had been educational and enjoyable. Much had been missing from his life, and he could try to do something about it, but there were other important things to do first.

He followed his usual Sunday routine. On the bus ride to the hospital, he realised the frustration of waiting for a message had gone when Monica told him about Kravitz.

Emily Tennant was sleeping on the third day of her chemo treatment, and Dave knew she would be out for up to eighteen hours each day as her body adapted to the poisonous drug, but he didn't leave. He sat in a chair beside her bed and held her hand for two hours. Sometimes, he let his mind wander to the past or an imaginary future; other times, although he didn't know if she heard, he spoke quietly to her about events in his life.

Talking about skating on his last visit to his mother had led him to think about that period. During his teenage years, he had been taller than any of the others in the gang. His being a gangling beanpole incapable of walking or running anywhere without bumping into things had been a handicap when they ghosted through darkened streets looking for mischief. So Dave had taught himself using the only affordable method—exercise. He ran in the streets—to school, to the shops—and lifted weights in the garden of a boy whose brother was a keen weightlifter. And Dave practised walking silently, melting into shadows, slowly at first, until he was better at it than the others, and they nicknamed him "The Shadow". When he left for university, he was the leader of the gang and had become its invisible and silent spy. Slowly, they became police informers, dropping a hint in a receptive ear whenever they spotted something they thought worth mentioning. They learned to like a copper who said, "Hello Tommy; nice evening tonight." It made them feel valued, and they had a lengthy list of tricks to stay out of trouble. A blow from a stevedore was inevitably painful.

He had also learned the dockside vocabulary and slang. However, at thirteen, he was often uncertain about the meaning of certain phrases, prudently not revealing his innocence until the expression "She's a tart" became clearer a year or two later in a dark street lined with women in tight skirts near the docks.

But he had escaped the port, followed the courses to a university degree, and then had begun work in a laboratory. It was tedious work, but he had continued his studies, and he became a member of the American Society for Clinical Pathology and eventually earned an appointment as Lab Manager at BaVir.

7

Meghan woke that Sunday thinking of Dave. She had enjoyed her Saturday with Hamish, although she wouldn't choose him as a date. He was a born politician, charming, and ready to expound on anything to keep a conversation going.

He never failed to call Meghan, for her family inevitably burdened him with goodies, and news, to deliver. She had learned that Rory had a new girlfriend named Kenna and deduced the family liked her.

"A nice quiet girl; good family," Hamish had said. "I don't know if she will calm Rory down, but one look at her voluptuous figure must have snared him."

Like she always did, her mother had sent a tin box of her homemade shortbread, and her father had sent her a bottle of Tullamore Dew, her favourite whisky, which she and Alice would drink. Meghan dreaded the day Hamish would present her with a haggis.

Between races, Hamish had told her about the various family members. When he mentioned her brother's latest passion, she remembered the intern, Barry, cut from the same cloth.

That evening, Hamish took her to a restaurant in Soho for

dinner; she thought it an arty place but realised, once Hamish had greeted one or two diners, that he had chosen it because of the political clientele.

Walking back to a taxi rank in the narrow streets, they passed the garishly lit Bang-Up Club; they could hear a muted-but-recognisable beat.

"I've never been in one of those clubs, Hamish."

"Well, I'm not taking you; you must be under twenty-five and wear earplugs, from what I've heard."

"Then I must get another man to take me."

"It's your funeral; if it doesn't make you deaf for life, you'll learn you're too old for that kind of club. I won't be the one responsible; I'm taking you home."

Meghan woke early. Lying in bed, she wondered if Dave would take her to a club. She thought he wouldn't—he was too calm and collected—but she didn't know him that well. She could ask.

She got up when she heard Alice in the kitchen. The only time she and Alice could relax, compare notes, and sort out housekeeping problems was on Sunday mornings at breakfast. They had agreed that Alice did their cooking, groceries, and other shopping, and Meghan did the rest, mostly cleaning and laundry, but there were always things that needed replacing or fixing. Their conversation became more personal after the bacon, scrambled eggs, and the week's job list.

"Have you seen Peter lately?" Alice asked.

"No, he said he would call, but he hasn't. I suppose he's still in Leicester doing a company audit."

"He's a dead loss; let him go and start looking."

"You might be right, but Peter and I haven't had much time to get to know each other, so maybe I should see him some more; he has interesting stories to tell and can be very funny."

"Has he asked you for sex yet?"

"No, I haven't encouraged him; we aren't even at the good-night kiss yet."

"Well, I would leave it at that; a man who can't find the time for you is not worth having."

"Are you still seeing Tim?"

"No, I broke it off."

"Why?"

"I spent a lot of time and effort working my way up to Third Assistant Chef, and I want to learn more. Tim's idea of the future is not mine. He might make a great husband for another woman, but I need someone who will partner with me in the kitchen, not with others in an office."

"How do you know?"

"I've been working out my recipe. Once you know what the ingredients are, you are ready to choose. A good husband is like a delicious meal; you will never have a good dish without the right high-quality ingredients. Just one bad one spoils it completely."

"No compromise?"

"Like with any dish, you can have different quantities, but not too much or too little of an ingredient."

"Don't you think that's limiting your choice too much?"

"Yes, the options are fewer, but no, because those I meet will already be my kind of person; I won't waste time finding out they aren't. I can check out ten definite possibles where I used to find one possible in ten."

Then Peter called.

"Meghan, it's Pete; I'm back in town for tonight. I must return to Leicester tomorrow. How about dinner?"

She agreed to seven-thirty pm.

Meghan's date started badly. Peter was outside the restaurant looking at his watch when she arrived only two minutes late. He tried to put his arms around her, with the clear intention of kissing her, but she pushed him back when she smelled a whiff of perfume on his jacket. She knew it at once, the unmistakable jasmine and neroli—Joy.

Peter led her to a secluded table, they chose from the menu, and then he set out to entertain her with stories about the people he had met during the last two weeks. The anecdotes were interesting, and some were funny, but when the meal began and Peter had his mouth full, Meghan had a chance to think.

She remembered what Alice had said earlier. Peter hadn't asked her anything about herself or her job. He had done all the talking; he wasn't interested in her. Yet, he only spoke about people he'd met but didn't say anything about himself, his colleagues, or what he did. He hadn't told her anything about his ambitions, past, or what he wanted in the future. He had *told* her he was an accountant, but he could be a clerk or a chauffeur.

Then she thought, *"I've only worked with Dave for a short while, and I know more about him than I do about Pete, and Dave knows more about me than Pete does."*

Peter realised he was getting nowhere as they finished their dessert, so he switched tactics. "Where would you live if you could live anywhere?"

"I don't know. I haven't thought about it. Where would you like to live?"

"Outside London, in the country, a house with a garden, roses, a swing for the kids. It could be anywhere, as I must travel to audits for the next ten or fifteen years. Wouldn't you like something like that?"

She felt disgusted by his obvious ploy. *Did he think her a simpering fool with tits? Only suitable for pleasing him in bed?*

"That sounds like every girl's dream," she replied.

"Would you like to share it with me?"

Her stomach turned. "I must think about it."

"Then please do. The restaurant wants to close; they do so early on Sundays. We must go."

As they walked towards the door, Pete put his arm around Meghan and said, "We could have a dream life. Will you come to my place tonight?"

Meghan felt a wave of nausea and removed his arm from around her as they stepped outside. "If you want sex tonight, I think you should go back to Leicester and your girlfriend who wears Joy perfume. There may be a late train. I'm sorry for her; you're an untrustworthy, egotistical liar. Don't bother calling me again."

She turned and walked away, leaving him open-mouthed.

It was still early when Meghan returned to the flat, so Alice was not back from the restaurant. Sundays, Alice worked a long day to let the married staff have a day with their families. Meghan made a cup of cocoa while waiting for her …

"Meg, why are you asleep in the kitchen?"

Meghan woke with a start. "Oh! Hi Ally. I made a cup of cocoa and fell asleep."

"And where's Pete?"

"I've no idea; I told him never to call."

"Tell me; I like juicy stories."

Meghan did.

"Good for you," Alice said. "I didn't like him, though I only met him once. Now you are free of him. Dave is a much better bet."

"You haven't met him, not even once."

"I don't need to; I can tell."

"How?"

"By the look in your eyes when you mention him."

"I told you—he's not going to have an affair with a colleague at work."

"Perhaps not, but would he marry one?"

Meghan's mind felt around the question. It would be nice if she could answer yes, but no, he was off-limits, but ...

"No, at least ... Not now."

"Then wait. You know he's worth it; the good ones are worth a wait."

8

Dave was cheerful when Meghan arrived at the lab and spoke to him.

"Good morning, Dave. We must recruit a DNA technician."

"Why?"

"For two reasons. If it's not permanently available, we can't offer a DNA service, and I might be away or ill. Also, if it's successful, I won't be able to do both QA and DNA."

"Ok, go and see Emma. Tell her I agree."

Dave had thought carefully about the American lab after visiting his mother. He had re-read the equipment list and decided he might be able to use what he'd learned about the American company to BaVir's advantage. When he entered the building, he didn't change to enter the lab; instead, he went to see Philip Jones.

At Philip's offices, Dave greeted Mrs Peterson and asked, "Can I get a word with Mr Jones before I go to the lab?"

"I'm sure you can, Mr Tennant. He should be here any minute. Take a seat ... Tell me, how's your new QA lady doing? I met her last week; she seems highly intelligent and quite pretty."

"Intelligent, yes, beautiful—especially when she smiles—and

very definite about things; she bit my head off the first day because I called her 'Ms'."

"Good for her; I think it's stupid when you know if a woman is 'Miss' or 'Mrs'. But are you getting along?"

"Yes, we are; she's very keen on her work and ready to help with anything. She certainly knows more about QA than I do."

Philip Jones came in at that moment. "Good morning to you both. Dave, I'm surprised to see you here."

"I wanted a quick word, sir, before changing for the lab."

"Well, come in then."

As they went into the office, Philip asked, "Is it about the complaint?"

"No, that's progressing normally; we've proved we didn't make a mistake, and we will receive another sample on Friday to do a final check."

Philip sat down behind his desk, and Dave took a seat opposite.

"Then what is it?" Philip asked.

"I was offered a job last week for the position of Director of Operations at a lab, and I went to an interview to get more details." Before alarming Philip any more, Dave explained that he was not interested in the new job.

Philip carefully kept his face neutral as he asked, "Aren't you happy here? Or did you go for interest's sake?"

"Interest's sake. I'm not looking for another job. It was only a first interview, and we didn't get to the salary negotiation stage."

"Then why tell me?"

"Because I think the lab is in trouble and will be closing. They gave me a list of their equipment. Some of the items would help with advanced procedures. The lab is in Belgravia."

"The American crowd?"

"Yes."

"I agree; now that the mass of Covid tests has dried up, they may fold. Do you have the equipment list with you now? And what interests you?"

Dave produced the list from his pocket and handed it to Philip. "Particularly the cell counter, sir. Currently, to count cells, we must look at a slide under a microscope and tally them manually. The eyepiece of the microscope has a reticle that allows us to see the cells through a grid of crosshairs. We count the cells in each grid square, then add them up. However, with cell counters, once you've identified the cell you're looking to count, the machine automatically tallies all the other identical cells. As you know, this will help us with some of our processes, such as when we must find the concentration of cells in a sample, giving us valuable information about a patient's health. The machine will help us get faster, more accurate results."

"Thanks, Dave. I'll pass it on to the right person and try to get you the cell counter."

Dave left Philip's office, changed, and began his Monday paperwork routine. He didn't see Meghan, so he assumed she was in the DNA lab.

When he finally finished the paperwork, he entered the DNA lab just before lunch to see how Meghan was doing. She was standing in front of a bench with cupboards on the wall behind it. The doors were wide open, and what looked like a hundred bottles of all sizes were on the worktop.

He stood at the door watching as she looked at a list, then selected a bottle and ticked it off.

As Meghan reached up to place the bottle carefully on the highest cupboard shelf, Dave was grateful there was no one else there. Lab coats made it impossible to identify the shape of the person hidden inside, at the most displaying a fleeting teasing crease when moving—a sexless environment. As Meghan reached up, raised on her toes, and leaned forward, he couldn't drag his eyes away from the way the coat, trapped between her and the edge of the worktop, tightened over her butt.

He was about to leave the lab, thinking Meghan hadn't seen him, but he hadn't noticed a mirror on the door; she had spotted him the moment he walked in.

With her feet squarely on the ground again, she stepped back, without turning, and asked, "Dave, what are you staring at?"

"Your feet."

She turned to face him. "What's wrong with my feet?"

"Nothing, they are nice feet, and the spider thinks so too."

Meghan jumped back, looking down. "Spider?"

"He's gone now, under the cupboard."

Meghan turned to look straight at him as he stepped towards her; he could see the laughter in her eyes.

"You caught me that time," Meghan said. "That's the best excuse from a staring man I've heard."

"Thanks, I'll add it to my book of excuses."

"Dave, you were about to leave the lab without saying anything. Why?"

"I thought I should."

"I can see you need lessons in sexual harassment. Looking at a girl's backside is not sexual harassment."

"Then what is?"

"Saying anything about it or grinning and licking your lips. Moaning and saying something like, 'Oh my God,' or 'What a beauty.'

"Oh yes, touching—definite harassment."

"Well, I didn't do any of those, so I'm clear, right?"

"Yes, but you must answer my question." Her eyes twinkled as she asked, "Did you like what you saw?"

"Are you fishing for a compliment? I only saw your back. I can gladly say you didn't look like an ice lolly."

Meghan laughed, a pleased laugh. "Next time you want to stare, don't be afraid of a comeback; most girls love it, and I won't complain—I'll tell you first if you cross a line." She added, "Where were you this morning?"

"I went to tell Philip about a job offer I received last week."

Meghan was shocked, she felt her skin was cold, and she was sure she had blanched.

Dave noticed that Meghan had paled, and assumed she might faint, so he reached out and put his arms around her. "Meg, what's wrong?"

For half a minute, Meghan remained with her head on his shoulder, leaning against him. She mumbled into his shoulder, "I've just started a new job, and you're telling me my new boss might be leaving."

Dave had to concentrate; the feeling of the two soft bumps against his chest and the smell of Meghan's hair distracted him. "I said job *offer*; I didn't say I had got a new job."

Meghan felt better. "If anyone comes in, we are in a compromising position."

"Bugger that; holding you is super. Do you feel better?"

She stepped out of his arms. "Much better. Are you leaving us?"

"No, but I think the lab I interviewed for will close, and they have some excellent apparatus. I went to tell Philip about it and put in my bid for a cell counter if BaVir buys their equipment."

Meghan felt a flood of relief.

"Did you enjoy the horseracing?" Dave asked her.

"Oh yes, and I bet on three horses that Hamish said were sure things. Two lost, but the third got my money back. That was exciting. We had dinner in Soho, and Hamish told me about my family."

"Oh, I didn't know he was from Scotland."

"Well, it's a Scots name, but I should have said he's my brother-in-law; he married my sister, Ella. He works for the Scottish National Party. My family always asks him to deliver goodies to me. He usually returns on a Friday but has a meeting today and will fly back tonight."

Dave wondered why he felt relieved.

Meghan then asked, "And you, Dave? Did you have a good weekend?"

For a moment, her question flustered him; he couldn't tell her about Monica.

"Mixed. I went to a nightclub in Soho and met a friend from my university days; he told me some interesting stuff. Then on Sunday, I made my weekly visit to my mother in the hospital."

As he had hoped, his statement about his mother diverted Meghan from asking for more details about the nightclub.

"Is your mother ok?" Meghan asked.

"She has cancer. Last Friday, she started a new chemo course, so she wasn't very talkative."

"Oh, you should have told me. Does she like having visitors?"

"Yes, when she's between treatments and isn't exhausted. Unfortunately, that's likely to be less frequent as the months roll on. Her oncologist is hardly encouraging as to the outcome."

"Tell me when you think she's well enough; I would love to come with you."

Then Meghan thought, *"There might be another job offer, and I'll only learn about it after Dave accepts,"* so she added, "and if you go for another job interview, tell me first."

"What, and spoil a chance to hold you in my arms again?"

"Well, I felt the blood drain from my face, but I would never have fainted—though it was a good excuse to be held by you." She winked.

It was only much later that Meghan wondered: *Had Dave been in the Bang-Up Club?*

Dave asked himself if Meghan had been in the restaurant next door.

Meghan made her weekly visit to the laundromat and wasn't surprised to find Barry Dickens. Visibly, she thought, *not waiting for her.*

He told her about his thoughts on specialisation; she decided he was either hoping for guidance or thought asking for help was a good ploy. He invited her for a coffee next door after their washing had dried. She accepted, then after half an hour told him that only he could decide on which specialisation to follow, and she had to go.

The advert announcing a new DNA-technician job appeared on the company noticeboards, and Jennifer, carrying a file folder, came to see Meghan.

"Yes, Jennifer?"

"Please, can I apply for the DNA job, miss?"

"Do you meet the qualifications, or do you want training?"

Jennifer handed Meghan the file, and Meghan paged through it in amazement. Jennifer had several certificates proving her competence.

"What sequencing machine did you use?"

"There should be a certificate in the folder for the one in your lab."

"Does Mrs Thompson know about these?"

"No, miss. I didn't think to tell her."

"Jennifer, *always* tell your employer about every training course you take and every formal qualification you achieve. You might study for pleasure, but if you don't tell your employer, how can we help your career? Now see Mrs Thompson and show her your file."

Later, Emma called. "Meg, do you want Jennifer?"

"Yes. She suits perfectly."

"Then I'll have to find a replacement for her current position; that will be easier."

Dave enjoyed his walk to work. The weather was milder than in previous weeks, and the sun shone from a blue sky. It augured well for the weekend; the Met Office forecast was as cautious as ever: expecting no rain tomorrow or during the weekend.

Everyone at work seemed cheerful, and when Meghan reported that the new lab was complete and they could move offices on Monday, Dave thought it was a perfect day.

Then she added something unexpected: "The electron microscope is up and running. I've done all the tests and calibrations. The suppliers can come and sign it off next week."

"Shouldn't you have done the DNA stuff first?"

"It's nearly finished. The microscope is a lot more fun, and I thought it might be helpful for Mr Kravitz's new sample."

"Meg, Mr Kravitz's sample will arrive late today from Doctor Morrison; the medical courier phoned and apologised about the lateness. I don't have anything scheduled, so I'll stay to receive it, place it in the blood-temperature store and come tomorrow to analyse it."

"Not without me, I hope."

"Do you want to spend *another* Saturday morning in the lab?"

"Definitely, and I'm going to look at slides of it under the microscope."

They completed the analysis on Saturday and found the results were identical except for a slight improvement since the last one.

"That proves it," Dave said, "there is remission."

Meghan replied, "I'll make slides from the sample and look at them."

She entered the new lab, prepared several slides stained in assorted colours, then put the first one under the scope and fiddled with the controls.

"Wow, there's a bacterial soup here. Look at the screen."

"Can you identify any of them?" Dave asked after taking a look.

"Not right away; I only know the most common ones. I'll take a photo of each slide and then compare them with data from the web. I can access my alma mater's database; I still have the password to log into the university's system."

"Will you do that now?"

"No, I'll do it at home tomorrow. I've got a hairdresser appointment now and a date tonight. I'll email the photos to both of us."

She busied herself with the task, then ten minutes later said, "There, you can also try to find out what they are. I must go."

Dave looked at the photos on his screen and then decided there was no reason to stay in the lab, so he went home and started again. Ten minutes later, he found he couldn't concentrate; he was thinking of Meghan, where she was going and who with. With a feeling of rebellion, he thought, *"If she can go off on a date, so can I,"* so he called Monica.

"Hello, Monica Beasley speaking."

Her voice sent a shiver down his spine. "Hi Monica, I thought I would call to ask you out for dinner."

"When, Dave?"

"Well, I suppose you are out clubbing tonight, so let me know when."

"I was to babysit for my sister tonight, but that has been cancelled. I don't have any plans. Tonight is ok."

"Great. I'll meet you in front of Ravenscourt Park Station. When can you get there?"

"Eight-thirty?"

"See you then."

Dave returned to the computer with renewed energy.

9

Meghan met Rory in the lobby of the hotel near Heathrow where he was staying for a conference. Like many siblings, they had clashed over anything and everything during their childhood and teenage years. Meghan had once thought that being an elder sister who didn't withhold a rebuke when it was necessary was an insult to the male ego. Nevertheless, they remained firm friends, and when she had left home, the fighting had died down, but she thought wryly, *"He now thinks he can give orders."*

Over a coffee, they discussed Kenna. Hamish had not told her much more than that Kenna was likeable, and Meghan wanted to know more. Rory waxed loud and long over her virtues and then, as his monologue ended, asked, "What about you? Any men on your horizon?"

"None at all. I had an accountant interested but cut him off when I decided he was a liar. Since then, no one."

"You're not getting any younger; you don't have much time left if you want to marry and have kids. Kenna is two years younger than me, so we still have time to tie the knot."

"Don't repeat what Mother keeps saying. I know."

"So why haven't you got half a dozen possibles queued up?"

"Because, firstly, I've spent much of my time since varsity

studying. I love what I'm doing and what I'm learning. And secondly, the men I've met might be good matches for some women, but not for me; they all have ideas of a future that don't gel with mine."

She thought of Peter and added, "The last one wanted a country house with a swing for the kids."

"What's wrong with that?"

"His vision included me staying in the house while he went off around the country for years doing audits. I was to look after kids, and when he came home, to do his washing and ironing, feed him, and open my legs for his pleasure. If you think that's a good marriage, I don't."

"Then what is your vision?"

"I'm trying to work that out. What's yours?"

"Kenna and I have it planned; she's completed several commercial courses and one on small-business management. When Dad decides to retire, I'll take over our pharmacy. I'm sure that, between Kenna and I, we can successfully build it into something bigger.

"But it's *you* that Mum, Dad, and I are worried about."

"Well, leave me to work it out alone."

"Ok, but please remember, we must make compromises. All my life, I've been learning that. List the good and bad qualities of a suitor, and accept those less-important faults."

It was enough to trigger her anger. "Rory, tell Mum and Dad that I'll never marry, and they must rely on you to produce the next batch of grandchildren. The man who asks me to marry him must meet *all* my requirements. I refuse to make compromises.

"Meanwhile, I'm going to keep looking. You never know what's around the corner."

"Why so stubborn, Meg?"

"Because I've seen the results of a marriage founded on

compromise: it's either a life of misery or boredom for both partners, or it breaks up when one of them finds a better compromise. When I marry, I want to feel and know inside me that I haven't made any compromises and to believe my partner hasn't either."

"You're destined to be an old maid."

"Better that than a dishrag, Rory. Meanwhile, I'll get on with my job, where I can enjoy what I'm doing and not spend at least half of my time as a servant to a man who doesn't appreciate me."

"Well, you haven't changed; you're still the stubborn Scots lass. I wish you the best of luck. Is there not even one?"

Meghan was about to say no when she thought of Dave. "Maybe one. We like each other, and he might be the kind of man I want, but he's busy with other things."

On her way home on the Heathrow-to-Paddington express, she had fifteen minutes to consider what she had said. She liked Dave, but was he the kind of man she wanted? She felt he was, but she knew so little about him.

Dave booked a table at a restaurant, changed, and was at the station entrance at eight-twenty-five pm. He watched the people walking by until Monica slipped her arm under his and squeezed it. "Hi, big man, feed me. I'm starving."

He turned to look at her. She had her giant bag.

"Hi, Monica. How about steak?"

"Lead me to it."

Dave was surprised to find the conversation interesting. Relaxed and open, Monica told him about her life. He had only to ask something or prompt her with a word, and she happily told him about her family, friends, and the life she led. When he asked how she had got the job with Doctor Morrison, she gave him the whole story. O levels, a secretarial college, and an ex-boyfriend who had also been a doctor's receptionist. Dave asked about boyfriends, and she said, "I don't keep one more than a few days. I want to have fun before getting to babies' nappies, laundry, and housework. I must get rid of boyfriends before I feel obliged."

They had a pleasant meal, and then, as they were leaving the restaurant, she said happily, "I'm sober tonight; take me to your flat."

Dave found that he had got everything wrong. Monica didn't give him a lollipop as thanks for the last time. She had come for a reason he couldn't have imagined from his limited experience. When they entered the flat, she went into the bathroom and came out a few minutes later wearing only a wisp of perfume.

"Your turn, Dave."

Minutes later, he joined her in bed, where he learned she had come for simple animal ecstasy and lots of it. Not for lovemaking. Like a jockey at the Derby, she was determined to ride a horse to the winning post in every race.

After Monica left in the morning, Dave worked through his Sunday routine, after which he took the bus to the hospital. His mother was sleeping; he knew she wouldn't wake. He took her hand and sat beside her, feelings of despair creeping into his mind and disturbing his thoughts. *"If only I could talk to someone."*

He didn't believe she would hear him, but he told her anyway while sitting looking at his hand, holding hers. "Ma, I mentioned that I have researched cancer since your doctor diagnosed it; I didn't tell you that I'd almost given up hope a few weeks ago. I found nothing that might give a clue as to how to save you.

"But one has appeared out of nowhere; I have done the sample analyses of a cancer patient for years, and now, his cancer is in remission for no known reason.

"Let me tell you about Boris ..."

Talking to his mother as he had done hundreds of times before eased the burden and the despair; he convinced himself that success in saving her life was on the horizon.

"Good morning, Dave," Meghan said. "Did you manage to identify the bacteria?"

Dave didn't reply but looked at her, especially her eyes, for what seemed ages. "Is this your Monday disguise?"

"Not especially 'Monday', but do you like it?"

"I'm not sure whether you look like a vampire or as if you're just exhausted after a weekend debauch. It suits Monday, but isn't the makeup heavy on the dark eyes?"

"So you don't like it?"

"I didn't say that. I must admit, I like having a different girlfriend each day of the week."

"Ok, I'll tone it down next time. Now you didn't answer my question."

"I identified most of the bacteria, but there is one that seems impossible to name, and another I cannot find in the references."

"Let me guess—the impossible one looks like cholera, and the other has a squiggly tail."

"That's right; so you came to the same conclusion?"

"Exactly, now we must look at the older samples under the microscope. This guy has been somewhere and gotten infected. Can we get an idea of when?" She added, "The wee beastie with the tail needs a name; I suggest 'Spunky'."

"Meg, you have a depraved mind, although the bacterium does resemble a spermatozoon. The tail is like a corkscrew, so I propose 'Corky'. I could never sign a report in which anything is named 'Spunky'."

"Right, 'Corky' it will be, although you need to loosen up;

Spunky is a far more adventurous bacterium than Corky. Can we look at the slides today or after work?"

"No hurry. Let's look at the slides later."

Dave couldn't wait. He held off until after lunch and then asked Meghan, "If you have the time, we can look at those slides now."

She smiled. "So you can't wait either? I'll get the samples and make slides."

An hour later, they had the first slide on the microscope screen.

"These two are from the sample taken when he left the hospital."

They studied them carefully. "Not a sign of Corky or cholera, Meg."

"I'll switch to the slides for the three-month analysis."

Fifteen minutes later, Meghan said, "Not a sign of them here."

"Agreed, switch to the six-month sample."

It took only seconds for Meghan to say, "Here they are: visibly fewer Corkys and more cholera than in the nine-month sample. What does that mean?"

"The Corkys are multiplying, and the cholera is dying away."

"Well, call Doctor Morrison. We need to meet Kravitz. He got infected three to six months after terminating treatment."

Dave made the phone call. "Monica, it's Dave. Can I speak to Doctor Morrison?"

"Indeed, Mr Tennant, I'll put your call through."

Dave felt miffed by the "Mr Tennant" but guessed he was now part of the discard pile. Then he thought he should be grateful; Monica had taught him a lot and cut off any relationship before it became painful.

Had he made a mistake calling Monica by her first name? Meghan had shown surprise. He hoped Meghan didn't think he was having a relationship with Monica.

"Good afternoon, Mr Tennant," Doctor Morrison answered.

"Doctor, can you arrange a meeting with Mr Kravitz? His analysis proves not only that he has cancer remission but also that he has a variation of a cholera bacterium and something else. We would like to know where he got it."

"Does it have anything to do with cancer?"

"We have no idea, Doctor, but we at once impose strict precautions when an unknown bacterium pops up in lab analysis. Cancer or not, we must find out what it is, where it comes from, and what it does."

"I can appreciate that; it sounds bad and dangerous. I'll call him at once. I think he's still in London. Thank you, I'll let you know."

Meghan and Dave were both in their new office when Doctor Morrison called back at five pm.

They listened as the doctor, on speakerphone, explained that Mr Kravitz could make a meeting at five-thirty pm on the coming Wednesday.

"Can you make it, Meg?" Dave asked.

"I wouldn't miss it for anything," Meghan replied.

Dave confirmed the meeting, thanked the doctor, and hung up.

Meghan considered going to the laundromat on a different day to avoid Barry, but then she thought, "*What the hell? I can do what I want.*"

Barry was there. He changed his tactic this time; he asked Meghan what she was doing at work. She explained she was trying to identify two bacteria. She didn't say why.

"Where have you searched?"

She gave him a list of sites she had tried.

"What about London University?"

"I don't have access. I would have to go there to register."

"Well, I do, so if you want to search on that site, we can do so."

Meghan looked at him sideways. "In your room?"

"No, it's your search; you decide."

"Well, I have the photos in my flat, and my flatmate is home, so I reckon we're more likely to get some work done there. Let me call Ally and see if she can feed us both."

When Meghan asked her on the phone, Alice didn't disappoint.

Meghan and Barry waited for their dryers to finish their cycles, collected their laundry, and then walked up the road to the flat.

Barry flattered Alice's chicken fricassee several times, and then he and Meghan huddled over Meghan's laptop as Barry logged in to London University.

They started with the cholera bacteria, reading one paper after another. An hour later, Alice went out; she had a date with an assistant chef who had come off shift.

Another hour later, Meghan said, "Yes! Look at this."

The research paper was about cholera in West Africa. Endemic in the area, the bacteria flared up from time to time, but the researcher declared the population had a high resistance to minor infections. The author had not identified why. He did state the cholera bacterium differed from the more common, endemic variant. The bacterium shown in the electron micrograph seemed identical to that in Meghan's photo.

"Yippee!" yelled Meghan. "That deserves a scotch."

One drink became three, and Barry got a kiss for his help.

Then another. Then Meghan thought, "*What the hell? I haven't had a roll in the hay for years.*"

Barry left, promising to research the other bacterium. Meghan felt a little guilty about the escapade but shrugged it off. She had no desire to bed Barry again.

Alice made breakfast in silence.

After ten minutes, Meghan said, "Ally, if you have something to say, then say it."

"You slept with him, didn't you?"

"Not exactly; we went to bed but didn't sleep, then he went home."

"Are you proud of yourself? He's a kid."

"Not a kid; he's twenty-six and will be a qualified doctor in six months. I'll admit I don't fancy him and won't take him to bed again, but I've not had a man in my bed for more than a year. Why are you upset?"

"I thought you were hot on Dave."

"I think so too, but it seems like a one-way street. I'm sure Dave likes me, and if I offered, like most men, he would come to my bed like a shot. But we work together. If we start, it must be long-term, or one of us must leave BaVir. Dave won't; he needs the lab for his research, and I don't want to; I'm enjoying the job. So it's better if we don't get involved."

Mollified, Alice asked, "And he's not ready for the long term?"

"I don't think so; he keeps the other lab girls and me at a polite arm's length. The other day, I caught him admiring my bum, but he wouldn't touch."

"Well, that's a good sign. But why's he not ready?"

"His mother. She's a cancer patient. Dave visits her in the hospital every Sunday, and he is committed to trying to save her. I think he'll only be ready when she gets better or passes away."

"You can't fight that, but Barry and his like are not for you."

"No, they're not, but they provide a distraction—" she smiled, "—and enjoyable exercise."

Philippa called. "Hello Meg, how are you? And how's the new job?"

"Fine, Philippa, I enjoy the challenge and have no complaints."

"I must ask: Are you still seeing Peter?"

"No, I've cut him off. It took some time to learn he's not what he appears; I don't like what he is. Why do you ask?"

"I'm glad you have done; I was worried you might be having a full-on affair."

"By 'full-on', I suppose you mean sleeping with him. I didn't let him get beyond a good-night peck in the street. He might be charming, but he's not what he manages to project."

"That's a relief; it makes it easier to tell you he has another young woman in Leicester. Craig says she's under eighteen, and she's pregnant. It's creating a stink—her parents want to sue for child support, and the company is not happy. I was dreading having to tell you."

"Thanks, Philippa, I'll remember you cared. Pete told me he was a chartered accountant; is that true?"

"No, he did a BCom. He works as an accountant but has not done articles, so he's very junior."

"I suspected as much."

"I'm holding a dinner party on Friday. Craig's new colleague, Colin Sturgeon, has just transferred from Scotland, and Craig is showing him the ropes. Three of their colleagues are coming with their wives, but it looks like Colin doesn't have a date. That makes an odd number, so I thought of you to even it up. If you can, would you like to join us?"

"Philippa, one good turn deserves another; it'll be a pleasure."

"I didn't do anything; you did it yourself."

"Yes, but you were ready to tell me."

Meghan thought doing a favour for Philippa was a minor, one-off thing ...

10

Monica was behind her desk when Dave and Meghan arrived at the surgery.

"Good evening, Mr Tennant." She was professional in her greeting, apart from a pleasing smile. Dave thought someone greeting you with "Mister" was problematic when they've seen you stark naked.

Meghan noted Monica's use of "Mr Tennant" and thought, *"Dave was just being friendly to her on the phone the other day."*

Monica didn't open the door for them this time around.

Doctor Morrison introduced them to Boris Kravitz, a tall, lean man with a severe expression whose body language conveyed worry as he fidgeted with his hands and crossed his arms to try and hide his agitation.

Dave took out a photo of the Corky bacteria from a folder and held it up as he explained how he and Meghan had named it. "When we saw it, we needed a name for it, so we adopted 'Corky' because of the corkscrew tail; we haven't found a reference to it in the literature, so we don't know what it is or does and whether it's contagious. In contrast, cholera is usually infectious. We found cholera bacteria in the sample, but they seem slightly different from the normal strain. There is one research paper that mentions them.

"Mr Kravitz, where did you go three to six months after terminating treatment, where you might have caught it?"

Boris took a small diary out of his pocket and paged through it. "Except for one-day trips to European airports, I went to Burkina Faso in West Africa four months after stopping treatment."

Dave asked him about who he had met and worked with and whether anyone had been sick or off work, but he answered in the negative.

Meghan, in her forthright manner, took the bull by the horns. "Infection can occur through the exchange of bodily fluids, and sex is a well-known mechanism. HIV is the most famous example of this. Mr Kravitz, it's your well-being, future, and possibly the health of millions that hangs in the balance. If you can remember anything that might have happened to give us a clue, say so."

Boris appeared guilty or ashamed. "Knowing one will die in the not-too-distant future is an excuse to throw all the normal constraints out the window. I went each night to a small local bar near the airport. I bought several drinks for a hostess on the first night, and after three rounds, she said bluntly, 'You pay me one hundred dollars, and I fuck you.' I took her back to my hotel room."

"Did you use a condom?"

"Why should I bother, miss? Aids takes more time to develop than I have left to live."

"Did you have sex only once?"

Boris sheepishly answered, "I was there alone for more than two weeks, training local maintenance staff. Although I got invitations on some nights to have dinner with local colleagues, on other nights, I was alone and went to the bar. I had sex five or six times."

"Always with the same girl?"

"All except the last time. I had sex with a different woman who said the hostess was unclean; I think she meant the first woman was having her period."

With them having exhausted the possible leads, Dave said, "It has been a helpful meeting, thank you. We'll continue by analysing your next samples. We'll also try to find out more about Corky from universities in Africa."

After Boris left, Dave asked Doctor Morrison to include a spinal-fluid sample in the following three-month samples.

"I'll do so if Boris agrees. I'd also like to suggest publishing something in the journal *Oncology*. Doctors involved with cancer worldwide subscribe, and help might come from anywhere."

"I agree, Doctor, that's an excellent idea. Meg and I will draft a report for your approval."

"Mr Tennant, you should split it into two reports and call them 'interim statements', since there are no conclusions to report," Doctor Morrison said. "The first will announce the cancer remission with no known cause. I'll co-sign it. The editor will put it in the 'Interesting Case Reports' section.

"Then the second will announce these bacteria. I'm afraid the scientific world will react negatively; many will laugh at the merest suggestion a bacterium can affect cancer, so you will likely get slated as an ignoramus."

Meghan drafted a report and sent it to Doctor Morrison, who made some changes and returned it. Dave took it to Philip Jones for permission to submit.

"Why, Dave; what does it do for us?"

"Sir, it gives Doctor Morrison a boost in his reputation, which is good for us, and, if anything comes out of our investigation, we will undoubtedly enhance our reputation. But if we don't publish, I think we're legally required to notify the Ministry of Health, and they are likely to close the lab until they have fully checked our safety precautions."

"Have you taken any?"

"Of course, sir, I've separated all the samples from the patient into separate storage. Only Meg and I have keys, and we wear appropriate gear when we do analyses. I don't think the cholera bacterium is a problem. Meg found a paper saying it's an endemic form in West Africa, and indeed, in Kravitz, it doesn't seem to be multiplying; why, I don't know."

"Ok, submit the article."

"Thank you, sir; the article should appear in the next issue of *Oncology*; it is short and doesn't need to be peer-reviewed, so it will be a helpful filler in the May edition."

As Dave was packing up for the day, he asked Meghan, "Is it too late to book a horseracing date with you?"

"Not at all; I've nothing planned for Saturday, but let me first check if there is racing somewhere."

After three minutes of looking at The Jockey Club site, she said, "Yes, at Kempton Park. That's not too far, near Weybridge. We could go by bus, but it takes nearly two hours. We should be there by one-thirty if we don't want to miss the first race."

"I can drive us there."

"Do you have a car?"

"No, but I'll hire one for the weekend. I'll pick you up at Chelsea Common at twelve. Afterwards, can you join me for dinner?"

"Yes, I'd love to; I'll book a table at a restaurant near my flat for seven."

When Philippa introduced her to Colin, Meghan's first impression of him was of a striking man, possibly nearing forty. Chestnut-brown hair, brown eyes, and a pale, unblemished face. He was no taller than Meghan, and her heels weren't high. Meghan thought he carried too much weight. Due, she felt sure, to a lack of exercise. His voice seemed younger; the extra fat might be deceiving.

Meghan wasn't impressed with his handshake; his hands were soft, and the shake was not a firm positive, but his smile seemed to light up his face.

"'Meghan', a nice Scots name. Do people call you 'Meg'? I know Philippa does."

"Yes, Colin, I've had to bear it since childhood, when the kids called me 'Meg the Peg'."

"Were you skinny?" He looked her up and down. "You aren't now."

"Yes, like most little girls, I was. And suggesting I'm fat is a statement that will land you in court for sexual harassment."

He laughed. "I'm qualified to argue my way out of it."

"Colin, any relation to Nicola Sturgeon?"

"No, Meg, no connections with the country's leading lady. I've avoided investigating my family's past, frightened to find that my forebears invested in slavery."

"That's a shame; I would have liked to introduce you to Hamish, my brother-in-law, who works for the Scottish National Party."

"You still can; I'd like to meet him."

Meghan had a funny thought: she remembered a scene from an old black-and-white Agatha Christie film in which the character Sir Wilfrid Robarts, played by Charles Laughton, was in a courtroom, dressed in his barrister's gown and wig. Colin would look just like him in twenty years.

Philippa seated them together. By the end of the meal, Meghan had learned the difference between commercial and criminal law. Colin was in the commercial branch of the law firm, and he often worked with accountants, especially when it came to mergers.

As they were preparing to leave, Colin said, "I've enjoyed the evening, Meg. Would you give me your number? I would like to invite you out sometime."

"I will, Colin, but I'm a working girl, all week and often Saturdays. What about you?"

"I can't go out during the week; lawyers work late, and they must spend too much time sitting in courtrooms and do their work afterwards. But a Friday or Saturday evening, perhaps?"

Meghan was reluctant; something about Colin's behaviour disturbed her. Nothing that she could pin down. "Well, you can try, Colin."

Alice came home after work at eleven-thirty pm.

"Hello Meg, how was the dinner?"

"I met a lawyer. I don't know much about him. He must be between thirty-five and forty, although he looks forty. He's quite handsome and wants to call me for a date. I'm going to the horseraces at Kempton Park tomorrow with Dave."

"Now, *that* I approve. You know my opinion. Don't bother with a lawyer, a doctor, or an accountant; don't waste your time. I should say nothing, but you will never be happily attached to a lawyer, married or not."

"Ally, if I can continue doing what I like, why should it matter? And I told you, Dave is off-limits."

"Continue then, find out about your lawyer, his life, and what he likes and dislikes, and then ask yourself if you want to live your life with him or with a man who loves doing what you love doing. For me, the answer is as clear as a bell."

"Dave, have you chosen a horse for the next race?" Meghan asked.

"Yes. April Rain."

"But that's twenty-five to one; it will never come in the first three."

"I like the name; if it wins, it will rain money on me."

"You have a lot to learn about horseracing. Take a tip. Bet on one of the lowest odds for a place or show. You might only break even over the day, but that's better than losing."

"I'll give the horse some encouragement."

"It's your money. Let's place our bets, then get back to our seats."

After the last horse crossed the finish line, Meghan stopped jumping up and shouting. April Rain had won.

"Dave, how much did you bet?"

"A hundred quid."

"My God. Win or place?"

"Win."

"So you've won more than two thousand pounds. Did you know something I don't?"

"No, promise. But I do know today's date."

"What's that got to do with it? It's April ... oh hell. April Fool's Day. You've been pulling my leg; I'll bet you didn't put anything on April Rain."

"What will you bet? How about four more horserace-and-dinner dates?"

Meghan was delighted. "Ok, show me your tickets."

He had three: his other two bets had come second and third. He *had* bet a hundred but had split it.

"I'll never bet you anything ever again."

"Never say never. I knew I had won when you made the bet. So I'll let you off."

"No, you won't. You won, and I'm glad you did; I get four dates."

"Win or lose; I wanted those dates."

"I thought you had never been to a horserace?"

"Quite true, but betting on the horses is a docker's third-favourite sport."

"And the others are?"

"Football is second."

"And first is?"

"The biggest thrill of all: sex."

Meghan, disconcerted, said, "I shouldn't have asked."

"Let's go and collect our winnings; I have enough now to pay for the dinners."

They were queuing at the booth when Dave noticed two young women a few places ahead of them. Dave thought he recognised the back of Angela. She was with a tall redhead, a striking figure wearing an outlandish dress and a large straw hat.

He had almost decided it was not Angela when she turned, saw him, and waved with a broad smile.

When he and Meghan had collected their winnings, he had no choice but to introduce Meghan to Angela, who was waiting for them, along with her companion.

"Meghan, meet Angela, an old flame from university days."

"Dave and Meghan, this is Susan, my partner in our veterinary practice," Angela said, then continued, "Can you join us for tea? I'd like to know what you've been doing since I last saw you, Dave."

The tea was awkward. Meghan said little as she studied the two women. Dave told them something about his progress to BaVir, and that he and Meghan were doing research work. Finally, they split up as the loudspeakers announced the next race. Meghan said she was not betting on the race, so Dave stayed with her as the others went off to a bookie.

"You told me Angela was your steady. Did you have sex with her?"

"If you must know, yes. However, we didn't have a passionate affair. Why do you ask?"

"Because she's now lesbian or bisexual. Susan is possessive."

"I didn't notice."

"You were looking at Angela, so you wouldn't have."

As they left the racecourse in a crush of punters, Dave felt someone come from behind and push something into his jacket pocket. He turned and saw Susan standing behind him. Angela was standing nearby.

"We thought we should say goodbye," Susan told him. "It's been a pleasure meeting you. Angela told me all about you. Can we get together with you and Meghan for dinner and something one day?"

"We might do, but we're on opposite sides of London now, and I've not set foot in Medway since I left. I wouldn't recognise it now."

"Oh, it hasn't changed that much. Goodbye, Dave; bye, Meghan."

The two women, holding hands, turned towards the train station exit as Meghan and Dave went out into the car park.

"I see what you mean now," Dave said to Meghan.

"Can I come to see your mother tomorrow?"

"She'll be sleeping. Perhaps another Sunday."

Dave took her home after dinner, parked his car a short distance from her door, and walked with her there.

"Dave, it's been a wonderful day, thank you."

"It's been super, Meg; it took my mind off everything. I could kiss you, but better not."

"Why not?"

"Because a kiss is a promise, and I can't make promises at the moment."

Meghan felt hurt but said, "I understand."

"Then you understand me more than I understand myself. Good night, Meg."

Meghan watched him walk away; the hurt had become sorrow.

11

After Dave got home, he fished in his pocket and found a folded slip with a telephone number, so he took his mobile out to add the contact. His hand stopped as he felt a small device—his old clamshell phone; compact, discreet, and modified by Tansy so that the battery lasted a month. It could only do calls and SMS messages, but it was off the electronic map, as it had a pay-as-you-go SIM card that Dave had bought in a supermarket when he was fifteen. Very few people knew the number. He carried it constantly, for someone might be in trouble one day. He removed his regular smartphone from another pocket and added the new number.

Dave followed his Sunday routine; repeating the tasks each week gave him the illusion that his mother would still be alive the following week. Although this time, a thought intruded when he was on the bus: *I would have liked it if Meghan was here with me now.*

Emily slept, and Dave sat and held her hand; despair grew again. He decided to tell her about the research.

"Ma, I told you about Boris; now I can tell you we have found some odd bacteria in his blood. We don't yet know what the bacteria do, but they are the only difference between Boris and an ordinary cancer patient.

"If we can find out what they are and what they do, perhaps we can save you. We have some clues."

Dave stopped. The despair had taken a step back as something from far deeper rose and gave it a smack. "*I said 'we'. Am I including Meg? Ma doesn't know about her, but it feels right.*"

"I said 'we', Ma, because a young woman has come to work in my lab; her name is Meghan MacDougal, and she's a microbiologist." He thought: "*Ma's a woman; she would want to know what Meg's like.*"

"She's got reddish-blonde hair, green eyes, and a lovely figure. She's slightly shorter than me and has the sweetest smile. But she's got a temper, Ma; I must be careful what I say. Meghan knows much more about DNA and bacteria than I do, so I hope we can solve the problems together.

"Trouble is, Ma, that we can't get too close, although I want to; I must keep our relationship professional, else BaVir will fire one of us. If they fired me, I couldn't continue the research, and I can't allow them to fire her; that would be unfair, as she loves the job too much."

"*Did Ma squeeze my hand?*"

Dave looked up at her face; was she smiling faintly?

Later, during his evening run in the park, it came again. "*Meghan could've been here running with me.*"

It rained the following day.

Dave accepted it as the other side of the coin he had won by betting on April Rain.

The phone rang at two pm. "Dave, William Morrison here."

Dave was immediately alarmed by the call. "Doctor, is there something wrong?"

The reply was a relief.

"Not at all; I'm calling to ask if you and Meghan could attend a conference on Wednesday afternoon at the Princess Margaret

Hospital. There are two visiting oncologists presenting papers. I'm not a regular attendee, but I thought if I took you along, your lab might get some positive publicity in return for the help you have given me."

"What time, Doctor?"

"Four-thirty to seven, with tea thrown in; get there at four, and you get tea before the presentations."

"I'll ask Meghan. I'll call you back or leave a message with Monica."

Dave walked over to Meghan's desk and said, "Meg, Doctor Morrison just called to invite us to an oncology conference on Wednesday."

"Why?"

"For some lab publicity."

"If that's all, you don't need me to come."

Dave was surprised; why was she so negative?

"Well, the other reason is that it's Doc Morrison's invite, and we owe him."

"No, Dave; if anyone owes him something, you do, but what do I owe him?"

"You seem upset; is something wrong?"

"When we left the races on Saturday, I told you I wanted to come to see your mother, but you turned me away. We must work together, and I want to continue researching the Corkys, but if you want to keep me at arm's length, it's best not to invite me to go with you unless I must go. And we should avoid contact outside of work. Perhaps I made a mistake, and you should call me 'Miss MacDougal'."

Her words left Dave speechless as she continued, "I'll consider the invitation and let you know before I leave tonight, but don't count on it."

She went into the DNA lab.

It took Dave more than an hour to think of his answer and pluck up the courage; he knew he was frightened by the situation but wasn't sure why. Finally, he went into the DNA lab to speak to Meghan. He stood just inside the door, hesitant.

Meghan turned to him and said, "Yes, Dave?"

"Meg, please listen; I think I've something to explain."

"Ok, I'm listening."

"The other night, when I took you home after the races, I said I could kiss you but that I better not."

Meghan remembered clearly, and his reminder hurt. Her voice was flat. "Yes."

Now it poured out: "Well, I don't know how you understood that, although you said you understood. What I meant then, and what I'll say now, is that the moment I kiss you, I fear I'll lose control; I'll spend every waking minute thinking of you and wanting to be with you. I've my mother to think of, and I know that if we get into a relationship, BaVir may fire you unless I resign first or you accuse me of harassment. Because of my mother, I can't risk either."

Meghan was already feeling more assured, as she realised she hadn't understood this complex man. "And why didn't you want me to see your mother?"

"It's complicated, Meg."

"I don't mind complicated; try and explain."

"For the last two years, I've used every spare minute to research cancer, and while I looked after my mother in my flat, I could talk to her, like I have done since childhood. I grew up without a father from the age of twelve, and my mother was the one who wiped my tears away when I hurt myself or encouraged me when I felt I would fail exams. Since she went into the hospital, that has gone. Others tell me their problems and hope for assistance, but they don't want to hear mine. So I've continued as before. I sit with my mother, and when she sleeps under the effect of the chemo, I hold her hand and tell her everything, believing that she's listening. I think it's my therapy time; I reacted instinctively at the thought that you would intrude.

"Last time, I told her about you; I don't know if she heard, but I'm convinced she squeezed my hand and smiled a little."

"Some senses never sleep; your mother hears everything said and converts the sounds into electrical impulses. The brain may refuse to listen to them, but I'm sure that sometimes the important ones get through."

"Meg, if you want to come, it will make me and her incredibly happy because I'm sure she will love you.

"You accused me of wanting to keep you at arm's length. Nothing could be further from the truth. You love your job; I have no right to ask you to risk it when I can't promise anything in return—that's why I said a kiss is a promise."

Meghan's heart was beating faster. *It takes enormous courage to say what he just said.*

She smiled. Dave thought it was so beautiful that he wanted to take her in his arms.

Meghan replied, "I understand what you mean about a kiss. I might feel the same, so we must both be careful. I'll come with you to the conference as a colleague in research."

Meghan thought his answering smile was tender; it slowed her heartbeat as he said, "Thanks for understanding, Meg."

Dave called Doctor Morrison's surgery. "Monica, Dave here. Can you tell Doctor Morrison we will meet him at the Princess Margaret Hospital at four pm on Wednesday?"

Monica confirmed that she would. Dave thanked her and hung up.

Then Meghan said, "Let that be a lesson to both of us; if we have doubts or feel hurt, we must ask immediately and give honest answers."

Just then, Emma called. "Meghan, I have three candidates to interview tomorrow afternoon. If you can make it, please join me."

"I'm sure I can, Mrs Thompson; what time?"

"Two-thirty."

Barry was not in the laundromat that night. Meghan wasn't sure how she felt about his absence. Had he found her inadequate? Or was he signalling that they should be no more than friends? She hoped it was the latter but decided it might be the former, as she didn't love him and had given him no more than a brief embrace.

After the interviews, Emma asked Meghan, "Well? What do you think?"

"Zoe is a level above the other two, and she has something else. I sense she will think about what she's doing, not just do it. For QA, that's important."

"Fine, then you'll accept her?"

Meghan didn't reply immediately, thinking of Zoe: twenty-six, as tall as herself, blonde, curvaceous, and vivacious.

Emma said, "I know what you're thinking. You wonder how she'll fit in with the others and, of course, with Dave."

Meghan's reply was sheepish. "Yes."

"Meg. You know little about Dave. He's a hard man to understand and has depths I cannot comprehend. I've worked with him for three years and am only halfway there.

"Zoe will disrupt things for a few days. She will throw herself at Dave like every girl in the lab has done and, after two weeks, will give up. So don't worry about her. I'm more concerned about you."

"Me? Why?"

"Because I hope you won't give up. Dave's a hard nut to crack.

But if anyone can, I think you are the woman who will do it, and he needs someone to support him, especially now."

Alice was home when Meghan arrived.

"What are you doing for Easter, Meg? Are you seeing Colin?"

"No, my sister has invited me to stay over. She's organising an egg hunt for the kids. Rory and my parents will also come. Colin hasn't called; I think he might be visiting his parents. He has such a tight schedule that he doesn't see them often."

12

Dave and Meghan thought they would learn nothing at the conference. They may not have understood some technical details, but they both realised that managing a cancer case was like piloting a boat in a rough sea, a battle to outwit an implacable enemy.

However, the tea sessions were more rewarding. Doctor Morrison introduced them to several oncologists as representatives of BaVir who were helping him with a cancer-remission case.

Dave recognised a name in a group of doctors and asked, "Doctor Trelawney, are you the author of a paper on cancer remission?"

"I am. Have you read it?"

"Yes, and several others. I found yours particularly interesting, especially the part about blood pH."

Doctor Trelawney and several others were impressed; they hadn't expected Dave to know more about cancer than the average lab technician did.

At the tea break after the first presentations, a tall, slim man with an upright posture and a crown of white hair overheard Doctor Morrison introducing them to another doctor.

The white-haired man approached them and said to Doctor

Morrison, "Doctor, I should know these two young people; I feel embarrassed that I don't."

"Doctor Sankewicz, this is Dave Tennant and Meghan MacDougal from BaVir Labs in Cromwell Road."

Dave at once knew who he was. Before joining BaVir, he had looked up the directors and knew that the doctor was a retired Cambridge Professor of Pathology.

Doctor Sankewicz shook hands with Meghan and then Dave, who realised the doctor's hair was styled to make him look taller than he really was. Sankewicz smiled. A smile, Dave decided, that did not extend to his piercing blue eyes, giving an overall impression of a severe schoolmaster. The high collar on his shirt also helped the image.

"Meeting you here is a surprise, but it explains something. You recently asked Philip Jones for a cell counter. I assume you want it to investigate Doctor Morrison's remission case?"

"That's correct, sir. We don't know whether we will discover anything of interest, but we want to pursue it. Spontaneous-remission cases are rare and poorly documented."

"True enough, and I think it's worth betting on the outsider from time to time. There must be a little-used cell counter in one of our labs; I'll try to get one for you."

"Thank you, Doctor," Dave said. "It will help us a lot."

"You're welcome.

"Doctor Morrison, I'm pleased BaVir is assisting you."

"Professor, I cannot adequately express my satisfaction. *Oncology* will shortly have an article on the case; hopefully, another will follow."

"I'll look for them. We must go now; the session is starting. I hope to see you again soon."

After lunch, Dave received a call from Philip Jones.

"Dave, I've some news for you: you will have a cell counter on Monday."

"That's wonderful; how did you get it so quickly?"

"I didn't. One of our labs has one they don't use. A bigwig at head office told them to send it to us. Do you know anything about it?"

"I met Doctor Sankewicz yesterday at an oncology conference with Doctor Morrison; Sankewicz seemed to know I wanted one and promised to help me. He seemed surprised by Doctor Morrison's opinion of BaVir."

"That's the other thing I must tell you; Marketing says they have had unusual queries from doctors who believe we have advanced skills in cancer analysis. Whatever you said at that conference, it must have stirred interest."

Dave recapped his conversation with Jones to Meghan.

She thought for a moment before replying, "Then, once I set up and calibrate the cell counter, we can do the Corky counts. Say Wednesday. Now, I must pack up; I have a flight to Edinburgh at seven. I'm spending the weekend with my sister."

"How was Edinburgh, Meg?"

"A lot of fun, Dave. Yesterday, the whole family was there for the kids' egg hunt. I'll tell you about it later; I have a backlog of work to catch up on."

Colin called. "Meg, I've an invitation to a cocktail party on Friday evening. Would you like to come as my partner? We could have dinner afterwards."

Meghan had nothing else to do, and despite not being keen, she agreed, thinking, *Maybe I'll learn more about him.*

Meghan had calibrated the cell counter as promised for Wednesday. Dave and Meghan were in the DNA lab that afternoon.

They loaded a slide—from the first analysis Corkys had shown up in—under the microscope.

Meghan did a manual count, finding that there weren't many Corkys, and then moved the slide to the cell counter.

It finished in thirty seconds, reporting the same number as their manual count.

"Well, the machine counts Corkys correctly; let's try the latest sample we received from Boris."

Again, Meghan did a manual count for a benchmark, and Dave added up the total. There were many more Corkys in this sample.

Meghan then took the slide to the cell counter, focused on it, and placed the crosshairs on a Corky. A moment later, the counter pinged and displayed a much lower number than the manual count—it hadn't found all the Corkys.

"Bugger, something's wrong."

"Try again; choose a different Corky."

Another moment, another ping, and another far-too-low result—although higher than the first.

"Not only wrong but inconsistent."

"I'll count another slide. The glass on this one might have a reflective defect."

Dave went to the microscope, used another slide, and did the manual count. Meghan added up the total. Then she used the cell counter. The numbers were different, but it was the same problem. The counter gave lower figures.

"Meg, it only takes a minute to repeat a count; do six or seven, and let me write the results down in a table. Choose a different Corky at random each time as the seed."

She did, and then they looked at the column of figures. There were seven: three were low, and four were higher, but the low ones were identical, as were the high ones.

In a very calm but strained voice, Dave said, "Incredible, utterly incredible; we must have two different Corkys. The machine can see the difference, but we haven't; let's go back to the microscope and switch to the highest magnification."

They stared at the screen in intense silence, moving the field a little at a time to see different Corkys, unaware that their faces were only centimetres apart.

They didn't spot anything until Dave, who had shut his eyes from the strain, looked again. "Meg, we haven't been very clever."

"What do you mean?"

"They are identical except in one characteristic."

"What?"

"There are left-hand corkscrews and right-hand ones; it's so obvious that we didn't notice."

Meghan looked and confirmed it.

Dave, who had picked up the list of counts, said, "If you add a high to a low, it matches the manual count."

"Why didn't we have a counting problem on the last analysis?"

"I don't know; maybe they were all the same helixes."

"I'll get the earlier slide."

It was true; the first Corkys were all right-hand ones.

"Meg, we must think this over; let's pack up, change, and go home."

"Not much to think over; we must talk to Boris again. Where did he get the left-hand Corkys?"

Dave called Doctor Morrison, who said he'd try and reach Boris right away.

Only a few minutes later, the doctor called back and said, "He's out of the country; he expects to be back in three weeks, and he'll confirm."

Colin called for Meghan with a taxi waiting. Alice let him in and had two minutes to introduce herself while Meghan collected her coat.

Meghan and Colin entered the hotel ballroom a few minutes after seven. It appeared to Meghan that the guests had come early to take advantage of the free drinks and snacks; a crowd was already there. Colin paraded her around the room like, she thought, a prize cow being shown off at an agricultural show. He introduced her to lawyers whose names she couldn't remember afterwards. Then he left her with a drink after introducing her to Madelaine, the wife of one of his colleagues. "I must circulate, Meg; there's no point coming if I don't."

Madelaine took pity on her. "Meghan, this is what they all do; see the man in the blue suit? That's my husband. He won't speak to me until we leave."

"Then why come?"

"Because having me around shows others he's a stable, trustworthy family man. Trust, or at least its appearance, is essential for lawyers."

"Can they be trusted?"

"Mine certainly can't; they know the law and how to bend and twist it to their convenience."

"I meant, personally."

"He's too smart not to give me whatever I want, Meg. He knows I would divorce him if he didn't."

"Then why did you marry him?"

"I was much younger and far more innocent back then. I had no idea what lawyers and their work were like. Most of the time, they decide to become lawyers because they are full of noble ideals and lofty words and think they will fight for justice; I thought it was romantic and that I would work with him to bring justice to the people. Then when they get into the system, young lawyers learn that all the others are fighting for themselves, money, and their careers, and they end up doing the same."

"So you didn't marry for love?"

"Of course I did, Meg. But that romantic love doesn't last long when your husband stops bringing you flowers and has his secretary send a bouquet on your birthday and wedding anniversary. I doubt he can remember the dates, but she's got it in her diary. Then when I get the bouquets, I show them to my friends; they admire them and say what a great husband I have while secretly being satisfied that they are not the only ones with flowers ordered by a secretary."

"Have you got children, Madelaine?"

"Yes, having them hides what's happening in the first fifteen to twenty years. The nature of lawyers' work does nothing to help; they're in a club together, spending long hours and days away. When they come home, they collapse into bed, and by the time the third child is on its way, they lose interest in sex with you; legal wrangling is far more exciting. You bring up the kids on your own, and when your children leave home, you find your husband is a stranger, that there's nothing left except politeness, separate bedrooms, and that your boobs, backside, and tummy hang too low when you're naked to attract anyone else. The only thing you have is money and security."

"So you think lawyers make for bad husbands?"

"Not bad, Meg, *bloody terrible*. If you were a lawyer, you could make a success of marriage, especially if you were better than he was. You would know how to keep him in line and share a common life."

"Madelaine, thanks a lot; you've given me much to think about. Tell me: What do you know about Colin?"

"Apart from his age, which is thirty-seven, and that the company promoted him from the Edinburgh office, which I suppose means he's a competent lawyer, nothing. You could ask about him in Edinburgh if you want any personal details. You might not find out much; lawyers are good at hiding what they don't want to be known.

"There's a lawyer, a woman I could introduce you to, who I think knows everything about the men."

Meghan thought she was about to continue when Colin appeared.

"Meg, do you want to have dinner, or have you eaten enough here?"

Meghan felt he had other plans, so she said, even though she had eaten little, "I couldn't eat anything, Colin; I'll take a taxi home."

"Good night, Madelaine. Good night, Colin."

"Good night, Meg. I enjoyed the evening. Thanks," Colin replied.

In the taxi on her way home, Meghan wondered again at her feeling that she wasn't the only woman in Colin's life.

Alice was still home. "You're back early. How was the cocktail party, Meg?"

"Boring, Ally. Colin showed me off to his colleagues and left me with a woman called Madelaine, the wife of one of the lawyers. She told me a few things about lawyers and living with them. Colin had somewhere to go afterwards. I didn't want to go with him to dinner."

"I don't like him."

"Why, Ally?"

"Because when I met him, I felt he thought of me as socially unacceptable because I work in a kitchen and don't have a degree."

"Ally, thanks for telling me; I'll watch out for his attitude."

"I'll be off to work then; I have the late shift until two tomorrow morning."

Oncology came out on a Monday. The May edition featured Dave and Meghan's first report.

Doctor Morrison received a dozen emails of encouragement, some from international readers of *Oncology*. None suggested a reason for spontaneous cancer remission. Four were from people who said that they'd had cases of remission but that their patients had experienced a reversal and eventually passed away, although they didn't say what the patients had died from. Three said the same thing, except that their patients had died after contracting a respiratory disease months or years after the cancer remission. They thought the patients' immune systems might never have recovered from cancer.

Later, there was a short letter to the editor.

Dear Sir,

The report on the cancer remission case does not merit the use of your paper. All cancer remissions eventually die.

Prof. D.M. Higgs

The editor of *Oncology* sent them invitations to attend the next conference sponsored by the journal. It was in three weeks. It appeared to Doctor Morrison that someone—he wasn't sure who it was—had suggested inviting them as a step toward obtaining sponsorship from companies.

Meghan went to see Dave on Monday. "Dave, can I have Friday off?"

"Making a long weekend out of the holiday, Meg?"

"Yes, I want to go to Edinburgh and see my folks."

"Well, everything's running fine, and we have nothing more to do about Kravitz until the next sample comes, and Fridays are slow, so ok."

13

Dave was in his office when Doctor Morrison phoned to tell him that Boris would come to the surgery next Thursday.

Meghan had left on the early flight, and during Dave's day at work, her absence brought on a growing feeling of loneliness. It seemed overwhelming to him that he would spend Saturday, Sunday, and Monday without seeing Meghan, or anyone, except his mother for an hour or two. He tried to bury himself in work. Then he remembered Susan had given him her number. He found it on his phone and dialled it.

Angela answered.

"Hello, Angela. I'm at a loose end this weekend and thought of you. How about coming out for dinner?"

"That would be cool, Dave. But how about coming here? Susan is a great cook, and we can promise to spoil you. Come tomorrow night at about seven. I have your cell number, so I'll send you our address. We live above the practice."

"Ok, thanks. I'll see you then."

On Saturday morning, Dave received a call from Meghan.

"Dave, my flight back arrives at half-past three on Monday, and I need exercise. Are you running on Monday, as it's a holiday?"

"Yes, will you join me?"

"That's why I called. Where shall I meet you?"

"The tearoom near Ravenscourt Park Station; I'll wait for you at five-thirty."

"Ok, what have you been up to?"

Dave decided to be frank; hiding things was difficult for him. "Yesterday, I worked late on the month-end reports. Today, I'm doing research, and later, I'm going to dinner with Angela. I've memories to put to bed.

"And you, Meg, the family all fine?"

"Yes, thanks; I'm going to a banquet tonight with my brother, Rory."

"Well, enjoy."

Dave found the food and wine as delicious as promised, and the two women kept him laughing at the stories they had to tell about their animal patients and the pet owners. Susan claimed that bulldog owners looked like bulldogs.

Angela disappeared, returned wearing a loose, diaphanous gown, and sat next to him on the couch. And then Susan did the same. It was when Angela started to unbutton his shirt that he realised.

Susan put a finger across his lips as he opened his mouth to protest. "Dave, being bi is difficult. Lesbian is easy, but for two bisexuals to stay together, we must share everything, including men. We will give you the experience of a lifetime, starting with a massage. Relax."

Dave did so. For a while, anyway. Having two women in his bed was a new sensation, and they were experts; they caressed, rubbed, and kneaded each other and him. Susan told him what Angela liked, and he did what she told him to. Finally, when he reached a height of arousal he had never experienced, for every nerve in his body tingled, Angela rolled onto her back, parted her legs, and said, "Now, Dave."

Susan warned him: "Slow and steady."

Five minutes later, he and Angela orgasmed together. Dave knew she had never had such an abandoned orgasm with him before. Then came the thought, "*I don't remember her having an orgasm.*"

Susan ordered, "On your back."

The two women continued to caress and massage every part of him and each other. He felt intense love between them. This time, Angela told him what Susan liked.

An hour later, Susan straddled him and began to rock. Angela didn't stop her caresses. When she caressed Susan, it heightened Dave's excitement; it took longer but was explosive.

In the morning, Dave awoke entangled in the two naked women. He slowly eased himself from the bed. He took a quick shower and dressed. He found Susan, still naked, pouring coffee when he came out of the bathroom.

"Dave, have a cup before you go." He accepted as she continued, "Thanks. We both needed that last night, and you did us proud. But don't call again. I don't want Angie getting ideas. We have a working partnership that's not worth destroying."

Sitting on the train back to London, he thought it had been fantastic, but he would have preferred Meghan in bed with him. Susan's last comment weighed heavily; working partnerships were not worth destroying.

Rory had told Meghan the banquet they would be going to was to mark the end of the conference he'd been attending at the hotel. He picked her up with his girlfriend, Kenna McTavish, a curvaceous blonde woman who was years younger and a good ten centimetres shorter than him. Her smile and cheerful voice made her attractive, Meghan thought. Rory introduced Meghan to Kenna and then to the second passenger in the car: "Meghan, this is Cameron, Kenna's brother. He's a doctor."

Rugged-looking, nearing forty, thought Meghan.

"GP or specialist?" she asked.

"Plain GP; I'm a country doctor. I treat people for anything and everything. I also treat animals, for vets are scarce." He laughed. "I must average one sheep for every two or three humans."

The evening went well. It was a large banquet, but the dining hall emptied rapidly when the final thank-you speeches began. Rory said he and Kenna were going home directly; Cameron could see Meghan home. He kissed Meghan and murmured, "He's a nice guy, Meg."

Cameron invited Meghan to the bar for a scotch. She went, knowing his intentions were more than a scotch, proven when he said, "I brought a bottle of Tullamore Dew with me. Would you like a wee dram in my room?"

A question confused her. Suddenly it became enormous. If Cameron had just said "come", she would have said no, but she had to think about her answer. First, she felt *no*, but then she thought, "*Dave is with Angela; he said he had memories to put to bed, and he might be doing that right now,*" so she would go with Cameron. Then she thought, "*Dave should not influence my decision. I don't want to go with Cameron; he doesn't interest me, I won't enjoy it, and if I don't want to, I should walk away from a catastrophe.*"

Meghan looked at her watch and said, "Thanks for the invitation, but no, I'll take a taxi home."

Disappointed, Cameron walked her to the taxi, and they said goodbye.

On the way home, Meghan thought it was the right decision. She remembered Barry and realised that she had wanted to go to bed with him; they had a rapport because they had worked together.

Then she thought, *"That damned brother of mine must have told Cameron it was my favourite whisky."*

Meghan and Dave warmed up with a light jog. The park was full of picnicking families on the spring holiday.

"How's your mother doing, Dave?"

"I saw her both Sunday and today. She's woozy from the chemo, so we didn't talk much."

"What's her name, and how old is she?"

"Emily, and she's only fifty-four."

"That's cruel. Can you explain the chemo programme?"

"The cycle is about three months long with this chemo cocktail; she sleeps as it takes over her system and fights her cancer for the first week or two. Then she starts to recover and eventually seems normal. When her cancer progresses again, she begins a new cycle."

"So they are keeping it at bay?"

"Yes, Meg, but with every chemo cycle, she gets weaker. It's noticeable; in the first cycle, she slept for a week, and now she's sleeping for three weeks."

"How long can they continue?"

"The oncologist thinks she can withstand two more cycles, and then we must accept she can't support it any more; her cancer will win six months later."

"Then we had better get to work."

"Did you have a good evening on Saturday, Meg?"

"Yes. Rory was at a pharma conference and brought his girlfriend, Kenna. He invited me to the banquet to meet her."

"So you were the odd one out?"

"No, he had a doctor friend with him, Cameron, who is Kenna's brother, so I made up the numbers. But before you ask, Cameron invited me to his room for the night, but I left and took a taxi home."

"I wasn't going to ask; it's none of my business."

"It is, Dave. I couldn't help thinking I would have accepted if it were you. But I wouldn't have enjoyed sex with Cameron McTavish; he didn't stir any feelings."

Then Meghan asked, "And how was your evening with Angela?"

"You mean with Angela and Susan."

"Oh, was she there too?"

"Yes, I learned how difficult it must be for someone to be bisexual. Angela and Susan are good people. They had a fund of stories about the owners of the pets they treat at their practice. I'm sorry for them, Meg.

"Susan said they must share everything openly to keep their relationship stable. When I left, Susan said I must never call, as she doesn't want Angela getting ideas."

"I suppose that means sharing men as well?"

"Yes, but I don't think they do so often."

"Did you put your memories to bed?"

"Yes, I now know that Angela and I were never in love, not like she is with Susan."

Meghan made her usual Monday trip to the laundromat. She had decided Barry might help further.

She was almost hypnotised by the rotating drum of the dryer when Barry disturbed her. "Hello, Meg. Did you have a good weekend?"

"Yes, Barry, and you?"

"It was great. I went to Brighton for the weekend. I took one of the foreign nurses with me. She had never been there, so I had fun showing her around my hometown."

"That's great, Barry. I wish you luck. You helped a lot with the cholera variant."

"A pleasure, Meg, and you helped me in return. I think I'm going to do Heart and Lung. My laundry is dry; I must go."

"So must I. I have a meeting tomorrow to prepare for."

"*Another man who has lost interest in me; I must have a disease or something,*" thought Meghan.

"Good morning, Doctor Morrison," Dave said.

"Morning Dave, Meghan. Boris Kravitz should be along soon; I've told Monica to show him in at once. What have you got to report?"

"Two things. First, the last sample has a much higher count of corkscrew bacteria. And second, there are two types of Corky: a left- and a right-helix one. The previous sample has a smaller number of right-helix bacteria, and the later one where the cancer count dropped has a much higher number of right- and left-helix bacteria."

"So you asked for a follow-up meeting with Kravitz because you suspect a second infection from another source?"

"No, Doctor, we know nothing and can expect nothing; we're trying to eliminate possibilities. The bacterium may be reproducing in both forms."

Just then, Boris Kravitz came in, and they all said good morning.

"Boris," said Doctor Morrison, "Dave and Meghan have found a second form of the bacterium that you might have picked up after the first one. They have much the same questions to ask."

"Doctor, I didn't go back to Africa; that I know." He took his diary out of his pocket and opened it. "After the Africa trip, I had a short, three-night trip to Dubai; I didn't go anywhere except the maintenance hangar and the airport hotel room. Then I had to tend to a breakdown of a tourist charter plane in the Far East; it was a four-night stay."

Hesitantly, Dave asked, "Did you ... um ... have another experience of the type you had in Africa?"

"No, not really."

Meghan posed the next question: "Mr Kravitz, did you have *any* sexual experiences there, and were they different in any way to the ones you had in Africa?"

"Well—yes. There was a tourist bar near the hotel, and I went there each night. Of course, several professional ladies hung out there. I agreed to join two of them on the second night in what they called a 'Bang-Bang'."

"So why did you say, 'No, not really'?"

Boris looked wretched. He sighed, committing himself to a confession. "It turned out to be what the French call a '*partouze*'; there were four girls and three other men, and each girl took on each of the men, so I had sex four times."

"Boris, you must be a superman in bed."

"No, miss, I might have had two orgasms, but no more."

"Thank you, Boris," Meghan said quietly. "You have helped us a lot. It is not my job to say this—I'll let Doctor make the case—but as a woman, I'll ask you to use a condom in future; you don't want the responsibility of infecting others, even though the bacteria may be benign."

"Miss MacDougal, I understand and will do so."

After Boris left, Dave asked Doctor Morrison if he would agree to another report for *Oncology*.

He replied, "I don't know; why do you want to do one?"

"For one specific reason, Doctor. We have found a corkscrew bacterium; just Meghan and I can spend years looking into it, trying to find out what it is, what it does, and where it comes from, but we don't have the research facilities that universities and governments have. If we publish another report, again neither argumentative nor conclusive, just informational, with micrographs of the bacterium, we might get a reply from someone with useful information. I think it's worth doing."

"All right, draft a report and let me see it; I'll add my name, but only refer to me in a final paragraph as a witness to the suspected origins of the bacterium. Make no mention of sex. You can be discreet; say the path to infection is unknown but could include the exchange of bodily fluids—that's a commonly used euphemism."

Meghan and Dave wrote the second report. It mentioned West Africa and the Far East, but no countries.

Philip refused to sanction it. "Dave, I can't agree to this. It's beyond my competence. What I can do is ask Doctor Sankewicz for his approval."

"Ok, Philip."

Dave and Meghan received a message to report to the head office at nine in the morning the next day. Dave thought it inconvenient; they could have started their weekend early if it had been in the afternoon. However, they agreed to it.

As befits a senior director, Doctor Sankewicz had an office on the top floor with a view over the Thames; his walls were decorated with awards and diplomas. Dave and Meghan were surprised by his friendly greeting; they had prepared themselves for a severe rebuke.

"Dave, Meghan, I'm impressed by your work and discoveries. It would be unfair to block the publication of the report Philip sent me, but I want to ask you to delay it for a week or two."

Meghan asked, "Why, sir?" Although he seemed open, she felt suspicious. *What was behind his request?*

"I think I've much more experience publishing technical articles than you, and I have also experienced the reactions that such an article will stimulate. I can, and will, make some minor adjustments to the language, but that won't help much. I propose to enrol you as research fellows at Cambridge. You are both professionally qualified but outside the research sphere, which is enough for the entire research community to pooh-pooh your results. If the article cites you as research fellows, that should help."

Meghan asked, "Won't that take months?"

"I still have adequate influence at Cambridge, so two weeks should be enough."

"Thank you, sir."

"You must meet me there for an interview. I'll try to arrange it for next Friday, in the afternoon. Three pm will work well because the committee will want to go home, so it might only take an hour. Afterwards, if you wish, you can explore Cambridge and its facilities. I can also arrange a tour of the Pathology department before the interview. Would you like that?"

"That would be interesting, sir, thank you," Dave said. "Meg, are you occupied that weekend?"

"No, I've no plans right now. I'll let you know if anything comes up, but count me in, Doctor."

"Good, then it's all arranged."

After they left, Dave asked, "Meg, shall we stay for the weekend? Come back early on Sunday? I must visit my mother."

"It would give us a break, and I don't know Cambridge. But separate bedrooms, and no kissing."

Dave was in two minds, so he said, "Ok, you make the reservation." He added, "What did you think of Sankewicz's proposal? You didn't seem delighted."

"I don't believe directors of major corporations make magnanimous gestures, so I was trying to find a motive for him enrolling us at Cambridge."

"And did you find one?"

"No, but I felt he was trying to gather us into his fold. We shall have to be careful about keeping our information secret."

14

It was a glorious May Day; the temperature was over sixteen degrees centigrade by two pm. After a morning of research unsuccessfully looking for something, somewhere, *anywhere*, that described a Corky, Dave decided not to waste the sunshine. Although he would run after seeing his mother the following day, he decided to go for a jog.

When Dave arrived home, he found Valerie in the entrance hall of his apartment building, sitting with her back to a wall. She had a Rubik's cube in her hands and was feverishly rotating the layers.

"Val, what are you doing here?"

"Waiting for you, Dave; let's go to your flat, and I'll explain."

Upstairs, she burst into a torrent of words.

Dave put his arms around her and said, "Slow down, Val, you're safe here." He rubbed her back as she put her arms around him.

She closed her eyes and said nothing, with her head on his chest. Dave held her, gently rubbing her back, for several minutes until Valerie said, "Thanks, Dave. I'm better now."

"What's the problem, Val?"

"I had two real bastards on Thursday. I don't think anyone can help them. They taunted me together. I almost kicked them in the balls. I couldn't go back to work on Friday. I didn't know what to do; I've walked in parks for the last two days, but it didn't help, then I thought of you. I couldn't call; my hands were trembling. I might have begun screaming, and you'd have to send an ambulance. So I came here."

"Come, Val; let's cuddle."

He found she was much thinner than he remembered her being.

They slept late, and when they woke, Val said, "Love me, Dave."

Later, she said, "I didn't eat yesterday. I'm hungry."

Dave thought that was a good sign, but after Val left, a worried Dave believed she would crack if she didn't resign soon. But what to do?

He went to Marco's. It was almost an instinctive reaction.

Marco said what a good friend should say. "I'm surprised to see you, Dave; you look worried. If you want to talk, play chess with someone until the rush ends, and then we can catch up. It should take about an hour for the place to clear out a bit."

Dave managed two games and lost both; he thought it showed how disturbed he was.

Marco dropped into the chair opposite him. "Ok, Dave, we may be disturbed if I have a customer, but tell me."

"It's not me, Marco; it's Valerie. If she doesn't give up her job, she'll crack and end up in a mental hospital."

"Why?"

Dave explained.

"So you are trying to think of a solution?"

"Yes."

"You're too close to her problem; what are her assets? I know she's good with children and plays chess at a high level. What else?"

"She's a qualified child psychologist, but she doesn't want to work in that speciality any more for fear of the same thing happening again. So I don't think there's anything else, Marco. Not that I know about."

"Ok, let's think about this. Where do you find children in groups needing supervision?"

"Playgrounds? Sports fields? Crèches? Schools?"

"Right. Which of these groups play chess?"

Dave said, "Mainly those in playgrounds and schools."

"So that's where you must look to find her a job. If you know anyone you can ask, that will help. I'll put out some feelers and place a notice on the counter. Someone might have an idea."

When Dave got home to change for his Sunday hospital visit, his mind repeated like a broken record: "*Chess, school, chess, school, chess ...*"

"Dave, you are very quiet today; did you see your mother yesterday?" Meghan asked.

"Yes, she's much as I expected."

"Then tell me your problem; maybe that will help."

"I don't think so, Meg; let me think about it."

It disappointed Meghan that he hadn't the confidence to tell her, but she decided not to push him.

That night, Ally said to Meghan, "Something's worrying you; you've been mooching around like a lost soul."

"I employed a woman for analysis work. She started on the second. She's young and sexy and is throwing herself at Dave. It's disturbing the other women, and I don't know if I should fire her. And Dave was worried today and wouldn't tell me why."

Ally looked at Meghan sympathetically. "Be honest, Meg; you mean she's disturbing *you*."

"I suppose she is."

"Meg, I learned something in high school. I had a crush on a rugby jock. Blake was big and handsome, and every girl in school was flirting with him. I hated them. I was over the moon when he decided to take me out one night."

"And you lost your virginity, Ally?"

"Not the first time. It was ten days of agony hating every girl that flirted with him before I gave in.

"Then he left me. I despised him. I decided to watch him, and learned it was his technique to get sex. Date an innocent and flirt with the others until the girl spreads her legs.

"You are watching this new woman. She's doing what comes naturally; she can't help it. You should be watching Dave. Is he flirting? Is he interested? Ignore her; *his* intentions matter to you, not hers."

Two days later, after taking Ally's lesson to heart, Meghan decided that Emma Thompson had been right. Dave showed no signs of interest in Zoe. However, she learned something else the following morning.

"Dave, you seem to be worried still. Do you think you can tell me?" Meghan asked.

"I can, Meg, but it won't solve the problem."

"Try anyway."

"Ok. It concerns a woman I met months ago at Pizza Out, a place where you can meet people and play chess while waiting for your meal order. This was before you joined BaVir. Valerie and I played four or five times. She's a child psychologist who works with troubled kids. They are rough, insulting, and sometimes impossible to handle.

"Valerie told me about some of her cases and said child psychologists who work with them don't last many years before they must give up. On Sunday night, I found her on my doorstep, exhausted and close to a breakdown. She slept twelve hours and has taken a few days off, so she should be ok for a week, but I think she's close to breaking point."

Meghan decided it was not the time to ask what kind of sleep, so instead, she asked, "Why doesn't she change her job?"

"She's an orphan with no family, no one to advise her, and she has no idea what she could do. But she's sure she doesn't want to work in any form of child psychology. I talked to my friend Marco about it. He pointed out that she was good at chess and working with children—and he suggested we try and find employment for her at schools."

"Why's it your problem? Can't you recommend that she see a psychiatrist?"

"I can, but with the delay getting an appointment, she might be in a mental hospital before seeing one."

"Can I meet her? A woman's viewpoint might help."

"Let me call her; she's not working, so maybe tonight."

Alice's lesson was still fresh in Meghan's mind when she and Dave met Valerie at a café near Marco's. As Valerie shared her life story, Meghan was rapt, but she watched for any reactions from Dave. By the time Valerie had come to the end of her story, Meghan was sure of two things: Dave was not in love with Val, but he cared very much for her, and that was what mattered. She would try to help Valerie.

When Valerie left, Meghan said, "She's a genuinely nice woman, and I understand why you care for her health. I'll try and think of something that might help."

"Thanks, that's very generous of you."

"Right, now take me to my flat, or call a taxi; it's dark."

He called a taxi.

On the way home, Meghan thought, *"Dave's not in love with Valerie, but it affects him to see her hurt."*

Valerie's problem had circulated in Meghan's mind all day yesterday, finally lifting from the depths a memory of learning to play chess at school. At sixteen, she had fancied a final-year student, two years older than her, who played chess. Unlike the other girls her age, she preferred the more intellectual boys. He didn't pay her any special attention until, one day, he noticed that she always came to watch the matches at the school chess club. He thought she was keen. She was, but not on chess. He took it on himself to teach her how to play.

Meghan smiled at the memory; she had scored because he'd met her to play a game in the school canteen where all her friends could see them. However, although she now tried every trick she knew to remember his name, one memory surfaced repeatedly: his pants, and the girls' nickname for him—"Bargepole".

On her way to work, as she took the escalator from the station platform, absorbed in the memory, she forgot to step aside to allow those in a rush to pass. A male voice behind her said sarcastically, "I grant you have the right to stand where you are, but do you think you might give some consideration to those in a hurry?"

Meghan stepped aside with one word shining in her mind: "Grant".

She went straight to Dave in the lab, her excitement bubbling over. "Dave, I have someone we can ask about opportunities for Valerie. When I was at school, a boy called Grant taught me to play chess. I later heard that he became a teacher at a school where he coached the chess team that won the Scottish Chess Championship."

"Do you have his number?"

"No, but it must be on the web; search for Scottish Chess Championship."

Three minutes later, Dave said, "He's at a school in Glasgow, and here's the school's number. Call and ask for him."

Meghan learned he had moved to a school in North London. Five minutes later, she had him on the line.

He answered, "Grant Starveling."

"Grant, I hope you remember me, Meghan MacDougal."

"How could I forget you, Meghan? I've often thought with regret that you were not a year or two older."

Meghan blushed as she remembered his nickname. The reddening intrigued Dave.

"Grant, I live in London now, and my boyfriend and I would like some advice. It's regarding a chess matter. If you can find the time, we'll meet you at a pub or the school."

"Meg, I'm a housemaster now; getting out is difficult, but you are welcome to visit in the evening. I've a bottle of scotch in my study. Just ask at the gate."

"Ok, thanks. When are you free?"

"It must be after the weekend. How about Tuesday the sixteenth?"

"That's great; we will see you then."

Dave and Meghan went to the faculty interview at Cambridge and, as agreed, spent the weekend there to investigate their new alma mater. Meghan had booked a bed and breakfast.

She enjoyed their tour of the Pathology faculty and listened attentively to everything the researcher who showed them around had to say. Dave felt the hairs on the back of his neck stiffen; he always gave such sensations careful attention. Their guide was just too insistent in asking questions about their research. Scientists respected the desire to keep research a secret until certain the results were correct. So he gave little away and added one or two minor falsehoods.

After the interview, Dave and Meghan went to the bed and

breakfast. They put their bags down in their respective rooms at opposite ends of a corridor.

After a walk around the city centre, drinks at a pub filled with students, and a sumptuous dinner, they returned to their rooms.

Dave said, "Good night, Meg, sleep tight," and leaned in to kiss her.

Meghan turned away as she said, "Good night, Dave." She had sensed he was hoping for an invitation but thought, "*No, I said no kissing. He'll have to live with it.*"

Dave lay in bed, thinking. He knew he had told her he couldn't kiss her. But it seemed everything had turned upside down. Now it was Meghan resisting a good-night kiss. Then he felt an open pit form in his gut. "*Is it because of Valerie? Or does she have another man in her life?*"

Meghan had booked a punt. The weather blessed them, and it was a wonderful day, apart from an initial struggle with the pole and snide comments from Meghan. They went leisurely up the Cam to a riverside restaurant. Meghan lounged on the cushions and fed the swans and ducks. Then they drifted slowly back. They avoided discussing work things. Relaxed in talking about what they had seen and would like to see in England and Scotland, they enjoyed the pleasure of each other's company.

Later, when they went to their rooms, Dave said good night, not expecting a kiss.

Meghan stepped forward and hugged him. "Thanks for a wonderful, wonderful day." She turned away, swung back, raised herself on her toes, and kissed him on the cheek. "Good night, Dave."

He stood in the corridor looking at her until she closed her room door, remembering the feel of her in his arms. It didn't answer his question. "*Does she have another man in her life?*"

15

Dave and Meghan took the early train back from Cambridge, and during the ride, Dave asked, "After I have seen my mother, I intend to run. Would you like to join me?"

"I'd love to. Call me later. If Ally has not left too much mess, and I've done the housework, I'll meet you in the park. But why don't I come with you to meet your mother?"

"If you want to, I'm sure she'd be delighted. She should be on the way to recovery from the chemo; she's stopped sleeping through the day. I take the bus from Ravenscourt Park at two, so you could meet me there, but I can take you to lunch first if you can make it for twelve or twelve-thirty."

"That's too soon for me. I must bring my running gear, as I don't want to wear it to the hospital. Can I meet you at your flat at quarter-to-two and leave it there?"

"Of course, you can change afterwards, and we can run."

Dave was right; his mother looked far better. She was wearing her wig and enough makeup to hide her paper-white skin.

"Ma, I've brought you a visitor."

"I can see that. Hello Meghan."

"Ma, how do you know who Meghan is?"

"You told me about her, and she's the only girl I've seen that matches your description. Dave, go and find another chair. Meghan, come and sit next to me."

Dave just stood bemused while Meghan took his usual place, and as she did, she looked at him and said triumphantly, "I told you so!" Turning back to the bed, she said, "Emily, call me Meg."

"What did you tell him, Meg?"

"That you could hear everything he said when you were asleep."

"Not everything, only the important bits. I think they must stay in my head until I wake up."

Dave fetched a chair from the corridor. When he sat down, Meghan told Emily of their punting in Cambridge, with graphic descriptions of his amateurish boat handling.

He sat back and let them talk, feeling overwhelming pleasure when he saw his mother laugh.

As they were about to leave, Emily asked, "Are you going to marry my boy, Meg?"

"That depends on him, Emily; I've told him not to ask until we have solved your cancer problem, so he's now got two reasons to work hard."

They ran in the park after the visit, and between breaths, Meghan said, "She's a lovely woman."

"And you are just the medicine she needed, thank you."

The rain belted down that Monday to prove, Meghan thought, that summer hadn't arrived.

Zoe came to see her.

"Yes, Zoe?"

"The reagent in batch 4578 is bad, miss."

"What's wrong with it?"

"It doesn't work right. I don't know what's wrong with it. I borrowed some from a different batch, and that worked."

"Then collect all bottles of that faulty batch and put them in a box. I'll send it back to the supplier."

"Don't you want to test it or something?"

"Zoe, I chose you when you applied for the job here because I believed you would apply your intelligence to your work. If you say it's bad, that's good enough for me."

"Thanks, miss."

"Sit down, Zoe."

Zoe sat.

"Now tell me. Are you settling in well?"

Zoe looked embarrassed. "I made a fool of myself at first, miss. I couldn't help it. Then when Marjorie told me I had no chance with Mr Tennant, I realised everyone was laughing at me. I told them all I was sorry."

"That was brave of you, Zoe. Unfortunately, Mr Tennant has that effect on women. He can't help it either. Thank you."

As Zoe was about to leave the office, she turned to look at Meghan. "Thank you for not firing me. If someone had told me he was yours, I wouldn't have been so stupid."

Meghan thought: *"They think he's mine. Would somebody please tell him?"*

Dave and Meghan met Grant at the school where he worked. After Meghan and Grant had caught up, Grant explained that he had little time to coach chess after his appointment as Housemaster.

Dave told Grant about Pizza Out.

Delighted, Grant said, "There are few safe places where you can get a walk-in chess game in London." He asked for the address and wrote it down.

Then Dave said, "I have a friend called Valerie who has a problem, and we were hoping you could help ..." He explained the situation to Grant, then added, "We wondered if there's an opportunity here, at your school, for her to see if teaching kids to play chess would be something she could do. If so, perhaps you could give her two weeks. But if after some time you find that you don't think it would work out, you shouldn't feel obliged to extend the arrangement beyond a few days."

Meghan added, "She's a lovely woman, Grant; I'm sure you will like her."

"I can appreciate her problems with anti-social children; we get them here from time to time. Let me ask for the Head's permission; I'll call you."

Later, Dave called Valerie. "Hi Valerie, can you take some leave?"

"Why? Do you want me to go somewhere with you?"

"No, Val. Meg's old schoolfriend, Grant, is a schoolteacher and coaches chess. We've asked him to let you spend two weeks teaching the kids chess. Is that something you think you'd like to try?"

"It does sound good."

"Between you and Grant, you will be able to see if it's worth you pursuing a job as a chess coach. While there are difficult kids at the school, they won't be as bad as the ones you've had to deal with, so you can apply your skills as a child psychologist, too."

"Dave, why would you do this for me?"

"Because you can't go on much longer before depression gets to you. I think you must try now."

"Do you love me, Dave?"

"Valerie, the answer is yes, but not passionately. I admire you and love your tenacity and desire to help kids, and I don't want to see you broken. There's no obligation. You can walk out of the school after one day if you wish."

"Ok. If you can arrange it, I'll do it for you. I'll need two weeks' notice to get a temporary replacement."

Dave told Meghan about his conversation with Valerie.

She replied, "See, two heads can find solutions where one struggles."

"Yes, and thank you for understanding."

"Don't answer this if you don't want to, but did you sleep with Valerie?"

"If I admit that, I must clarify it."

"How can you clarify sleeping with a woman?"

"Well, one night after playing chess, she asked me to take her to my flat and comfort her. She was stressed out, and I thought comfort meant sex. I stripped and got into bed, and she did the same, snuggled against me, wrapped her arms around me, and then went to sleep for eleven hours."

Meghan broke into peals of laughter. Then she had a thought, "*I think I'd like that too.*"

When Grant called and said the Head had agreed, Dave told Valerie and gave her Grant's number.

The *Oncology* conference had sixty delegates—most of them cancer specialists from various fields. During the tea break, a spectacularly shaped woman approached Dave. She had long, black hair and was dressed in a jersey knit dress that had no intention of hiding anything.

"Mr Tennant, your report in the journal does not indicate the research you are doing. Will you be producing a new drug?"

"Not at all, Ms ...?"

"Ramirez. But call me Ysabel."

"The lab I work for doesn't manufacture drugs. I don't have the skills and facilities to produce them. Why do you ask?"

"It's my job to visit doctors and persuade them to use our medicines and not those of a competitor."

Dave blatantly looked at her bust and hips. "Well, if I were a doctor, I would be thrilled to have you visit."

She laughed.

Dave asked, "How many hours a day do you spend in a gym?"

"An hour three times a week, then I run twenty kilometres every other day."

"Well, I run in Ravenscourt Park if you want to join me on a Sunday. From five-thirty in the evening."

"Oh, I've run there before. From the tearoom?"

"Yes."

Meghan was coming back from the bathroom and was about to join Dave when a man approached her. She thought him outstandingly handsome. *About forty*, she guessed.

"Miss MacDougal, I'm Redwin Beltgood, a cancer specialist like my colleagues here. I read your article in *Oncology*—a most interesting report. I couldn't discover much about remission cases. How is the patient doing?"

"Very well. The remission is ongoing. But we have no idea why. As it says in the report, I'm a microbiologist, but I'm more interested in the DNA of microbes."

"That's a coincidence. I'm interested in the DNA change when a cell becomes cancerous.

"We should get together and compare notes. Can I have your phone number?"

He was so charming; she gave it to him.

When he walked away, Meghan looked over to where Dave was standing. He was talking to a woman she immediately classed as a predator, so she walked over to interrupt.

Dave introduced her. In Meghan, he sensed the same iciness she'd shown when they'd first met Monica. Ysabel did, too, so she excused herself and left them with a cheeky grin at Meghan.

"Wow. You do affect women."

"I don't try; I think they just like me."

"That one looks to me like a praying mantis."

"Why do you say that?"

"The mantis female eats the male when they have sex, so watch out, Dave."

Dave laughed. Meghan almost missed the innuendo.

"But human males eat the female," Dave said.

She blushed.

Although Dave kept an eye out for Ysabel at Ravenscourt Park, he didn't see her and soon forgot about her.

Meghan didn't get the expected call from Redwin, so she forgot about him.

Dave and Meghan finished their second report, with modifications to the wording by Doctor Sankewicz, and sent it to *Oncology*. Now Dave and Meghan would both be credited as "Research Fellow (Cambridge University)".

Doctor Morrison took new samples from Boris on Friday, twelve months after Boris terminated treatment. The blood arrived in a warm box at blood temperature, so Meghan put the sample into heated storage.

Later, when she told Dave the sample had arrived, he said, "Oh good, this will tell us if Boris is still recovering or not. Do you want to do the analyses with me?"

She replied emphatically, "If you dare do it without me, beware of involuntary sterilisation."

On occasion, Dave lapsed into dockside slang; he was, after all, from Tilbury. "Never heard of that; I suppose you mean you'll cut my balls off."

"Regretfully, yes."

"Well, I won't take the chance. Tomorrow's Saturday, and there won't be any distractions. Are you free in the morning?"

"As it happens, yes. Nine o'clock?"

"It's a date."

The next morning, they prepared the fluid samples and slides.

Three hours later, the analysis showed continued cancer remission.

"Let's look at the slides."

Meghan focused the microscope on the first one. "Dave, I can see many Corkys and very few cancer cells."

"Yes, right- and left-helix ones, and not many cholera." He pointed at the screen. "That cancer cell is dead; the nucleus is not showing. Can you try to count the Corkys and the cancer cells?"

Meghan took a slide to the cell counter. A moment later, she read off the cancer cell count. Then she did the same for the left- and right-hand Corkys.

Dave continued studying the first slide. "Meg, can we get a photo sequence, like a video, of a Corky moving?"

"I don't know; let me try a different light frequency or another angle. Take a clean slide, wipe it with the neutral surfactant, then put a small drop of fluid in the middle; it should spread slowly."

Dave did as Meghan had asked and handed her the slide; she put it in the holder and fiddled with the controls.

"There, is that what you wanted? I've set it up for time-lapse imaging. Whatever's there, we'll have a video of it."

They both stared at the viewscreen; after a minute of scanning it carefully, Dave said, "We have something new. Top right, just off centre; tell me what you think."

Meghan was silent as she watched. Then she said, "The wee beasties are humping; we have the first-ever porn video with bacterium actors."

"Bacteria are asexual."

"Well, these two are humping and have different helixes; it looks to me like sex."

"You think that's bacterial intercourse?"

"Looks like it; what would you call it?"

"I don't know if it's humping; they seem to be joining, merging, into one, and doing so while attached outside a cancer cell."

"That means humping to me."

"Ok. Oh, look, the Corkys have somehow breached the cell wall; they're going in. Wow, something is going on in the cell. Meg, blow up that part of the screen."

She did. "Dave, that's a scene of wild sex under the covers; they are bumping around inside the cancer cell."

"You've got sex on the brain; bacteria reproduce through binary fission."

Meg was angry. "They might be fissing, not fucking, but it's sexual; they can only do it together, and it needs a left- and a right-helix Corky. Believe what you see, Dave."

"Speculation, Meg."

Her voice cracked as she said, "And here are the babies."

Dave was silent for what seemed ages. "They aren't baby bacteria; they look to me like bacteriophages. Turn up the magnification, slowly.

"They *are* bacteriophages. The original two Corkys are now exiting the cancer cell, which seems to have died."

"It certainly looks like it."

Meghan reeled back the image sequence to the beginning, and they watched silently through to the end.

"Dave, phages are viruses that attack bacteria; they don't live long unless they invade a bacterium. What bacteria do you think they attack?"

"I haven't a clue. I can take a wild guess, but it's purely speculation."

"What?"

"We have two new forms of bacterium, both of which we've never seen before we stumbled on Boris's case, and they are in the same person—it seems reasonable that there must be a link. Perhaps the phages attack the cholera bacteria. And kill them."

"If they are virulent, yes, but temperate ones—those that don't kill bacteria immediately after infection—might be lysogenic, meaning they would be absorbed into a cholera bacterium and participate in gene transfer."

"With what result?"

"I don't know; it would make a modified bacterium. We must experiment to find out. We have a chance to separate the phages and both the left- and right-hand Corkys for a DNA test. Let's do it now—I'll do the separation; you can then store the three separately in a bit of the fluid."

As they finished, Alice called to tell Meghan she had prepared a steak-and-kidney pie but wouldn't stay for dinner, as she'd received an unexpected invitation. She said, "I'll put it in the oven to keep it warm. I've left some boiled potatoes on the stove, for you to mash. Don't forget butter and pepper."

Meghan replied, "Thanks, Ally. I'll be late anyway, as I'm still in the lab."

Alice answered, with a dash of hope in her voice, "There's more than enough for two; bring him home to eat it."

Dave and Meghan managed to separate the cells and phages, then packed up, got changed, and went to Meghan's flat.

The pie was in the oven as promised; it just needed more warming. Meghan laid the table and gave Dave a bottle of wine to open. "The glasses are in the top of the cupboard in the corner."

"Meg, this is delicious. I've never had a pie like this; the herb mix is fantastic. You can tell Alice if she makes it again, she has a dedicated client."

They drank too much wine while discussing Corkys, wondering what the phages would do and why the immune system didn't destroy the Corkys. They each took turns to propose ideas and shoot the other's theory down. In the end, all they had was speculation and questions.

Dave stood. "Meg, it's late, and I must go."

Meghan was silent as she struggled with something. Then she said, "Dave, that's not what I want right now, but it may be the wine talking, and I think it's best if you do go."

The next day, Dave found he couldn't concentrate after having spent hours unsuccessfully searching the net for any reference to a bacterium identical to Corky. He needed a diversion like the one he'd had on the night at the Bang-Up Club when he had met James. He thought of Meghan but then concluded, *"No, she's off-limits and perhaps has another man to take her out."*

The thought of the Bang-Up Club was enough to remember Monica, but since she had called him "Mr Tennant", he knew he was on her discard pile. It brought the memory of Fluffy and her invitation to teach him about something called "breakbeat". He gave her a call.

"Hello Fluffy, Dave here; we met at the Bang-Up Club when I went with Monica."

"Dave, nice to hear from you," she said. Her voice had an undertone of warmth and was clearer without the insistent bass that had marred it when they'd met in the club.

"You offered to teach me about techno music, or was that just politeness?"

"If you take me to my old club, I'll teach you all I can."

"That's great; when?"

145

"How about this Friday? Fridays are safe nights at the club."

"Why 'safe'? Is it dangerous?"

"Saturdays, there's often a football crowd, and they've been drinking all afternoon and evening, so it's rowdy and unpleasant."

"Friday is fine for me."

"Where do you live, and have you got an extra bed for me at your place?"

Dave thought, "*Good, she doesn't want to sleep with me.*"

"Ravenscourt Park, and I've got one in the study; why?"

"Then give me your address. The club is too far for me to get home late. I'll come to your place and take you to the club, then spend the night and return to my home in the morning."

"If you come before eight, I can take you to dinner first."

"Ok, see you then, and thanks."

"Bye."

16

Meghan was unaware of the grey-suited men who stood on street corners, watching her in reflecting shop windows, or who followed her down the steps to the Underground and boarded the same train as she did. Men whose lives depended on invisibility. She and Dave didn't know that the records of their studies and careers had been copied into reports.

But Dave was a member of the "look-at-people" club. He was always on the lookout for imminent danger. His mind stored snapshots of the people he saw, and when—for the third time—he spotted a stranger following him, he took action. He used the Underground to a nearby station. There, he rode the long escalator to an upper level, but he quickly switched to the down-escalator at the top. He knew that the man following him would be riding the up-escalator. They passed each other at the halfway point. The man tried desperately to avoid looking at Dave, but Dave stared directly at him until the stranger risked a glance and saw his wide grin.

When Dave arrived at the office, he told Meghan: "Men—spies of some sort—are watching me. I caught one at it this morning."

His calm words alarmed her. "Who are they?" she asked.

"I don't know, and it doesn't matter; let them waste their time. I'll check if anyone's watching you."

"Are you going to do anything dangerous?"

"No, I can't go roaming around your flat. I'll get some invisible help. Now, let's do some work."

"Dave, please explain. Saying they don't matter worries me. What if you're wrong? Who are they?"

"Professional surveillance men; call them private detectives if you wish, but that's flattering—the man who followed me this morning is a professional tail."

"But who's he working for?"

"The Big Pharma companies like to know of any developments that might affect their business. They must have noted the article in *Oncology* and put us on their watch list. For the moment, it's not dangerous, just a damned nuisance, and it may become a problem if they try to prevent me from saving my mother. I must stop climbing through your bedroom window at midnight."

Meghan laughed. "*He has the gift of making scary things seem normal.*"

Later that afternoon, Meghan asked, "Have you ever been fishing, Dave?"

"I've been many times. Before my father left, I often went fishing with my friends at a pier."

"Did you catch anything?"

"Little ones usually, but sometimes we caught a whopper and had it for dinner."

"Have you ever been fly-fishing?"

"No, have you?"

"My dad would go on a Sunday. He tried to teach me how to cast when I was thirteen. All I ever caught was Rory, who wouldn't keep out of the way and always gave me unwanted advice. While

Dad fished, I often walked up the stream. The countryside is lovely in the Highlands. At uni, a guy who fancied me tried to teach me but lost interest when he discovered I was a duffer."

"And you haven't tried coarse fishing?"

"No, never."

"Well, how about I take you coarse fishing at the Thames on Monday? It's a bank holiday, and the weather forecast is good. I know a spot upriver that's quite active. It calms the nerves and allows thinking. I used to go regularly before my mother fell ill."

"What did you catch?"

"Only a few little ones. And one or two pike. That was exciting. But I threw them all back to catch another day."

"Dave, you continue to amaze me. I'm looking forward to Monday; it sounds like it'll be fun."

Fluffy arrived at Dave's flat. He took her bag to the study and asked, "Do you have another name? 'Fluffy' must be a nickname."

"Yes, I'm Karen Dickson, but my parents called me 'Fluffy', the kids all followed suit, and it has stuck. I'm so used to it that I tell everyone to use it. Don't you like it?"

"I think it's sort of affectionate; I like it."

"Then use it. Where are we going for dinner?"

"Depends on you. Do you have a preference: meat, fish, vegetarian?"

"Fish."

At dinner, Dave was surprised to learn Fluffy was a qualified physiotherapist.

"I didn't manage to get into med school, and I didn't fancy emptying bedpans as a nurse, so I studied physio."

"Do you enjoy it?"

"Yes and no. I enjoy working on patients who need help recovering from injuries such as a sprained knee or ankle, or a broken or fractured bone. But I don't look forward to working on patients with chronic back pain or bad circulation requiring repeated treatment. Especially those who complain or don't bathe or wash. Sometimes the stink is terrible."

"That I can understand. Do you get harassed?"

"You mean sexual harassment, don't you?"

"Yes, Fluffy; you're an attractive young woman."

"In the first few months after I started working, I had three requests for masturbation and a dozen wandering hands. Now all professional masseurs have cameras. If it's a male patient, I tell him about the camera, so they don't try.

"The bedridden cases that need circulation massages are the worst. It's depressing seeing them fade until the day you are told you don't have a patient."

"I can imagine, but doctors have the same problem. I never thought physiotherapists did too. So techno is your release?"

"Yes, and we should go. We'll take the Underground to Elephant and Castle and then walk to the club."

That night, Dave learned about breakbeat music; he was surprised to find he enjoyed some of it, and he began to understand what Fluffy called "transcendental". When she asked when he wanted to leave, he replied, "I'm not in a hurry, and we'll take a taxi back, so you decide."

They left before one in the morning, quite sober.

At Dave's flat, Fluffy said, "Dave, in the morning, you will have stiff calves and a stiff neck; if you like, I'll give those muscles a work-over so they'll relax. Strip to your shorts and lie face down on your bed."

Dave felt her surprisingly strong hands probing and pulling for half an hour. He could feel the muscles relaxing as she manipulated him.

She did his neck and then said, "Turn over, Dave."

She worked on his upper thighs. "There, that should do it."

"Thanks, Fluffy, but what about you?"

"I'm used to the dancing. Since the practice sessions at school, I haven't needed anything."

"Well, I'm not as good as you, but I've spent many hours working on my mother; she was bedridden for months. So, lie on the bed; it's your turn."

She stripped to a string, and before she lay on the bed, Dave thought that lots of dancing had given her the muscles to avoid sagging breasts. He did the same for her calves, thighs, neck, and back.

She turned over with her eyes closed. "Dave, you're excellent. You can massage my breasts; the muscles get a workout from dancing."

He obliged and then moved across her stomach to the upper thighs as she had done. When she groaned, he stopped, looked up, and saw her nipples had swollen.

"Dave, don't stop." She parted her legs so he could continue inside her thighs. After another three minutes, she spread her legs wide and gasped, "Dave, touch me there."

It happened quickly. Fluffy's legs snapped together, trapping Dave's hand as she raised her hips. He didn't move until finally, she relaxed.

"Dave, that's never happened to me before. You are exceptional. I'm tired; let's sleep."

Dave woke the following day, relaxed, with Fluffy still asleep beside him. He didn't move, letting her sleep.

When she opened her eyes, she said, "Good morning, Dave."

"Morning. Are you ready for breakfast?"

"I am, but do you realise we've slept together all night and haven't kissed?"

"True, Fluffy. Do you want to?"

"Yes."

The kiss lasted, and Dave unconsciously cupped one of her breasts and felt a hardening nipple.

"Dave, I don't know what's wrong with me; I've never made love in the morning."

"Nothing wrong, Fluffy; more like *right*." He caressed the nipple, then felt a wave of heat and Fluffy's hand on his member.

"Oh God, I need you."

It was hard to believe she was the same woman he had met in the Bang-Up Club.

As Dave walked Fluffy to the station, she said, "Dave, last night was transcendental. If you want to call me again, please do."

As he walked back, he wondered if he would call her. Why did he feel guilty? What would he say to his mother tomorrow, if she was awake? He had no feelings for Fluffy except for friendship; he hadn't expected sex, so why had he invited her for the evening?

He thought back to when he had called Fluffy last Sunday night: he had visited his sleeping mother for two hours, run in the park, and become bogged down in his research. He'd been late with Meghan on Saturday, and she'd refused to allow him to stay. Was that the reason he'd ended up calling Fluffy? But had Meghan rejected him? He recalled her words: "Dave, that's not what I want right now, but it may be the wine talking, and I think it's best if you go."

What if it hadn't been the wine? Did she want him? It gave him a warm feeling that she had wanted him to stay but had sent him away because of the lab's policy against colleagues being romantically involved. Then he felt a gut-wrenching pain; he loved her but had to remain silent.

The next day, Dave spent another two hours with his mother, who slept through his visit. Dave didn't need a blood analysis to tell that his mother was worse; the battery of electronic monitors displayed her condition clearly. As always, he noted her vitals in his notebook. Her state was steadily regressing.

17

After two train rides and a bus, Dave and Meghan chose a spot on the grassy riverbank. Dave assembled their rods and lines, then handed one to Meghan and demonstrated with his. "No need to cast; use the rod to throw the hook and float a little way out—the fish prefer swimming near the bank."

Meghan, cautious at first, began to enjoy her day after catching three small roach and a chub. Dave caught a good-sized dace. They lounged on the bank and ate the picnic meal Meghan had brought. Their conversation stayed off work. Instead, they each spoke about different things, trying to judge reactions and learn about each other.

"Meg, I'm going to catch a pike. I'll change my hook and lure."

"Change mine too; I could be lucky."

They both had drifter floats, and they needed only to watch them going back and forth as gentle puffs of wind brushed the water. They continued to talk.

Suddenly, Meghan's reel screamed. She grabbed the rod, and Dave shouted, "Strike, Meg, seat the hook!"

He reeled in his line and turned to her to assist. "Meg, he's too big for you; let me help."

"If I need your help, I'll ask. I want to catch this fish myself."

Dave couldn't resist giving some advice. "Let him run to get him tired. You won't land him until he's exhausted."

"I don't need your advice either; you remind me of Rory."

Dave sat on the grass behind her and said nothing, watching as she fought the fish.

The sun was setting behind the trees, casting a shadow over the river. Several anglers had packed up as the temperature dropped, but Meghan, absorbed in the fight, continued.

"I think I've got him. He's tired now."

Dave said nothing. He knew pike. He decided she needed a lesson; the comparison to Rory annoyed him.

Meghan began reeling the pike into the bank; the fish gathered his remaining strength, letting her pull him along. Meghan leaned over the bank to look down at the languidly moving fish. "He's a monster, Dave. Bring the net."

She let the line slacken. The fish got the signal and burst into a run. Meghan, overbalanced by the sudden jerk, belly-flopped into the water.

As she surfaced, Dave asked politely, "Do you need help now?"

Her immediate reaction was to say no, but the cold was too much. "Yes, get me out."

He reached down, grabbed a proffered hand, then another, and lifted her onto the bank.

She wrapped her arms around her chest as he got his fishing bag and removed a parcel from the bottom.

"What do we do now? I'm freezing." Her teeth were chattering.

"Face me and raise your arms." Dave lifted her shirt over her head and then released her bra. She grabbed it before it could fall. The parcel contained a terrycloth beach robe that Dave wrapped around her. She pushed her arms into the sleeves, letting her bra fall to the grass, and pulled the robe closed. Dave reached in, undid her pants zip, and pulled everything down in one move. Then he used a small towel to dry her legs.

"Sit on the bag, Meg. I must dry your feet."

He removed a pair of socks from the bag. As he finished drying each foot, he put a thick sock onto it. After a minute, her teeth stopped chattering, and warmth started to build.

"Why have you got socks and a beach robe in your bag?"

"All fishermen carry socks and a towel; we get wet feet. A beach robe is a survival necessity, and I've read the *Fisher's Guide to the Galaxy*. Now just get warm while I wring out your clothes and try to dry your shoes."

Half an hour later, Dave said, "You can put these shoes on. We must go before it gets too cold."

"Where to? I'm naked except for a robe. Are we taking a taxi?"

"We'll walk across the park. On the other side of the street, there's a laundromat where we can dry your clothes and shoes. Then we'll return the way we came; it will be far quicker."

In the laundromat, a stout housewife took one look at Meghan and asked, "Did you fall in the river, or did he throw you in, my dear?" Then seeing the wet clothes Dave carried, she added, "Here, sir, put the clothes in the washing machine for a spin-dry first." She took them from him and loaded them. She couldn't miss the bra and panties.

Dave grinned. "We were fishing, ma'am. Meghan hooked a big pike, and it pulled her in. I had to pull her out."

The woman smiled. "If I tell my hubby there are naked mermaids to catch in the river, he'll be out fishing every day!"

As Meghan opened the front door to her flat, Dave said, "I'm sorry you fell in the river, Meg. It doesn't often happen when fishing. But I enjoyed the day."

"It was my fault, Dave. I'm glad you were there to rescue me."

"Meg, ask me tomorrow about Rory. Good night, *Mermaid*."

Meghan told Ally the whole story. Including that he had called her "Mermaid".

"That's a good sign. You know you've hooked your man when he has a loving nickname for you."

"Hooked maybe, but not caught, Ally; I've learned they can get away."

Nevertheless, her heart was singing, "*Mermaid, Mermaid, Mermaid ...*"

Meghan, fully recovered from her swim in the Thames, didn't waste any time when she arrived at work. Dave was already working.

"Good morning, Dave. You said I must ask about Rory."

"Morning, Meg. Yes, I did. Tell me: when I offered to help yesterday, you said, 'You remind me of Rory'—why?"

"Because he always tried to order me around or give me advice. Trying to make me feel incapable or inferior."

"Think about yesterday. Was that what I was trying to do?"

Meghan remembered the moment. Up until now, she had been too preoccupied with the fish to analyse it. She pictured Dave's worried face. Tritely, she replied, "No, Dave."

"You must control that blind reaction; it can be dangerous. An angry person doesn't think clearly, is unaware of the surroundings, and might do stupid things. If you feel that anger, ask yourself why. I'm not Rory and will never put you down. I don't mean you should meekly accept an order or advice. Analyse it first, and accept it only if it's good, but never get angry."

"I understand, Dave. I'm sorry about yesterday."

"You couldn't help it. Don't be sorry; you got a dunking, and I felt like a spider, but we are still alive."

"A spider, Dave?"

"I got a close look at your feet."

Meghan laughed. *"Incredible; when I screw up completely, he can make me laugh."*

Meghan knew he was right. But how could she control a reaction established in childhood? It might take some time ...

Dave spent two nights walking the streets around the Chelsea area to recruit the help he sought. He spoke the language of his dockside youth.

Scarp, short for "Scarper", christened as "Tony Benton" by doting parents—although it's doubtful how long they remained doting—was idling along the pavement under the streetlights, desultorily kicking a small stone. A voice stopped him as he passed a blind alley where the lights didn't penetrate.

"Hey Scarp, I wanna talk to you."

He couldn't see anyone in the alley as he backed up a step, ready to run like hell—something he did well, hence his gang name. "Who's talking?"

"Guy looking for some help."

"What? And what's it worth?"

"Mebbe thirty quid, Scarp."

"Tell me."

"You know the lady that lives in thirty-four, a young woman with reddish-blonde hair?"

"Yeah. Miss MacDougal." Scarp thought it a stupid question; of course he knew the lady—this was his territory, and he knew everyone living here.

"I want to know if a guy is watching her."

"Ain't seen one."

"Then go look, Scarp. If you follow the guy, do it with three or four of your gang. Take turns following him so he doesn't get suspicious. My number is on the paper under the rock by the pillar. Send an SMS when you know something, and I'll meet you here."

Scarp asked, "Mister, why do you need me?"

"Your territory, Scarp; gotta respect a guy's turf."

Scarp felt an incredible sense of pride. "What's your name, mister?"

"The Shadow."

The name struck a note of fear into sixteen-year-old Scarp; he had heard it somewhere. He hid, then waited fifteen minutes, but nobody left the alley; when he went to look again, he found no one.

The SMS came.

Dave went to see his informer. "What do you know, Scarp?"

"There's a guy who comes in the morning, early. He follows her to the station and goes on the same train. Then follows her back after work."

"Thanks, Scarp, the thirty quid will be under the rock. Keep watching."

Dave spoke to Meghan in the lab: "A man is watching you. It's not a problem, but we had better ensure we keep our data safe. Also, give me the serial numbers of any notebooks or tablet computers in your flat. They might get stolen."

Dave got another SMS on his shadow phone, so he met his helper again.

Scarp told him two men were now sitting in a car up the road from Meghan's flat, that the car dropped off a man at the station when she went to work, and it came back when Meghan returned. It was a different car each day.

"Scarp, you sure it's not the same car every time?"

"Yeah, I've got a list of the plate numbers; here, look."

"They may be pinching a new car every morning. Do you know any of the coppers on the beat in Chelsea?"

"Yeah, one—he owes me."

Dave was impressed.

"You wanna tell me why, Scarp?"

"I don't mind. There was this girl I fancied, younger than me, under sixteen, but she wasn't interested. Two of the gang and I found her fighting off a boy bigger than her one night. We gave him a beating, and I took her home. Her dad saw me, and the girl told me when I saw her at school that she had told her dad about it."

"What's that got to do with the cops?"

"Her dad's a cop; he gave that boy a warning. And now he says good evening to me when we see each other on the street."

"Give that list to the copper, Scarp; tell him about the men and that you think they are using stolen cars. They'll check those plate numbers."

The following evening, two imposing figures in boots came from behind the waiting car, one on each side, to stand at the front windows. One of them tapped on the driver's window. When it wound down, he asked politely, "Good evening, sir. Waiting for someone, are you?"

"Yes, Officer, he should be along soon; why do you ask?"

"Just a check, sir; we check on anything suspicious."

"What's suspicious, Officer?"

"Two men, sitting in a stolen car."

"Bloody hell!" The driver started the engine and began to pull out but was blocked by a police car.

Dave met his helpers again and thanked them.

Scarp said, "You're a cool guy, Mr Shadow. We never thought of using the cops. We'll keep an eye out for the lady from now on."

Dave replied with some advice: "It's more fun fucking up the bad guys, and if the cops are on your side, they are put away and can't get back at you. It can be more dangerous, so watch out; some crooks are bastards."

160

Dave got another beep on his second phone and met his helpers again.

"They got a stakeout, Mr Shadow, a room across the street. I borrowed my brother's bird-watching binocs, and I got a look when the curtain moved—they have a telescope and other gear set up."

"Good thinking, Scarp; leave it to me."

"Meg, who lives in the other front flats in your building?"

"On my floor, the neighbour is Mr Jenkins; he's about sixty, nice and polite, and reticent. Two old widows, a very nosy pair, Mrs Coolidge and Mrs Watkins, are on the ground floor. I've seen them on the common with other elderly women who live in the street."

"Well, go see one or both, take your horseracing binoculars, and tell them that men are watching them from the house opposite, the upper floor on the right."

"Is that true?"

"Yes, they may be planning a break-in; tell the widows that you are worried they'll break in when you and Alice are out."

As Dave had expected she would, Mrs Watkins reported the peeping Toms to the police. Only to be told that no law prevented people from looking out their front window. So she set up her personal watch, convinced the men were planning a robbery. She sat quilting in a chair in her front room, behind drawn curtains with a narrow gap through which she could see her house's front door. Her patchwork quilt steadily grew.

On the second day, she saw Mr Jenkins depart for work, then Meghan appeared, followed by Alice at ten am. Shortly thereafter, she watched a nondescript man leave the house opposite and unhurriedly cross the road carrying a tool bag. Mrs Watkins picked up her phone and tapped the police number. When the man arrived at the front door, he didn't ring the doorbell but fiddled with the lock, so Mrs Watkins pressed the "Call" button.

"Police, can I help you?"

"Mrs Watkins here. I complained two days ago about potential thieves. Now they are breaking in at thirty-four Manresa Road."

She was relieved when the officer didn't hesitate. "Police are on their way, ma'am. Please stay on the line. Tell me when you hear a siren."

A few minutes passed. Mrs Watkins heard it and said, "I can hear a siren now, and someone is walking above me in number four."

"Thank you, ma'am; the police will take over. Please stay in your flat. Goodbye."

The first police car arrived, and an officer ran into the building just in time to arrest the man who—warned by his partner in the house opposite—was running down the stairs. Seconds later, an officer from a second police car caught the partner, who had run outside. The officer pinned him down and cuffed him.

Mrs Watkins had stayed in her flat but called Meghan. Dave and Meghan were already en route to her when the police called.

"The thief stole nothing, Ms MacDougal, but we think he was planting listening devices. There is recording equipment in the flat opposite."

18

Meghan and Dave's second report was published in the June edition of *Oncology*. The magazine *Popular Medicine* carried an article titled "Home Cures for Cancer are Possible". It was mostly a list of quack medicines, but it cited the *Oncology* report in a faint attempt at credibility.

Dave had been thinking about the men who'd been watching Meghan. He worried that they'd planted listening devices in Meghan's flat. Only an expert would know what to look for and where to find them. Fortunately, he knew someone, so after struggling with his conscience, he called Tansy after Meghan went into the lab. He hoped Tansy still had the same number.

"Hello."

Dave recognised her melodious voice; he got a knot in his stomach as he remembered the past. He replied, "Tansy, it's Dave."

"Dave, nice to hear from you; I thought I never would."

"No hard feelings, Tansy. How's your boyfriend?"

"Greg? I threw him out long ago. He may be an electronics genius, but he was nowhere near as good as you in bed. He thought of me as a defective circuit board that needed re-soldering."

"I'm sorry to hear that, Tansy. Are you unattached now?"

"No, my boyfriend, Brian, is also an electronics fanatic. An

Asimov fan, he calls me 'Dors' or 'My Beautiful Robot'. I think he will propose, and I'll marry him. Don't ask me to come back, Dave; I need an electronics geek to live with, although I guess a communications guy might fit."

"I wasn't going to ask you to come back, Tansy; I called because I need someone to search my flat and my partner Meg's place for bugs."

"Partner as in girlfriend?"

"No, Tansy, as in work colleague."

"Working together is a good start for a relationship. Where?"

"My flat near Ravenscourt Park, and hers in Chelsea."

"Ok, when?"

"I'll check with Meg and call you back, Tansy. And thanks."

"Dave, do you keep computers or tablets in your flats?"

"Yes, of course."

"Then, when you call, give me the serial number, make, and model of each. We've been partners in one way or another for years; it's my pleasure."

When Meghan returned to their office, Dave said, "I want to check out your flat and mine for listening devices."

"Can you do that?"

"No, but I know a woman who can; she's an electronics fanatic."

"What's her name?"

"Tansy Roper."

"Interesting; a girlfriend?"

"A long-time friend, and ex. I was fifteen, and she was thirteen, when we met. Then I went to university, so we lost touch until we met again in London.

"She came to work in town, and I had just moved to BaVir. We had a short, passionate affair, probably because we didn't know anyone else, then she left me cold for an electronics nut."

"Ok, what's your plan?"

"First, you give me the serial number, make, and model of each computer and tablet in your flat. And second, I bring her to your flat and take her to mine."

"No, I've got a better idea. I'll come to your flat and meet Tansy while she checks out your place, then I'll take her to my flat."

"Meg, she's expecting a marriage proposal from her boyfriend. Do you think she'll go to bed with me for old time's sake?"

"No, but at my flat, I get to ask her about you and your past without you being there. You are the most mysterious, uncommunicative, and un-ordinary man I've ever met. Every day we are together, I'm surprised." Then she thought, "*And he thinks I'll be upset if he goes to bed with her. What does that mean?*"

Tansy swept Dave's flat for bugs, opening his computer and tablet devices and fiddling inside them. She found nothing. Secretly, he was relieved, as Monica had been noisy. But Tansy did find a bug in his phone.

When she was finished, Dave asked, "Tansy, what all did you do?"

"I cleared out any data that a hacker would be after, such as your search and location histories. Then I installed whatever tracking devices and software I could. Keep that list of serial numbers somewhere safe; then, if anything gets stolen, call the number I'll give you. Just tell the guy the stolen item's serial number, then do the police report."

"And if we don't have the serial number or know what has gone missing?"

"Call him anyway and give your name."

"Who's the guy, Tansy?"

"It will be one of our employees who answers. We ensure someone is available twenty-four seven. Brian and I run a business to track stolen IT equipment. We tell the police where they can recover the items. But we cannot publicise our business. Please, if you sell or give away this gear, call the guy."

Tansy went to Meghan's flat as planned, without Dave.

The search yielded a collection of electronic bugs. Meghan hoped they had not been there when she had entertained Barry. Tansy deleted some of Meghan's sensitive data and installed tracking software on her devices.

Then Meghan asked Tansy, "How did you meet Dave?"

"I was thirteen when my mother died, leaving me with an alcoholic father who didn't care. I had no friends. The parents of the other kids my age didn't want me around. To avoid my father, I went out and wandered, sometimes for hours. Dave was fifteen then and belonged to a street gang. He must have seen me several times. One night, as I was walking, I heard a voice from an alley. It shocked me because I hadn't seen anyone there. It said, 'Hey, girl, I've seen you around. You got nowhere to go?'

"My name is Tinsley, but Dave shortened it to Tansy and took me to one of the places where the gang met. When they asked, 'Who's the chick?' he replied, 'Tansy. She's one of us.'" She smiled at the memory. "I remember it well.

"Meg, they're all grown up now. Some were rough kids. They had girlfriends, but there wasn't much love, and when they got older, sex was just physical—a fuck. But they all assumed I was Dave's girl, and I never had one try to fuck me.

"If Dave had asked, I wouldn't have hesitated. Please understand: not because I was in love with him, but because I thought I belonged to him after he rescued me. I thought he was my man.

"Dave gave me some back copies of *Popular Electronics*. He got the gang to go out and find me a soldering iron and old radios and electronics to take apart. I started because he wanted me to, not for any other reason. Then I caught the bug. By age fifteen, I had a workshop at the end of an abandoned shed. He sensed what I needed.

"By the time he went to university, he was the gang leader, and they called him 'The Shadow'. He made a lot of changes, and the gang became respectable."

"Why 'The Shadow'?"

"When I met Dave, I thought he was a werewolf, a teenage fantasy. Have you noticed how quietly he walks?"

"Yes, it's uncanny. When you walk beside him, it's as if you're next to a ghost."

"Centuries ago, when the legends began, there must have been men who could glide silently through a forest like a wolf. When Dave walks at night in lonely streets, dogs don't bark at him, for they don't hear normal human sounds. If you're walking beside him and you look away for just a moment, when you look back, there's no sound to guide your eyes, and he momentarily vanishes.

"But it's a handicap too; people feel he can help them with their problems. That means that strays—just like I once was—who need help gravitate to him."

"Were there any other girls in the gang?"

"No. I was the only one."

"What happened to the other members?"

"I've heard that one has become a schoolteacher. Another is an art dealer. One is now a stockbroker. And then there is a bio-lab manager."

"Tansy, he said you had a passionate affair?"

"Not truly. When I came to London, I felt lost again and thought of Dave, so I called. When we met, I instantly thought I wanted him, so I asked him to take me home. It was terrific; he's the best lover I've had and might be the best I ever will. But it wore off as

I realised he made love to me like he would stroke a pet. He never gave himself to me; we had nothing in common except our past. I never had a father to love, Meg; I loved Dave. Today, I think part of it was that he took my father's place when I was thirteen.

"You're a lucky woman, Meg. You've got a fantastic man who loves you."

Meghan thought, "*Another one who thinks Dave and I have a common destiny.*" She said, "I wish he would say so. If it weren't for the employment policies at work ..."

"Yes, that's it; he can't say so because he's afraid of losing his job. He needs the lab. Without it, his mother would have no hope."

"But he could say so; nothing more."

"Would it stop there? I think not. Do you want to lose your job or him to lose his by breaking your employment rules?"

Meghan turned away, despair in her heart.

A day later, Meghan came into the office with a smug look. Alone with Dave in their office, she said, "Good morning, Shadow."

"Oh God, she told you my nickname?"

"And *much* more." Her smile became a grin. "And some of it was quite *personal*."

Dave didn't know what to say.

"I've always felt safe with you. Now I know why."

"Do you want to play chess sometime, Meg?"

"Are you trying to change the subject?"

"No, it's just that if I can't put you over my knee and give you a spanking, I can try to beat the pants off you at chess."

As he said "spanking", she felt a shiver but decided to ignore it. She would think about that reaction later.

"I'd love to play, but you'll win. I would prefer that to a spanking."

"Then we will go to Marco's tonight."

"Is that the place called Pizza Out?"

"Yes," Dave grinned, "it caters for those few unusual women who prefer to lose at chess than be spanked by their boyfriends."

The word "boyfriend" generated a funny feeling in Meghan.

When they turned in to a passage, Meghan saw the sign, "Pizza Out", the warning about people tagging there, and the medieval gate. "Dave, that gate looks like it came from a castle; it has *spikes*."

"Marco's idea of security seems to work."

They continued down the alley until they entered the restaurant. The red-cheeked man behind the counter and in front of a pizza oven looked to Meghan like a pizza himself. Meghan thought he must be one to enjoy his food.

"*Ciao*, what'll it be?" He grinned, looked at Meghan—she could tell it was a mischievous grin—and added, "And are you playing with the lady tonight?"

"My grandmother, Marco."

It stunned Meghan into silence.

But not Marco. "Good genes in your family, Dave."

Meghan was about to protest when Dave, straight-faced, said, "I'll play her if she's here, Marco."

It deflated Meghan long enough for Dave to add, "Marco, this is Meghan, a work colleague."

"Hi, Meghan, nice to meet you. Dave's an old friend, and lovely ladies can come any time, especially grandmothers."

Meghan liked Marco at once. "He can play chess with me, but nothing else. I'll have a small Regina with extra olives, and an apple juice. No pips in the olives; my false teeth can't handle them."

Marco chuckled. "A feisty lady. For you, Dave, your usual *Quattro Stagioni* and beer?"

"Yes please, Marco," Dave replied.

They went into the adjoining room and picked a table already set up with a chessboard and pieces. There were six other players. One pair seemed absorbed in their game—they had a timer to tap after every move and didn't look up—although the others glanced at Dave and Meghan curiously. Two nodded at Dave. The drinks arrived at once.

Remembering that Meghan had mentioned she thought he would beat her, Dave took the black side.

Meghan started with a classic pawn opening.

The game didn't take long; they had reduced the board to ten pieces within fifteen minutes. Although Meghan soon realised she would lose, she fought until Dave called "checkmate".

They re-arranged all the pieces on the board for other players, then followed another pair out of the room to find Marco putting their pizzas in cardboard boxes.

"There you are," Marco said. "Meghan, I should have warned you; Dave always plays forward on the left of the board."

Meghan asked, "Can you put my box in a bag? I don't have three hands."

They left, and outside, Meghan thanked Dave.

"That's the most stimulating half hour I've had for years and the first time I've had to fight off my host on a chessboard. A chess game can tell you a lot about a person."

"Like what?"

"Have you played with someone who knocks over the pieces he takes before removing them?"

"Yes, I have."

"That kind of person doesn't mind hurting others; he has no consideration for them."

"I never thought of that; I'll watch for it in future."

"Any time you want to play again, say so. I also liked Marco; he seems like a happy guy."

"Marco's always like that. Although he's English, his mother was

Italian, and he was born in Italy; he came to England a few years later."

Tansy called Meghan that night. "Meg, will you wear a gold cross around your neck constantly? Even in bed, when you bath, and in the shower? I want to give one to you and another to Dave. The crosses contain a GPS tracker and an emergency-assistance trigger."

"Sure, Tansy. Is there anything we should be worried about?"

"I don't like those bugs I collected. The UK-sourced ones had flat batteries, but the others were foreign and newer. You and Dave may be in danger. Also, I want to replace your phones. I'll give you ones where the locator stays on even when the phone is off."

"So someone will be watching our every move?"

"No, Meg, you must trust me; I won't watch unless there's a report of you missing or you press the cross to trigger the alarm. Can I come around tonight?"

"Tansy, you'll be in danger too if we're in danger. Let me talk to Dave."

Tansy didn't tell Meghan that not watching didn't apply to the computer; it would record their every move.

Scarp collected the crosses and phones from Tansy on a street corner that night and gave them to The Shadow in a dark alley.

19

Doctor Morrison received a deluge of emails about the second report published in *Oncology*. He didn't have time to read them, so Monica forwarded them to Meghan.

Meghan printed out and sorted the emails into four files: *Encouragements, Insults, Stupid ideas,* and *Nut cases*.

When Dave first looked at Meghan's files, he asked, "What are your sort criteria?"

"Well, the first file contains emails from people qualified in biology or a medical field; the *Encouragements* are just that, level-headed and pleasant. The *Insults* file also has messages from qualified people, but they all say the report is far-fetched bullshit that deserves to be in the science-fiction genre. The *Stupid ideas* file includes notes from people with little knowledge of biology, most of them telling the story of Jimmy, who recovered from cancer because he drank vinegar mixed with the sap of one plant or another. *Nut cases* has emails from the people who believe anything, claiming things such as that Corkys are aliens sent to invade Earth."

"My God, I certainly didn't expect this. And we didn't put forward a single conclusion or theory, only the facts."

"We didn't, but just saying we found a bacterium with a

corkscrew tail in a man's body is enough to trigger hysteria among the nut cases. There are eighteen times more mails from them than all the others, and they are all conspiracy theorists."

"Let me read one."

Meghan popped an email up on her screen.

Dear Mr Tennant,

It is a proven fact that the Earth is under attack by aliens. Every night you can see their missiles arriving as they glow with unholy light and then vanish as they explode and shower us with their poisons. That bacterium is the sperm of an alien trying to infect our race. The only cure for your patient is exorcism before the devil's spawn infects him.

"Holy shit, how can people believe this stuff?"

"You would have to consult the experts. You can tell he's not a logical thinker; a fact does not need proving. Many of these include an appeal for cash to help battle for the truth. We can ignore them."

"What about the insults?"

"Although they seem to be from educated scientists, the writers don't appear to be open to new things; they seem determined not to read what we wrote."

"What do you mean?"

"We wrote twice for each helix that 'the bacteria may not be a factor in cancer remission'. They read this as 'I suggest the bacteria is killing the cancer cells'. You should have written, 'The bacteria have no link to cancer unless otherwise proven.'"

"Hmm, give me an example."

Dear Mr Tennant and Ms MacDougal,

Your report is unworthy of publication. The waste bin is its proper destination. Suggesting that bacteria can affect cancer is utterly ridiculous. Before publishing such trash, you should have studied the hundreds of worthwhile papers by other researchers in the cancer field.

Professor I.M.A Parkins

"He fails to make any specific suggestions. I imagine any papers he has published have a hundred references in a bibliography, whether he has read them or not, to prove he knows his subject. I *have* read hundreds of papers on cancer since my mother got it. None of them has made much progress towards a cure; however, the drug manufacturers have made a difference with improved chemotherapy and immune-system drugs."

Meghan said, "It's the kind of thing I've heard in microbiology meetings; step on anyone's pet theories, even a feather-light step, and they explode like a firework."

"Like having an orgasm?"

Meghan felt a rush of heat. She replied, "Now it's you with the depraved mind."

"Right, Meg, is there anything worth reading?"

"You will enjoy the encouraging ones. Most are congratulatory, like, 'New thinking in a field that has made little progress for years is refreshing.' They don't offer ideas or suggestions; a few have comments on specific parts of the report. I think you must read them, for there may be something that jogs your memory. I might be a microbiologist, but you have studied cancer."

Dave's mobile rang. "Dave Tennant, good morning."

"Tiger, it's Michael Jenkins. I had a devil of a job tracking you down."

The name didn't ring a bell for a moment, but "Tiger" did.

"Mike, where are you?"

"In South Africa. I manage a game farm and lodge here. I just got married, Tiger, so I'm coming to the UK on an extended honeymoon. I'm going to show my wife around Britain, and I want to see you again when we are in London."

A thought wormed its way out of the depths: "*He's not stuttering any more.*"

"It will be a pleasure, Mike. I don't hear the stutter."

"It hasn't gone completely. If I don't get excited, I'm ok. You are the person who taught me that."

"I can't remember doing so. Will you call me when you head for London?"

"Yes."

"Is there anything special you want to do?"

"Yes. My wife is dying to see a London musical."

"Then I'll get all the info on what shows we can see, and you can tell me what you would like to see when you call."

"Thanks, Tiger. See you soon."

The name "Tiger" brought back memories Dave thought he had forgotten—Kathleen.

At fourteen, he had met her in her father's off-licence. Even at that young age, he was strong. Dave had gone to fetch the weekly box of booze an alcoholic neighbour paid him to bring.

Taller than Dave and with long blonde hair, she took no apparent notice of him, but it was love at first sight for Dave. His crush lasted until he left school. Sometimes, the pain in his heart—and, he admitted, his groin—was almost unbearable when he saw her. He had changed the routes he walked, hoping to catch a glimpse of her, and he had dawdled where she might appear.

Two years later, when old man Jenkins, impressed with Dave's physique, had offered him a Christmas job delivering booze, Dave thought God had intervened. He accepted, and learned a lesson about women. Kathleen was on the other side of the railway tracks. A cherry too high on the tree for him to reach. She called him

"Tiger", as her dad did, but never showed the slightest interest in a boy with well-worn clothes. He kept what little money he had for his shoes.

Kathleen's brother, Mike, was four years younger than Dave, and he stuttered. He was ok until the first stutter; then, embarrassment worsened it. Dave let him talk about animals at a pace that kept the stutter from taking over. Mike had adored him and followed him around the shop like a dog. Since Dave's first day at work, Mike had sat with him outside in the wintry sunshine and talked about animals while Dave ate his lunchtime sandwiches. Passing schoolkids took note, and Mike noticed that the kids didn't tease him any more about his stutter. They didn't call him "S-S-S-Stupid Kid".

Dave couldn't help the thought, *"Is Kathleen married now?"*

By Friday, the deluge of mails had become a trickle, and Dave had read everything Meghan recommended; he decided to read the others at home.

When Grant called, Dave realised it had been a month since he had given Valerie his number.

"Dave, Valerie is superb. The school has never had a resident child psychologist. She's taken to it like a duck to water, and her chess level is far higher than necessary. We are making her a job offer."

"Thanks, Grant, we must play chess sometime."

"She says you can beat her; that puts me below you, so it would be embarrassing."

"A little tip, Grant: focus on the chessboard and ignore distractions, especially when she sits further from the table and leans forward, showing her cleavage when making a move. Check every move she makes; many of them are decoys, and the attack will come from somewhere else."

"Fascinating. I never noticed. Playing against Valerie will be interesting now."

Valerie called. "Are you in tonight, Dave?"

"Yes, Val."

"Then expect me at nine."

When she rang, he let her in and asked, "Why the visit, Val?"

"We had an agreement, and I wanted to say this in person."

"Say what?"

"I don't think I'll be calling again to play chess at Marco's."

"That's fair, Val. I hope everything works out for you."

"I should have given up my job before meeting you. Things might have worked out differently. Meghan's a lucky woman, Dave."

"How do you know, Val?"

"I don't. I'm a psychologist and can feel it. Invite me to the wedding."

Dave's visit to the hospital was depressing; his mother was still sleeping in the fourth week after the chemo infusion. Dave knew this would happen but had hoped it would take much longer to manifest.

Worried, he called Doctor Morrison as soon as he knew the doctor would be at the surgery. "We were expecting the Boris Kravitz sample last week, Doctor; is there a problem?"

"No, Dave, he's on a training programme on the West Coast of the USA; he has promised to come in as soon as he returns, about June the twenty-eighth."

Dave updated Meg. "Boris is in the USA, so we will have to wait a bit for the next sample. We need to know if his cancer remission is still ongoing and what the Corky and cholera counts are like. I hope he is still in remission. We have a lot more research to do."

20

Dave asked, "Meg, what are you doing on Saturday?" Meghan thought he was about to ask her out, but then he added, "I'm entertaining an old friend."

His words were like cold water poured over her. He paused, but she didn't give him the chance to say anything else as she felt the anger rise within her. "I have a date, Dave, for a show and dinner."

"Fine, another time."

His reply left her wondering, *Another time? Had he been about to invite her?* She would have cancelled Colin instantly. Meghan walked past Dave's computer and saw on the screen a website that displayed available shows in London. Apprehension started to build. *"Is Dave taking an old friend of his to the theatre?"*

She made several unnecessary visits to her desk from the DNA lab, picking up a piece of paper or putting one down, hoping to overhear in passing something Dave said on the phone. By the end of the day, she had only heard one fragment of conversation: "I have the tickets, eight o'clock." Rejection replaced apprehension.

She remembered Ally saying, "Ask." But she couldn't, fearing the answer she didn't want to hear. She left the office depressed, feeling she might have lost an opportunity that would never return.

Dave was surprised when Monica called. "Hello Monica, is there something wrong?"

"I don't know, Dave. I'll tell you if you invite me for a steak again."

"Ok, Monica." Dave had an engagement for Saturday. "Today or tomorrow?"

"Today's good for me. Seven-thirty at the station?"

"See you there, Monica."

Dave found Monica subdued as he guided her into the steakhouse. Once they had ordered, he asked, "What's the problem?"

"I don't know. Since we went to the club, I've not had a boyfriend. I've been back there twice: the first time, the guy took me home, and the second time, he went off with another guy, so I left early and went home. He cancelled our last date. That's when I called you, and now we're here ..."

Dave laughed. "So you chose a gay guy to take you to the club. That must be a record."

"Well, it's never happened to me before, and the guy seemed nice, with big muscles."

"They usually are. I've had numerous gay friends. The guy who took you home; was he younger than you?"

"Yes, a year or two."

"How long have you been going to clubs?"

"Since I was eighteen."

"And now you're about twenty-six? That's eight years."

"Not twenty-six, only twenty-five and a half."

Dave grinned at her. "I'll bet that five years ago, you told people you were twenty-one just after your twentieth birthday.

"Monica, I don't know you well enough to give you advice. But you are growing up, getting older, and the clubbing scene is much younger. Within four years, you will look at babies and say 'coo-coo'.

"The young guys are afraid of you, and I'll bet there are very few men over thirty in the Bang-Up Club. Start looking for an older man. Choose something else to do in place of clubbing."

"Like what?"

"Well, you could start by going to art galleries. They have evening expos. You get free wine and cheese. Act dumb and say you want to learn about art."

"That won't be difficult. I don't know anything about it."

Dave was silent for a moment, trying to find alternatives. "Would you like some dessert?"

"Yes, some ice-cream would be nice; chocolate flavour, please."

"Look up art galleries and museums. If you go to an art gallery and look at a painting with a puzzled expression, a guy will come and ask if he can explain it. Find a girlfriend who can go with you."

The ice-cream arrived before Dave finished. "And stop jumping into bed first thing and discarding the men. You'll find sex is much better when you know something about each other and he wants to please you instead of himself. Try to find out enough about them to see if they are worth trying. Men love talking about themselves. Don't keep them if there's anything you don't like, but give them a chance."

Monica finished her ice-cream in silence. Then she said, "I'll think about it. Now, I need reassurance. Please, take me to your flat."

It was different. Monica enjoyed the much slower and longer rides to the top of a higher mountain, an experience she had never had. Dave had learned much from Angela and Susan that helped.

As Monica left in the morning, she kissed Dave as before and said, "Thanks. I think I know what you mean. I wish you were available."

"How do you know I'm not?"

"When I see you and Meg together, it's obvious, and I'm jealous."

Dave watched her go. Was it obvious? There was more to Monica than he had first thought.

When Dave sat at his computer on Saturday morning, an idea surfaced. He searched for art galleries around South Kensington, found Graham Tookbridge's gallery, and went to see it late that morning. When Dave entered the gallery, Graham was talking to a client.

Graham glanced at Dave, frowned, and turned back to the client. Two minutes later, he hurried over and greeted Dave with a handshake. "Dave Tennant, after all this time, how are you?"

"Fine Graham, healthy, as you can see. I'm a bioscientist. John Miller told me about you, so I came to have a look. It seems you are doing well. Have you married?"

"The business is so-so. I can't complain. My reputation as a dealer is growing, but I've been too busy to waste time dating. Hunting for good art is time-consuming. Can I sell you a painting?"

Dave wasn't there to buy art, but knowing he was about to ask a favour, he thought showing interest was the thing to do. "Not right now, Graham; I came to see you, but if you have the time, show me around—you never know."

"Ok, I'll give you the grand tour."

They walked around the gallery. Between recollections about their past, Graham would tell him something about every painting.

Then Dave stopped in front of one. "Graham, what's this one called?"

"'Life'. Painted by a doctor some years ago."

"How did he make it seem so alive?"

"There's a target. At the top left, there's a partially visible egg. All the spermatozoa point towards it—they are fighting to get there against the other cells blocking their way. The movement comes from knowing where they are. You can sense the ones trying hardest by how bent the tails are and the swirling shadows made by them. Technically, it's a masterpiece, but the subject doesn't appeal to the public. I bought the painting because I like it." He added hopefully, "It would suit a position in your lab, Dave."

"Can I take a photograph? I'll show it to my boss."

"Sure."

"Graham, I need a favour, though you are probably too busy."

"What?"

"I know a young woman—a doctor's receptionist—who says she knows nothing about art and would like to learn. I don't know anything about art, so could she come and talk to you to get an idea of how to study it?"

"I'm always ready to talk about my favourite subject. Tell her to call me, and we can agree on a time."

Alice was dressing for work; her Friday shift was a long one.

"You're going early, Ally?"

"Yes, I've got a double shift tonight, but the chef has given me tomorrow night off, and I only have lunch to do. Are you in tonight?"

"I'm going to wash my hair. Colin has invited me out tomorrow night."

"Will you be back tomorrow?"

"I intend to be. Colin may have invited me out several times over the last three months, but only when it suited him. I can't think of him as a boyfriend. Nothing has developed between us with such infrequent dates, and I've not felt any physical attraction.

"But I'll definitely be back late, as we are going to a cocktail party and then the theatre before dinner."

"I don't like Colin."

"Why?"

"He's too proud of himself, too egotistical and cocksure. I had a rude thought when I met him."

"You can tell me; I'm not an innocent girl."

"Well, I thought he tried to give the impression that he had a whopper in his pants when it was really a tiddler."

Meghan shrieked with laughter. "Ally, sometimes you say the darndest things."

"Well, now that it's in the open, has he?"

"Has he what?"

"Got a whopper."

"If I knew, I wouldn't tell you, but I don't know."

After Alice left, Meghan had a stray thought, "*I wonder if Dave has a whopper.*" Then she felt confused. "*Why would I ask that?*"

21

When Meghan and Colin entered the hotel ballroom a few minutes after six pm, it seemed to Meghan like the same circus she had attended previously with him. She thought a later arrival would have been better, as they had at least an hour and a half before the theatre performance. Colin did as he had before, leaving her with Madelaine with the same excuse: "I must circulate, Meg; there's no point coming if I don't."

Meghan thought, "*He must say the same thing to any woman he invites to a cocktail party.*"

Madelaine asked, "How have you managed to stay with him so long, Meg?"

"I don't know. Perhaps it is because there aren't many men who invite me out. He is at least presentable."

"Do you see that group over there?" She pointed, and Meghan looked.

"Yes."

"Well, the only woman you see there is a lawyer, and she doesn't associate with the wives. She discusses law with the men and keeps a close watch on her husband."

"What's her name?"

"Gwendoline Allbright. I told you about her. Before you decide about Colin, I suggest you talk to her."

"Why?"

"She knows every man in the company and any secrets he might have. She deals with the cases of sexual harassment, rape, and violent marital disputes, so she has years of experience dealing with men."

"But Colin isn't like that."

"I don't know. But Gwendoline will know if he has any skeletons in the closet, and you should find out first."

Meghan remembered Pete, who had appeared to be a chartered accountant but was not. "That's good advice. I'll think about it. Thanks."

Colin returned to her and said, "Meg, we must go. We must be in the theatre when the bell rings, or they won't let us in."

The show was uplifting and the music inspiring, and when Colin and Meghan rose to wend their way between the seats, she had buried her confused thoughts under the layer of happiness laid down by a talented cast. She was, if not happy, at least cheerful.

Dave, Michael Jenkins, and two women came out of an auditorium exit only half a minute before Meghan and Colin came from another.

As they walked towards the lobby, Meghan recognised Dave, opened her mouth to call, and then shut it with a snap. She didn't want Dave to see her with Colin. The man with Dave had his arm around a dark-haired woman. Dave was talking to a statuesque blonde in a tight dress. Meghan could feel a ball of ice forming in the pit of her stomach while, oblivious to Colin, she watched as the crowd urged them forward.

She couldn't hear what they said. But they were *laughing*. It seemed like a knife to the gut as she sensed their happiness; it gave her a stomach cramp.

"Colin. I must go to the ladies."

"Ok, I'll wait by this column."

The route she took to the toilet allowed her to pass behind Dave and the others, only one or two other theatregoers hiding her from view. She heard, "Tiger, where are we going next?"

Only one word had any meaning; it filled every nook and cranny. *Tiger.*

She sat in the toilet cubicle for what seemed ages. Trying to stem the tears that formed in her eyes as she thought, "*The woman called Dave 'Tiger'.*"

After redoing her makeup, she left the bathroom. When she got back to Colin, she told him there had been a queue.

Meghan was quiet at dinner. She hardly heard a word that Colin said, for the image of Dave laughing with that woman wouldn't leave. Colin, however, was convinced she was hanging on his every word.

Meghan only came back to the present when Colin had paid the bill and asked, "Meg, it's been six weeks now. I've enjoyed every minute of our time together. Don't you think it's time you came home with me?"

Meghan hadn't expected him to ask. She knew she wasn't ready but wasn't sure why. There had been no spark between her and Colin, only some pleasure in each other's company. She had learned much but realised he had asked nothing about her profession.

They had laughed together, but something was missing. Meghan convinced herself she should say no, and talk to Gwendoline.

Then despair got the upper hand. Was Colin, or his like, the only choice? Dave didn't need her except for research work. He didn't want her. To add to that, he had a voluptuous blonde calling him "Tiger". Was Rory right? Was compromise the only solution? Meghan thought, *"Will I find the missing something in bed?"*

"Yes, Colin, I'll come."

Colin's foreplay was detached and short, and then he ejaculated after four strokes, leaving Meghan far from the pleasure she had last experienced with Barry. Then, instead of helping her achieve the heights her body wanted, he turned away and fell asleep with his back to her.

As her body shut down, she lay there thinking, mentally summing up her time with Colin. She had no desire to be a lawyer's wife, attending cocktail parties as a decoration to advance her husband's career—she had her own career. She would not be a stay-at-home wife waiting for her husband to come home from work late or return from a meeting in another city, only to part her legs to satisfy him. She would not sleep with a man who did not consider her needs once he satisfied himself.

Then he snored.

It was the last straw. Meghan slipped quietly out of bed, dressed, and exited after leaving a card on the table that read, "DON'T CALL". She almost added, "You're a lousy lover", but she didn't because "lousy" was an inadequate description.

It was not yet midnight. She took a taxi. The whole experience with Colin had taken less than an hour. Feeling sad and depressed, she slipped silently into the flat to avoid waking Alice if she was home.

She had a shower, scrubbing furiously to remove any trace of Colin, then slid into bed. She heard a man's voice coming from Alice's bedroom. *"Ally must have company,"* she thought. The wall only muffled the sound slightly, so she could have been in the room—watching. *"It must be Devlin ..."*

Weeks ago, Alice had come home as happy as a lark.

"Why are you so happy, Ally? I've never seen you like this before."

"I went to a cooking demo by a top chef, and I met a super Irish guy, Devlin O'Toole, a third assistant chef like me."

"And you swooned in ecstasy?"

"I don't know how to do that, but I wanted to be in his arms as soon as he said hello. It's the first time in my life I could have gone to bed with a stranger."

Alice had gone out with him repeatedly whenever their work schedules allowed. When they were too busy to meet, they called each other, and the first to come off shift would go to the other's workplace for a few minutes together and a good-night kiss.

But now Alice had brought him home. They spoke quietly, but Meghan could hear most of what they said.

Then Alice squealed, "Oh God, Devlin, more, please more!"

Meghan buried her head under a pillow to block out the sound, a sob in her heart and tears in her eyes. *"Why can't it be me?"*

Meghan hadn't drawn the curtain closed, and she was awoken by the daylight streaming in through the window. She heard whispering in Alice's bedroom and then the sound of someone going to the bathroom. A little later, there was movement, and the front door opened and closed before there was the clank of pans in the kitchen. Meghan got up with a heavy heart.

"Good morning, Ally. Why didn't Devlin stay for breakfast?"

"I asked him to, but he must go right across London, then change for work, because he's on shift at ten. I wasn't expecting you home. I invited him to cook our dinner here, as his flat doesn't have a proper kitchen, and we made a super meal together, then I told him he could stay.

"Things didn't work out for you? I saw your bag this morning when I got up for a pee."

"They didn't, Ally, certainly not as well as for you. Colin invited me to his flat, and I thought I might find what was missing in bed, so I accepted."

"Then why are you here?"

"A turnoff, Ally. It was like a horserace where I didn't get my horse out of the box, and he fell off after five metres. I didn't even have a chance to warm up, and instead of doing something about it, he turned over and went to sleep. I regret having gone to bed with him—it was a total waste—but in the end, that's the final test. I realised then that I don't want to be a lawyer's wife—they aren't my kind of people—so I left a card saying don't call again, and I slipped out. As you suggested, he doesn't have a whopper.

"From the sounds I heard last night, Devlin seems to have passed the test."

Alice had a satisfied expression as she smiled. "Yes, he did. He got three hundred per cent."

"Then bring him home again; I would like to meet him. What are your plans?"

"We haven't made any. Like me, he's Third Assistant Chef, but as soon as he is promoted to Chef, he wants to open a restaurant. It will take a year to get there, but I'll enjoy finding a place, planning menus, choosing decorations, stuff like that."

"What if he doesn't ask you to marry him after all that?"

"I'll know long before, but even if he doesn't ask when he opens the restaurant, I'll have learned how to do it and can start my own."

"Why are you so confident, Ally? I'm older than you but still struggling to find someone."

"The man you want will be like Devlin is with me; a man you will work with every day, achieving something together. You might not know it—maybe Dave doesn't—but he's your man. Tell him."

"What, Ally?"

"That you don't care about marriage and the rest, and that you want to work with him. Talk about everything, and learn about him. Meg, don't think about it, *feel*. I didn't go to bed with Devlin to find out something. I went to bed with him because I wanted to from the moment I met him.

"Look me in the eyes and tell me that you don't want to feel Dave's arms around you when you're with him. Then accept your feelings.

"I'll cook us a lunch, and then I must go to work."

Alice had the middle shift; she arrived home at seven-thirty pm. Meghan was sitting listlessly in their small lounge.

"Meg, you look thoroughly miserable, and you've been crying. Is it because of Colin?"

"No, Ally. Dave."

"Has he had an accident? Is he ok?"

The tears started again. "Dave's ok. I saw him last night."

"Where?"

"Leaving the theatre. He had been at the same show and was ahead of Colin and me in the passage on the way to the lobby."

Alice put two and two together. "And he was with another woman?"

"Yes, a tall, sexy blonde, and another couple. I heard her call him 'Tiger'."

"Now I understand why you agreed to go home with Colin. You've just done it again. Don't you remember the Zoe lesson?"

"It's not the same, Ally."

"The same, exactly the same. Why didn't you call out and say hello? Instead of imagining the worst, you might have found out she was his sister."

"He doesn't have a sister."

"Doesn't matter; she could be anyone."

Meghan looked a bit more cheerful, and the tears had dried.

"You think so?"

"Definitely, and you are going to find out."

"How?"

"Ask him how he enjoyed the show, and don't burst into tears when you do."

"I'll try."

Meghan couldn't hold back the question that had been on her mind since Sunday. "Dave, did you enjoy *Mamma Mia!?*"

Before answering, Dave paused, studying her. "Very much, it was a great show. Were you there?"

"Yes, I saw you from behind afterwards."

Dave just looked at her and smiled—tenderly, she thought. It annoyed her: "*Is he patronising me?*"

Dave reached for his phone and said, "Wait a moment, Meg."

He dialled a number and put his mobile on speakerphone. It rang for half a minute, then someone answered: "Hello, Dave."

"Hi, Mike. Can we have a drink or dinner tonight? I want to introduce my girlfriend to you. I'll bring her to your hotel."

"Sure, Tiger, come at seven."

Perplexed, Meghan understood nothing but had the beginnings of that feeling, *You've been a complete and utter idiot, my girl.*

Dave put down the phone. "I'll pick you up in a taxi at a quarter to seven."

"Just like that, Dave?"

"Yes, if you don't come, you will never know what you want to know."

She said nothing until he changed the subject. Instead, she remembered, "*He referred to me as his girlfriend.*"

Meghan had difficulty concentrating all day, continually asking herself, "*Who's Mike?*"

At a quarter to seven, Dave held the taxi door open as Meghan slipped in, then he climbed in himself.

Fifteen minutes of silence later, they entered the Holiday Inn in Bloomsbury to meet a man with a deep tan, smiling blue eyes, and a broad smile.

Dave said, "Meg, this is Michael Jenkins."

Mike took her hand and held it, his sparkling eyes looking into hers. "Meg, I wouldn't have let you go if I had seen you first. Nandi will be here in a second or two. You're a lucky man, Dave."

A voice behind Meghan said, "If you don't let her hand go, you lecher, I'll have you arrested for harassment."

Meghan turned. The Afro hairstyle gave her away; it was the woman Meghan had seen in the theatre with Mike.

Mike said, "Let's go into the lounge. I've reserved a table for seven-thirty so we can have a drink first."

By the time they went to dinner, Meghan knew she was a fool, and what was worse, she was sure Dave thought so too. As the party sat down to dinner, Meghan said, "Excuse me for a moment; I must go to the ladies."

Nandi went with her. When they left the bathroom, Meghan had learned everything about Dave and Mike's history and that the statuesque blonde was Mike's married sister. Ironically, the latter had been with her brother and Dave because her lawyer husband was working.

When the two women returned to the table, Meghan felt like confessing, but Dave adroitly introduced a new topic: "Mike, do you know why women always go to the ladies in pairs?"

"No, I've always thought it's so they can discuss their partners privately."

"Well, they might do that, but the real reason is that it's in their genes, something they can't help after a million years of evolution."

"Explain, please."

"Before the modern toilet, humans had to pee in the bush. Men can do so by standing up beside a tree while watching for predators. Women crouch down and need a guardian standing watch."

Meghan was recovering. "Mike, if you listen to this guy long enough, you'll find he has a long string of ridiculous ideas; where he gets them from, I don't know. Why do you call him 'Tiger'? To me, he's like a big pussy cat."

Mike and Nandi both laughed.

"Tiger, she's got your measure," said Mike. "Meg, you got it right the first time; he walks just like a cat, and when I was fourteen, I loved the tigers in the zoo. My father called him 'Tiger'."

Meghan thought, "*Yes, the smooth, silent walk.*"

The ice, now broken, melted completely, and Meghan thoroughly enjoyed the evening. She accepted another invitation to join Mike and Nandi—on their last night in London.

In the taxi, she was silent until Dave asked, "Did you enjoy the evening, Meg?"

Meghan stared straight ahead. "Very much; they are both lovely people."

"And have you learned what you wanted to know?"

Meghan turned to face him. She could feel her eyes filling with tears. "Yes, Dave, I've learned I'm a jealous fool."

Dave slid across the bench seat and put his arm around her. "Meg, come here."

She leaned against him and rested her head on his shoulder.

He said nothing more until the taxi entered Chelsea Common. "Meg, trust me; I don't know how many men have hurt you, but

I never will. That's not a promise I can break; it comes from deep down, and I cannot change it.

"I told you once it was better not to kiss you, and I told you why, which hasn't changed, but I want to add something.

"When I'm free to give you my every thought, I'll ask you to marry me. I know you might say no, that you might not wait for me, but that's the chance I must take. My mother had no life of her own after my father left us. She worked to support me, and I couldn't live with myself for the rest of my life if I kept thinking that I hadn't done the best I could for her. I hope you'll accept this.

"I'll also be honest: I need the support you give me daily."

Meghan had listened silently, a warm glow filling her. "Dave, I'll wait, no matter how long it takes."

Dave paid off the taxi and took Meghan to the door. She turned to say good night, but he had vanished.

22

Dave was running in the park when Ysabel, an effortless runner, caught him up. She said hello, and ran with him for an hour. When they were back at Dave's starting point, the W6 Café, she said, "I'm staying at the Premier Inn, across the road. I dislike eating alone. Could you join me for dinner? The hotel restaurant is nothing fancy, but if you like Vietnamese food, we can go just up the road to Saigon-Saigon."

Dave accepted, went home, changed, and met her in the hotel lobby. She wore a sheer silk dress, with no sign of underwear. They went to Saigon-Saigon. Dave was curious about coincidences. Ysabel had appeared after the first report was published in *Oncology* and again now after the second.

Although he asked about her work, she avoided saying anything suspicious, except once. When he asked what medicines she sold, she named two, seemingly unaware different manufacturers made each one.

On returning to her hotel, she said, "It's early. The hotel has no bar, but I've got a stocked bar fridge and a magnificent view over the city. Come up and have a drink with me."

"That's an attractive offer, but my mother told me, 'Never enter a woman's bedroom alone.' My flat isn't far. You're welcome to join me there for a drink."

Ysabel hesitated, then agreed. "Ok, if you insist."

Dave walked her back to her hotel near midnight. He had learned nothing more, for before he could think of a way to ask, she stood up, slipped off her dress, and said, "I didn't come to talk, Dave." For a moment, he gaped, then realised an expert surgeon had created the high, firm breasts, although running and exercise were responsible for the narrow waist and curving hips. If asked later, he would have said she performed as a polished professional without the amateur abandonment of Monica, the love and passion of Angela and Susan, or Valerie's desperate need. But he did learn Ysabel had muscles he had never felt before.

Dave spoke to Meghan the following day. "Meg, that woman I met at the *Oncology* conference, Ysabel, popped up running in Ravenscourt Park yesterday. I'm suspicious about her because she has appeared just after each publication date, and I wonder why. Someone might have sent her to ask questions."

"And did she invite you to her nest?"

"Why 'nest'?"

"Spiders always have a nest."

"She did invite me to her hotel room, but I refused. I told her my mother wouldn't like it."

Meghan chuckled. "You do come up with lovely excuses. Your mentioning her reminds me that when you met Ysabel, a doctor approached me. He introduced himself as Redwin Beltgood and said he was a cancer specialist. He asked for my number, saying he might want to discuss DNA. He might be a colleague or a competitor of Ysabel."

"Has he called?"

"Not yet."

"Well, be careful, Meg."

At three pm, Meghan's phone rang.

"Good afternoon, Miss MacDougal; Redwin Beltgood here—we met at the *Oncology* conference. I'm in London again, and I wondered if we could get together for dinner, say Wednesday night?"

Meghan looked over at Dave. "Doctor Beltgood, that's very kind of you. Where do you want to go?"

"The Strand Palace, where I'm staying. Please, call me Redwin."

"Redwin, can you call back in twenty minutes? I have an international call coming in that I must answer."

"Certainly, Miss MacDougal."

Meghan rang off and said to Dave, "That was Beltgood; he wants dinner at the Strand Palace on Wednesday."

"Don't go. When he calls, say you can't make it."

She was about to agree with him when she felt an annoying doubt. Dave had said he hadn't gone to Ysabel's room but hadn't said Ysabel had not come to his. Ysabel was none of her business, but it was none of his whether or not she went to dinner with Redwin.

"Dave, I'm an adult woman; I can handle a man like Beltgood. If he has a room and invites me, I can say no; I'm not a pushover. I'll try to find out more about him at dinner."

"If Beltgood is working for someone, he can be dangerous. I don't know what he might do. It's best if you don't go near him."

Her Scots stubbornness took over. "Sorry, you aren't my keeper. I'll accept and find out what I can. At least I'll get an expensive dinner."

"Then don't drink too much wine, Meg."

"I'll drink whatever I want, Mr Tennant."

Her calling him "Mr Tennant" hurt. He turned away.

She felt ashamed.

Meghan and Dave didn't speak to each other for two days—not even a "good morning" or "good night". Meghan didn't know how to undo the hurt she had done to Dave, and Dave didn't want to rekindle her anger.

Dave, however, decided to investigate. He looked up Redwin in the medical register. There was only one Redwin Beltgood. He was a doctor, and the reference did say he was an oncologist associated with Manchester University. There was no age or birthday, so Dave looked up his graduation date. He had to be dead, or over seventy. He couldn't be the Redwin that Meghan had met.

A few minutes later, Dave had the doctor's phone number. He called.

"Redwin Beltgood, good morning."

"Doctor, my name is Dave Tennant. I work for BaVir Labs."

"I know them. What can I do for you, Mr Tennant?"

"Doctor, a man who professes to be Redwin Beltgood approached one of my colleagues at a conference sponsored by the journal *Oncology*. I'm naturally suspicious, so I looked up Redwin Beltgood in the medical register, and you are the only entry, so I called to check if the man is genuine."

"Well, it's certainly not me. I haven't been to an *Oncology* conference in years, although I read the journal every month. That reminds me; there was an article in the last one about cancer remission, and I think it mentioned BaVir and David Tennant. Is that you?"

"It is, sir."

"I see; it was an interesting report. Regarding this man you speak of, impersonation of a doctor is illegal, and it puts my reputation at risk, so I must do something about it. Will you cooperate with the police?"

"With pleasure, sir. The imposter has invited a female colleague for dinner on Wednesday night, and I suspect she might be in danger."

"I'll have an inspector call you at once. What is your number?"

Dave gave it. "Thank you, Doctor. Perhaps we'll meet one day."

"I look forward to it. Goodbye."

Dave said nothing to Meghan. He would look a fool if she said goodbye to Redwin in the hotel lobby and came home.

After the inspector cross-examined Dave on the phone, he asked for photos of Meghan. Dave had none but then thought of her lab-personnel record and sent it to the inspector. It included her height, weight, age, and two good photos—face and profile.

On Wednesday morning, the inspector called. "Mr Tennant, please come to the hotel tonight. I suggest you arrive early and remain opposite the entrance. Make sure you have cell phone reception. I'll send you an SMS once the two parties—your colleague and the imposter; and two undercover officers—are seated at their tables, and then you can enter the lobby. Stay out of sight but with a view of the restaurant entrance. Someone who knows Ms MacDougal should be there if I arrest the man."

Later, from his place in the shadows opposite the hotel, Dave watched Meghan arrive. Then, after a short wait, he received the SMS: "Seated".

Redwin, the imposter, had turned his charm up to high as he'd greeted Meghan and led her from the reception area to the restaurant, where the maître d' had shown them to a table.

After they'd taken a detailed look at the menu and exchanged comments about the weather and polite enquiries about each other's health, the imposter asked how her research was progressing.

Meghan replied with something she had thought of: "I'm studying the DNA changes in phage attacks."

"That's interesting."

Meghan thought he knew nothing about it and was about to reply when she felt a flush of nausea. "Redwin, I think I should visit the ladies."

She stood up, took one step, and fainted. The imposter, who had also risen, caught her before she collapsed on the floor.

A diner at the closest table stood and asked, "Can I help?"

"No, we'll be all right. My wife needs to lie down. I'll take her to our room. I'm a doctor, so I know what to do."

"I thought I recognised you. Doctor Beltgood?"

In a hurry to avoid this unwanted interference, the imposter didn't ask how the man knew him. "Yes, that's me. Now I must take her up immediately."

"I'm afraid you won't, sir, as you are not Doctor Beltgood, and she's not your wife. You are under arrest for impersonation of a doctor under Section 49 of the Medical Act. You do not have to say anything. But, it may harm your defence if you do not mention when questioned something which you later rely on in court. Anything you do say ..."

The imposter ran before the detective finished the warning. Uniformed police arrested him as he exited the hotel.

Dave saw him run out of the restaurant and immediately dashed in, terrified that Meghan was hurt.

"She's ok, sir," said a woman cradling Meghan in her arms. "Can you help me get her to the hotel's emergency room? I'm Officer Naidoo."

The restaurant's manager, who was by now standing nearby,

said, "I'll call for a gurney and the hotel doctor," and disappeared. He came back, followed by a porter who pushed a gurney.

Dave and the porter lifted Meghan onto the gurney and wheeled her to the hotel's emergency room, followed by Officer Naidoo.

"Ma'am, thank you for your help," Dave said.

"My pleasure, sir. I'll wait for the doctor to examine her."

The doctor came in, and Dave introduced himself as Meghan's fiancé. Then the doctor began examining Meghan. After checking her pupils and listening to her heart, he declared, "An anaesthetic or a date-rape drug; she needs three or four hours of sleep and will be fine."

"Can the police have a blood sample, Doctor?" Officer Naidoo asked. "And should I call for an ambulance?"

The doctor was conscious of his obligations to the hotel and knew that, at every hospital emergency, an eager young reporter was waiting to record every case and write a story. He was annoyed and showed it. "What the devil for, Officer? For this woman to get shunted around London in an ambulance, then manhandled into a hospital corridor where she will lie on an uncomfortable stretcher until she wakes up and goes home? The hotel will provide a room where she can have a comfortable sleep and breakfast in the morning. I'm sure her fiancé will look after her far better than she'll be handled in an overworked hospital emergency room. As a doctor, that's what I'm ordering."

They moved Meghan to a hotel room on the ground floor, and then the porter left. With Officer Naidoo's help, Dave lifted Meghan onto the bed.

"Do you need my help, sir? You should make her as comfortable as possible. The longer she sleeps, the better."

"No, we'll be fine, Officer, thank you."

Officer Naidoo left.

Dave kicked off his shoes. He undressed Meghan and hung her

clothes in the cupboard for the morning. Then he covered her with a sheet, stripped down to his underwear, and got into bed beside her. She was sleeping peacefully on her back. He turned off the lights.

Meghan opened her eyes to pitch darkness. When she moved her head, it spun, so she remained still and listened, trying to make sense of her surroundings. Fear and terror slowly built as she identified breathing from close beside her and realised she was in bed, naked. She tried to shout but only managed a squeak: "Where am I?"

The person beside her switched the bedside light on. "You're in bed with me in the hotel," a familiar voice said.

"*Thank God, it's Dave,*" Meghan thought. The flood of relief defied description. She slowly turned her head to see Dave looking worriedly at her, then closed her eyes as her head spun.

"Meg, are you ok?"

She opened her eyes and blinked. "If I don't move my head."

"Do you remember coming to the hotel to meet Redwin?"

Meghan tried to remember. "Yes, I do." She added, "We were seated at our table, talking, and I felt nauseous, then everything went black." After a pause, she asked, "What happened?"

"He spiked your drink with a drug and, when you passed out, claimed you were his wife, and said he would take you to his room."

"Oh God, so he did take me to his room."

"No, a detective tried to arrest him on the spot, and he ran, but he was nabbed at the hotel door by uniformed police."

"How did all that happen?"

"I called the real Redwin Beltgood after our tiff, and when he learned an imposter was using his name, he called Scotland Yard."

"Oh God, I've messed up big time, haven't I? But how did I get here?"

"I was waiting in the lobby in case something happened, and when Beltgood ran out, I panicked, thinking you were hurt, so I ran into the restaurant. You lay stretched out on the floor in a policewoman's arms. The officer told me you were ok. We took you to the hotel's emergency room, and the hotel's doctor said Beltgood had given you a date-rape drug or something similar and that you must rest.

"The hotel gave us the room, and we brought you here."

Meghan's mind was still whirling and branched off in a different direction. "Did you undress me?"

"Yes. Your clothes are hanging in the cupboard, ready for you for breakfast."

"Did you look?"

"Of course, and I copped a good feel. You have lovely breasts."

Meghan's dizziness had improved. She thought he must have looked, but she knew that the feeling bit had been a joke. "Ok. What now?"

"We sleep, and the hotel gives us breakfast. You'll feel better in the morning. Good night."

"Good night, Dave."

Meghan could tell by his rhythmic breathing that Dave had fallen asleep quickly, but she spent a long time thinking about the evening, before the comforting thought that Dave had rescued her finally brought sleep. It helped when she snuggled against him.

Dave chose a full English breakfast. Meghan only had fruit and yoghurt.

Dave asked, "Meg, did you find out anything?"

"No, but I don't think the imposter knows much about DNA. I

said I was studying phage-induced DNA changes, and all he said was, 'That's interesting.'"

"Well, the police will let me know if they discover anything. I think he will be in jail for some time."

She looked into his eyes earnestly. "Do you forgive me?"

"Yes, Meg, I stepped over the mark and upset you, but I got a reward."

"What?"

"A night with a beautiful naked woman in a hotel room."

Meghan had no reply, but she managed to say, "Thanks, Dave, just don't tell anyone."

"Why not?"

"No one would believe I spent a night in bed with you and that nothing happened."

Dave reflected that between Valerie, Monica, Fluffy, and Meghan, he was accumulating more sex-less nights in bed with naked women than the average bachelor.

Two days later, Dave got a call from the inspector. "Mr Tennant, we may need Miss MacDougal to testify that the man, a wanted French criminal called Pierre Touchall, used Redwin Beltgood's name and invited her to dinner. I understand she works for you, and I would appreciate if you could ensure her cooperation if we need it."

"I'll certainly try, Inspector. You may assume she agrees if I don't call back. Did you find anything interesting in his room?"

"We did indeed, Mr Tennant. Miss MacDougal is fortunate to have you watch over her. In the room, a video camera had been set up, and there were props used in bondage and sadomasochistic films. We believe he intended to blackmail her."

After hanging up, Dave told Meghan the news, and she snarled,

"Testify against that twisted individual? Of course. Will you come with me?"

"You couldn't keep me away."

23

Dave saw the email in his inbox when he got to work. It came from Africa and was signed by Moussa Traore, a pathologist. It provided two contact numbers, explaining that Moussa could be reached on WhatsApp or satphone.

Dave looked up Moussa's profile. He was thirty-six, had been educated in the USA on a US Aid scholarship, and had done two internships at US hospitals before returning to Burkina Faso to assume the post of Pathologist at a teaching hospital in the capital city of Ouagadougou.

Why Moussa needed a satellite phone, Dave couldn't fathom.

Dear Mr Tennant,

I have a spinal-fluid sample taken from a patient and have seen the bacteria mentioned in your report. The patient has no recorded medical history, so there is no indication of the source of the bacteria. Your paper is the first thing I have seen mentioning these bacteria, and I would welcome collaboration if I can help.

Dave didn't hesitate—he checked the time difference, found little, picked up his mobile, and dialled the WhatsApp number.

"Moussa Traore."

"Doctor, this is Dave Tennant in London. I've just received your mail."

"Mr Tennant, it's a pleasure to hear from you. Call me Moussa. How can I help?"

"Moussa, please call me Dave. Is the patient still living?"

"I don't know, Dave, this is Africa; when you tell a patient you cannot cure them, sometimes they disappear into the distant countryside, where they see a traditional herbalist."

"That's a shame. Is it the only case you have come across?"

"For the bacteria with the corkscrew tail, yes. The cholera is common, endemic, and we have never recorded an outbreak. The epidemics we have are of the more common, infectious strain."

"Can you send me slides, Moussa?"

"That will be difficult since they belong to the university. We keep them in a cold room, and export authorisation will take time. It would be far quicker for you to hop on a flight to see them here. Discussing what we can do to identify the source will also be much easier."

"Right, Moussa, I'll see what we can organise. Could we come over a weekend?"

"No problem. Fridays are for religion, but we operate normally on the other days."

"I'll call you back."

Dave discussed it with Meghan. They agreed they would go at their own expense if Philip authorised their time off.

Philip had another idea: "Yes, you can go, but I suggest you keep an expense account; I might be able to wangle reimbursement."

"Meg, do I book one room or two?"

"Why do you ask?"

"I've ceased making assumptions about you, although we have already slept together. Asking is safer."

"I'll answer, but you won't like it."

"Go ahead."

"In a strange hotel in a strange town and country, I prefer to share a bedroom. But without intimacy. We must work together. Sharing a room will encourage that, but sex won't. I've seen a dozen office marriages and divorces, and in every divorce case, one of the partners has left the office. They can't stand seeing each other at work every day.

"If we continue researching this problem, we must decide: either no sex or a permanent liaison. Not necessarily marriage and children and everything that goes with it. But fidelity and life together. No girlfriends for you. No boyfriends for me. Is our work more important than a roll in the hay?"

"Thanks for being honest. I agree with everything you've said. I hadn't thought it through like that. I can promise to stay in my bed, so I'll book one room if you agree."

Meghan said nothing for thirty seconds, just looked into his eyes. "And if there's only one bed?"

"Then I promise to stay on my side."

Meghan had observed him as he said it. She grinned. "Ok, Dave. Like the last time? I do have an out. Try anything, and I'll start screaming!

"Oh, and don't forget your pyjamas."

"I don't have any, and you've forgotten: the last time you had none, and you snuggled against me."

Meg chose to ignore the last bit. She remembered it too well and treasured the memory. "Then buy some."

Dave grinned. "I'll buy ones with the most garish colours the shop has to offer."

When they got on the plane, neither Dave nor Meghan noticed the man who boarded last and sat in the first row of economy class.

By the time they had passed through the arrival formalities, the man was sitting in a nondescript car near the terminal exit.

They checked into the hotel and went to their room. It had twin beds.

"I get the one nearest the bathroom, Dave."

"Fine."

Meghan was a long time in the bathroom. Dave knocked on the door and asked, "Are you ok?"

"No, I've been bitten by something. I'm trying to put a cream on it."

"Meg, come out here."

The door opened, and Meghan came out wearing panties and bra. "It's on my back; I can't reach."

"Lie on the bed. I'll get the insect cream I brought. It's in my toiletry bag."

Dave came to the bed. Meghan was lying on her stomach, and there was a red mark in the middle of her back.

"I can see a bite. If you want me to check for others, I must unhook your bra and pull down your panties."

"Oh hell, a girl can't keep her modesty."

"I've seen naked women, including you, and I'm sure other men have seen you."

Meghan unhooked her bra and pulled her panties down. "Only a finger to rub on the cream, Dave."

He found four bites and rubbed cream around them. Meghan thought he rubbed a bit longer than necessary. "Done, Meg, you're fine." Before she could pull up her panties, he smacked the attractive globes.

"Ow! That's taking unfair advantage of an injured woman."

"Tomorrow, you spread on the insect-repellent cream. I'll do your back for you. Mozzies might not have bitten you if you had done it on the plane."

Meghan slid off the bed, holding her bra over her breasts. Then just before she entered the bathroom, she turned to face him, let her bra drop, and said, "Ok, you can do my bum, but I'll do these."

Moussa collected Dave and Meghan—both visibly covered in sunblock—from the hotel at nine am.

"You must be Dave and Meghan. I can't see another couple that would fit. I'm Moussa."

Meghan at once thought him an attractive man, well built, and around Dave's age, but the smile on his finely chiselled face drew her attention. "You don't look anything like I expected," Meghan said.

"Most Africans don't fit the stereotypes broadcast on TV. It will be long before Europeans differentiate between Africans from different countries and ethnic groups. I'm a *Peul*, or Fulani; my ancestors came here over two thousand years ago when they migrated from the north. Traditionally, we're nomadic pastoralists.

"But we will have time to discuss such things. I've warned the university we're coming, so we should go. My car is outside. But if I can suggest it, buy some floppy bush hats from the hotel boutique. The sun is unforgiving to pale skin."

It took them a few minutes to get the hats. Then Moussa drove them to the university. Meghan was delighted with the streets lined with shops and curb-side stalls selling anything and everything.

The endless stream of cars in each direction, repeatedly hooting at hundreds of motorcycles swooping and swerving between them, fascinated Dave, who expected a massive accident at any moment.

A hairdresser in a small, patchwork tent with one wooden chair drew an exclamation from Meghan: "Moussa, can we stop so I can photograph the hairdresser?"

"Meghan, I'll take you to a market after our university visit; you can photograph all you want."

"Oh, good, I want to buy one of those lovely colourful dresses. But please call me Meg."

At the university, Dave and Meghan agreed that the Corkys on the slides were the right-hand ones, and the cholera slides corresponded perfectly.

"Moussa, they are here, and we're grateful for the proof," Dave said. "The question is: Where do they come from, and how do they infect humans?"

"You pose tough questions. I'd like to propose that we join the rector, who has invited you for a snack lunch, then I'll take you to the central market. After that, when the temperature has dropped, we can have dinner at the hotel's rooftop restaurant, where we can discuss how to answer your questions."

The lunch was far from boring, for the rector knew how to fascinate his guests with the history of Burkina Faso and its people. The visit to the vast market took their breath away. Some stalls were makeshift, such as the one with an upturned bucket with little piles of peanuts on it. Others were more permanent, built with hand-made cement bricks and with a tin roof and shutter. The pathways and passages seemed to exist by accident, for no city government had laid out a plan. The smell was impossible to identify, an overwhelming mixture of human, animal, vegetal, and mineral scents.

Soon though, they left the odour behind as they followed Moussa in single file along a winding route through the packed crowds.

Dave said, "It looks like you can buy anything here."

"I'm sure you can, and if they don't have it in the stall, they will get it for you."

"But how do you know where to go?" Meghan asked.

"Well, let's ask that woman selling vegetables. I'll find out where we can get women's dresses."

They pushed through to the woman, and Moussa spoke to her in Fula. Meghan retained only "*Dan Fani*" and "*Tuntun Fani*" from the discussion and gestures accompanying directions.

"So," said Moussa, "for *Dan Fani*, or plain cotton dresses, we must find Mama Aziz, and for a cotton-silk mixture, Mama Idalina. We must go in that direction—" he pointed, "—to the side of the market, for clothes are over there."

"Marvellous. I'll get a dress of each."

"But you will probably need to hold your noses, as we'll be going past the meat market, and the stench can be terrible on a sweltering day."

"Lead on. For a new dress, I can stand anything."

Moussa grinned. "I hope you still feel the same way later."

For a dozen metres, the din from tinsmiths banging to make pots was deafening; then, as the noise died away behind the natural soundproofing of a dense crowd, the smell from the meat stalls filled their nostrils. They couldn't hurry; half of the dense mass of people was stationary, looking at wares or negotiating with stall owners, and the other half split equally between those going with them and those headed the other way. Dave scrutinised the stalls and the plethora of odd chunks of meat for sale—many with the skin, hair, or feathers still attached. Meghan kept her head down, following Moussa, convinced that if she didn't see anything, she wouldn't smell it, but Dave continued his scrutiny until he called, "Moussa, stop, please."

"What is it, Dave?"

"What's that woman selling? Over there." He pointed.

"Bushmeat. I'll explain it later."

"Yes, but is that *monkey* she has for sale?"

Moussa looked, then said, "Yes, I think so."

"Can you ask? And find out if it's fresh?"

"Probably killed last night; meat doesn't last long in these conditions."

"Then please ask what kind of monkey, what sex if she knows, and buy a small piece."

As Moussa approached the woman, Meghan said, "That's disgusting; are you going to taste it, Dave?"

Moussa came back with a small newspaper-wrapped packet. "Green Monkey. It's fresh, killed last night, and she thinks female. What will you do with it?"

"Not me; I hope you will agree to some tissue slides."

Moussa was a man of action. He raised an arm and beckoned someone over, and a moment later, a man—taller and heavier than Moussa but with the same broad smile—was beside them. "Dave, this is my brother Celso."

There followed instructions in what Dave supposed was Fula, then Celso took the packet and disappeared into the crowd.

"He will take it to the university and have them put it in the sub-zero fridge for me."

"Moussa, I admire your efficiency, but why was he nearby?"

"Dave, you have no idea how you stand out in this crowd. I don't think there's any danger, but in Africa, anything's possible, so a little help can sometimes be useful. Let's go and buy those dresses."

Meghan, to whom the crowds were overwhelming, felt a little safer. Dave wondered how many other brothers might be around.

Meghan bought two dresses, and long necklaces made from the seeds of wild plants interspersed with ivory beads. Moussa assured her they were made of tooth ivory. Dave bought a light cotton shirt and loose trousers. Then they returned to the hotel. Moussa promised to join them later.

The man had tailed Dave, Meghan, and Moussa to the university and then to the market. But he had lost them there, for he was too noticeable in the crowd, had been thrown off several times by someone bumping into him, and been obstructed by a large man who stood dumbly in front of him, waiting for him to move.

He decided to return to the hotel but didn't notice a young man on a motorbike who took the same route.

"Why did you buy that monkey meat, Dave?" Meghan asked.

"I'll tell you, but I want a cold beer to drink right now."

"Call room service. I'll have an iced tea—lemon. I'm taking a cold shower."

Dave also showered. Then they sat in the air-conditioned room with their drinks.

"Meg, you will think I'm irrational, but when I saw that bushmeat stand, I got a crazy idea. I'll give you the clues; you try to make sense of them.

"Kravitz, we think, was infected by a woman from this part of Africa or nearby. Moussa's slides of the sample taken from a local woman show the same Corkys and cholera.

"We don't know how the woman got them. It might have been through a long chain of contacts, but there have never been reports of a disease caused by Corkys, and Moussa did not say they are endemic in humans, as is our cholera variant.

"Corky's origins could be animal. It has infected humans, but we have no idea how.

"The Green Monkey is our nearest genetic relative in this part of Africa, and people are eating it."

Meghan replied, "Ok, you jump to conclusions; it's unscientific, but given the smell, the crowds, and the chance of getting a piece of Green Monkey bushmeat, I'll accept that it was a good decision." She swallowed the rest of her drink in a single, long draught. "God, that was good. I didn't realise how thirsty I was. Finish your beer before it gets too warm, and get me another drink; one was not enough."

"Ok."

Meghan sat in thought until the drinks came. She asked, "Why did you want to know the sex of the monkey?"

"That's just me; get as much information as possible. If I had thought she might know, I would have asked for its birthdate."

Meghan had been observing him as he answered. "Excuses, Dave; I know you too well. What's the real reason?"

"The only two humans from this region we have heard about who have Corkys, are females."

"That's a massive jump."

"I know, but what else can I do?"

Meghan thought about it, remembering his mother, then replied, "Ok, you jump to conclusions, and I'll prove them right or wrong. Now I'm going to do the female beauty thing and then dress in my new cotton-silk gown for dinner. You can have the bathroom afterwards."

Dinner on the rooftop was delightful. It was pleasantly warm, and the glow from the city lights was not as bright as that in London, so the stars were visible in thousands. Dave thought it would have been romantic, if only …

Moussa joined them. As soon as they had ordered, he gave them unsettling news: "A man followed you today from the hotel. He lost you in the market, then came back to the hotel, where he watched for your return. I've no clue who he is or why he is following you. Do you have any ideas?"

Meghan replied, "In London, there was a man who was trying to find out how our research was progressing. He claimed he was an oncologist, but we discovered he was an imposter."

"Do you think it's industrial espionage?"

"Yes, we assume so."

"Then you must be careful. I know, as it was a subject commonly discussed in the USA. I can tell you he must be employed by either American, British, or European pharma conglomerates."

"Why not Chinese or Indian?"

"Dave, they and the rest of the world mass produce existing medicines and only try to find out about the drugs that are about to enter the market. The three or four big ones in the USA and Europe do the research, and they want to know if your actions will wreck their plans to make money from a new drug that's cost them millions in research. They don't do the espionage themselves but employ contractors who hire sub-contractors. They can be ruthless because of the money involved. They may not be like the KGB and use torture, but they can do you much harm, professionally and physically.

"Now, can you explain what you'll do with the slides we'll make from the bushmeat sample?"

"A Corky count and cholera count. If there are none, then we must think again. If they are present, the Green Monkey might be the carrier in this part of Africa. We would like to know how widespread it is and get an idea of the number of monkey-to-human transmissions."

"That would be an expensive project."

"I agree, but the WWF might fund a monkey count and testing to avoid a cull if the university is behind you. The UN might fund a human survey. Both organisations will want to prevent another pandemic. I'm sure you could produce a superb paper. We'll keep you in the picture with whatever we discover."

"Then use my satphone number. Get one for yourself. Calls between satphones have unlimited talk-time, and you can reach me wherever I am."

"I wondered about the satphone number."

"Cellular coverage is poor here, limited to cities and a few larger towns, and consequently awfully expensive for foreign calls. My people are nomads, and cellular phones are useless to them. If I want to talk to my father, I call his satphone. There are thousands in the country. It's also secure; no one can listen in."

"Ok, I'll do that. Aren't emails and calls secure from pirates?"

"WhatsApp between phones is encrypted, and you should be fine as long as you use a Wi-Fi link and switch off mobile data."

"Ok, we'll remember that."

"You've booked your flight back to London for tomorrow night, so if you agree, I'll take you into the backcountry tomorrow to meet some of my family."

"Will we be followed?"

Moussa grinned gleefully. "I hope so; then, when the tail gets lost, unless he has a GPS transponder, he might have a long wait for help."

24

Moussa collected Dave and Meghan with the same car and driver at nine-thirty am the following day. He handed them two lengths of cotton cloth, one white and the other dark-blue. "Here, Dave, the white one is for you. Wrap it around your head, like I've done with mine. Meg, you can put yours over your hair like a headscarf, and across your face. These are desert scarves. They have many names, but they are commonly called 'cheches'. We will meet people from my family, followers of Islam. Although it's not mandatory, keeping your head covered shows respect. The cheches also keep the fine sand and dust from your mouth, nose, and hair."

They drove out of town, and as they left the outskirts, Moussa's satphone buzzed in its dashboard holder. He answered, listened a moment, and then replaced it. "We have a tail. I think it's the same guy as yesterday. He's with a local guide. Today will be fun."

They drove for forty minutes. Their tracks soon faded, covered by fresh sand blown by the wind. Then they were in a pristine desert, following an invisible route, sometimes between dunes or over them, and sometimes skirting a rocky patch.

Meghan asked, "Moussa, how does the driver know where he's going?"

"Do you know that cab drivers in London must pass a test to prove they know the city intimately to get a licence?"

"Well, I know they used to. They called it 'the knowledge'. My dad told me that in his day, you could give an address anywhere in London, and the driver would take you there."

Dave added, "No longer completely true, Moussa. With the ubiquity of GPS, the hackney-cab drivers now have a more limited test; they only learn the principal routes and landmarks, but like in the past, it can take two years of riding a bike around London to get the in-depth knowledge they need. Private-hire cab drivers, like those who work for Uber, don't need to pass a test."

"Well, for the nomads of the desert, it's much the same thing; the boys begin young, travelling with their father. It may take years, but we know every track, dune, wadi, gully, and canyon."

They crested a massive dune and rolled down the far side into what looked like an old riverbed; the sheer wall on one side, scoured by water or wind, revealed different-coloured layers laid down over millennia.

Moussa said, grinning, "Now we'll lose our tail."

After driving a short way on the flat bottom of the riverbed, they stopped near the wall.

"We'll get out," Moussa said, "and I'll wave my arms around to show you the interesting geology as if you're tourists. At the same time, our driver will watch in the rearview mirror for our tail, who should stop before the crest and take a peek before continuing."

"And your driver will see him?"

"Of course. He may only see a puff of dust, but like the other desert men, he has the eyes of a hawk."

A minute later, Moussa gave an excellent performance as a tour guide. "This is where you can find dinosaur fossils," he joked.

Dave couldn't help a chuckle, echoed by Meghan. "You should be on the stage, Moussa."

219

"Thanks for the compliment." Moussa glanced at the driver and said, "Our tail is watching; now we saunter around this rock and into the gully it hides."

They did so while Moussa continued his performance. In the gully was another car with another driver.

"Moussa, you are full of surprises."

"My people are primarily peaceful pastoralists, but we have family feuds and occasional disagreements about grazing or water rights. It's rare that bloodshed results—more usually, an opponent is captured, and he must work for a while in reparation. Our families are tightly bound and haven't forgotten the tricks for survival.

"Now, we have a thirty-minute drive. I'm taking you to an ancient well still in use; very few visitors have had the opportunity of seeing it."

Dave asked, "What about the first car and driver?"

"The driver will lie in the shade of a rock until sundown, then say his prayers, get in the car and drive back. We're good at waiting; we have learned patience from herding goats."

As they drove, Meghan asked, "Are there any trees, Moussa?"

"Very few. We never cut them down, as their shade is of immense value. There are palm trees—where there's water in a small oasis—and they provide us with dates."

"So, what do your animals eat?"

"What you can see about you; they are all browsers, eating the shoots and leaves of small bushes and tough grass that grows in the shade of rocks or shrubs. The animals never eat everything; they nibble a bit then move on to the next, leaving the plants to regenerate, so they need huge grazing areas."

Dave mentioned, "I read about acacias that produce tannin in their leaves to discourage grazers."

"Yes, some of the plants here do the same."

They crested a dune.

"There's the well," said Moussa as they coasted to a stop just short of it.

Amid a scattering of stunted acacia trees, there was a group of men, a herd of goats, and a dozen camels.

After much handshaking accompanied by *"Salaam Alaikum"* and *"Wa-Alaikum Salaam"*, Meghan and Dave got to see the well.

It was only a metre in diameter, just enough, Dave thought, for a man to go down and dig. It was surrounded by a low wall and a trough made from sun-dried bricks, with a cement-like lining. Gnarled, forked wooden posts stood on each side of the well, with a hardwood pole placed across them. A hand-carved hardwood pulley rolled on the beam in the centre above the well, squeaking as it turned.

One end of a rawhide rope disappeared down the well. The rope passed over the pulley, and the other end was attached to a camel that plodded away from the well in a deep groove worn in the hard-packed sand.

As they watched, a bulging goatskin bag appeared, the camel stopped, and a man—Meghan thought him ancient—swung the bag over the trough with a practised movement, emptied it, and then threw it back into the well. The camel turned and plodded back. Then the man grinned at them; he had sparkling blue eyes and three front teeth.

"Dave, this is fantastic; I'll never forget this place," Meghan said. "How does the camel know when to stop?"

"He counts the squeaks of the pulley wheel."

After a pause during which his reply sunk in, she exploded into laughter. "Dave, where do you get those ideas from?"

"I don't know; they just come."

Moussa had heard Dave's reply and translated it for the ancient. His cackling laughter was infectious.

"I won't forget it either; that well is over forty metres deep. What a feat to dig it with hand tools."

Moussa replied, "Dave, this well is several thousand years old. There may have been an oasis that dried up here, and the inhabitants started the well, but hundreds of others, over centuries, dug it a bit deeper as the water level dropped. My family are the keepers of the well today; we dug an extra metre out seven years ago."

"I must have a video of the camel pulling up the bag," said Meghan as she produced her camera. "Moussa, that man emptying the water seems too old to do that."

"He's a great-grandfather, as tough as nails, and will continue doing that until he loses his strength. It's not a matter of choice, it's a matter of survival, but pride is involved."

"Can you ask if I can take a photo of him? He's a splendid subject."

Meghan took the photographs and a video, not only of the great-grandfather but also of everyone there.

Moussa announced, "We must go; it's getting hot, and my family will be waiting for us."

Ten minutes later, they went into a valley between two dunes. A man was there with four kneeling camels.

"The car can't make it over the dune, so we will proceed on camels. Have either of you ridden one?"

"I haven't," said Dave, but Meghan answered, "Once, when I was a little girl, at a zoo."

"Then you'll find this interesting."

They mounted the camels, all dromedaries with a wood-and-leather seat on the hump. The herder voiced a command, and the camels rose with their characteristic loud groans and rocking movement—forward, with all the weight on the knees, then up and back as they stood. Meghan shrieked. Dave remained tight-lipped as he held on desperately.

They rode over the ridge and down a long slope to a tent between the dunes. The roof—made of a multi-coloured patchwork of woven camel-hair cloth—was held up by ten poles and two central ones and covered as much area as a small house. The sides of the tent were rolled up to allow the air to pass.

As the camels stopped, Meghan asked, "Moussa, can you take pictures of us before the camels kneel? I want a photo of Rudolph Valentino here."

"Of course. But wait a minute." He dismounted and went into the tent.

"Meg," said Dave, "Valentino rode a horse in the film."

"Ok then, Lawrence of Arabia. Although Rudolph was far sexier."

Moussa returned with a short, curved sword in a decorated sheath with a leather shoulder band. "Here, Dave. Sling this over your shoulder."

When Dave had it on, Meghan exclaimed, "Wow, you look dashing; no girl could resist you."

"Then can I carry you off to my tent?"

Meghan clasped her hands, fluttered her eyelashes, and said, "Yes, my hero."

The moment rapidly degenerated as Moussa translated, and everyone began to laugh.

Meghan thought the men approved of the idea Dave should carry her off to a tent, and the women seemed to agree.

They lay on mattresses in the tent, drank goat's milk, and ate dates, asking questions about anything and everything while the heat built until the sands outside shimmered.

Moussa told them, "This is the time for a siesta. We will move again just before sunset."

Meghan joined the women on one side of the tent, and silence fell during the inactivity.

As the sun neared the horizon, they could feel the temperature dropping.

Moussa said, "Dave, we must say prayers now. Either stay in the tent or join us; just sit or kneel behind the men."

Dave sat to one side, on his haunches, and followed the prayers. Somehow, the devotion seemed far more appropriate than that in a church or mosque. When the prayers ended and the men said the Taslim, Dave couldn't help doing the same, turning his head once to each side and saying the Arabic "*As-Salaam Alaikum Rahmatullahi.*" *The angel who records my wrongful deeds is to this side.*

On turning his head, one of the men had glimpsed Dave performing the Taslim. After the prayer, the man spoke to Moussa about it, and Moussa asked, "Dave, do you know the prayers? You aren't Muslim?"

"No, I'm not, Moussa. I shared a room for a year with an Egyptian student of Archaeology at university. He said prayers every night, and I learned a little. Somehow, out here it seems fitting, as if the desert is the right place to pray. I couldn't help repeating the final words."

Moussa told the others. Later, Dave felt he was a member of the family.

"Dave, we'll eat our evening meal—just couscous, dates, and roasted mutton—then drive back."

After two hours, they reached the hotel. Dave and Meghan thanked Moussa, promising to call as soon as Dave had a satphone.

Once in their room, Dave and Meghan changed and packed.

"This has been a fantastic day," Meghan said. "Let's go onto the rooftop terrace for a short while."

At the terrace, they walked to the far end, where it was darkest,

224

and Meghan said, "Dave, stand behind me and put your arms around me."

He did. She leaned back against him. "Don't move; just look at the stars and feel."

Ten minutes later, she said, "Dave?"

"Yes, Meg?"

"I'll never forget this place. I don't know what gets to me, whether it's the people, the stars, or the endless space."

"All of them. I feel the same. When the men prayed, I understood what total belief is for the first time. I felt like they did. This sky and the endless space is what does it; it transcends humanity."

"I'm sorry to go, but let's get on that flight."

Dave bought a satphone. Then, remembering what Moussa had said about security, he got one for Meghan.

Two days after they returned to work, he called Moussa to find out the results of the analysis of the bushmeat sample.

Moussa said, "Dave, I've good news for you. I did a DNA sequence on the sample. It was female. The tissue slides show both the right-hand Corky and the cholera bacterium."

"That's great news, Moussa. Are you going to do the surveys?"

"Well, I'm trying to write a project specification and justification for the university. Have you any suggestions that I can include?"

"You could say that you suspect a symbiotic relationship where Corkys keep cholera under control; it's probably far-fetched, but you have enough elements to sow seeds of doubt in the mind of anyone who says it's rubbish."

"Thanks. I'll keep you updated."

"Likewise, Moussa."

Dave told Meghan, and they discussed what they might do.

Meghan summed it up well: "Dave, what you said to Moussa was jumping to conclusions again. We know the Green Monkey is the possible source of Kravitz's Corkys. We don't have the means to study the relationship between the monkeys, Corkys, and cholera, so how do I prove your imaginary symbiosis without monkeys?"

"I'll ask Doctor Sankewicz; there must be a lab using animals in Britain."

Doctor Sankewicz was in a friendly mood. "Dave, what progress have you and your lovely assistant made?"

"Sir, not as much as I had hoped, although we have learned the Green Monkey, common in West Africa in the region Kravitz visited, is at least one likely carrier of the Corky bacterium. Kravitz's cholera strain is endemic in West Africa.

"A cholera vaccination lasts no more than two years, sometimes less, and Kravitz spent two years getting chemo treatment, so he never thought of renewing his vaccine. I feel sure he caught it there."

"Excellent detective work. How did you find this out?"

Dave explained.

"So, a university pathologist is collaborating with you on this?"

"Yes, sir, he's hoping to study how widespread the infection is and how it can cross to humans."

"Excellent. I assume you came to see me because you need some help?"

"I need the assistance of a research lab that uses the Green Monkey. Meg and I need to know if the Corky and cholera interact in the monkeys and how they move from one individual to another."

"Well, I'm sure there are labs in Britain. I don't know where or how many. I'll investigate and let you know; it may take a week or two.

"Who paid for your trip? I didn't see a request."

"We did, sir. It seemed best, as it's not the lab's business."

"If you have the receipts for your expenses, send them to me. I think it's about time we paid for some original research."

"Thank you, sir."

25

A week later, Moussa called. "Dave, I've something special to report. I have a Vietnamese friend I worked with as an intern in the USA. I communicate regularly with her, and I told her what I was doing and why, and referred her to your *Oncology* reports.

"She called me back this morning. She is dating a pathologist who has found the helix bacteria and a cholera bacterium in one of his slides. She also uses a satphone to call me, and you could reach her on it."

"Moussa, that's fantastic. What's her name and number?"

"It's Ylang. Tran Ylang—they put the surname first. I'll send you the number by satphone SMS."

Dave called Ylang immediately.

"Hello, is that Ylang? I'm Dave Tennant."

"Yes, Ylang here. Moussa said he would speak to you. I don't know more than I told him, but I'll send you my boyfriend's satphone number if you want to talk to him. I now have yours."

"That would be great, Ylang. If my research partner, Meg, and I visit, I hope we can meet you."

"I look forward to it. Bye, Dave."

A minute later, a message popped up from Ylang containing her boyfriend's name, "HOAN Danh", and number.

Dave called Danh. "Good morning, Doctor Hoan Danh?"

"Yes, you must be Mr Tennant. Ylang said you might call. How can I help?"

"Doctor, what's the sex of the patient with the bacteria, and does the bacterium have a left-helix tail?"

"Female, and the bacterium has a left-helix tail, Mr Tennant."

"Then I think my research partner, Meg, and I must visit you."

"You're welcome, Mr Tennant, but for reasons that I'll explain, if you do, would you please liaise with Ylang and not me to make a visit?"

"Certainly, sir; I hope to see you soon."

Dave made the bookings. This time, he didn't ask Meghan how many rooms he should reserve.

Dave and Meghan arrived in Hanoi after lunch on a Saturday and took a taxi to the Acoustic Hotel. The roads weren't filled with cars but with thousands of motorbikes. During the drive, they sat fascinated at the variety. Dave thought "culture shock" was an inadequate description of what he felt.

"Meg, look at that one; there's a family of five on it!"

"That's nothing; look over there."

A woman sat behind the rider, facing the rear, with a barbecue that seemed alight as she brandished a fork. Meghan exclaimed, "I'm sure she's cooking."

They continued spotting motorcycles with odd cargos. Meghan had to admit Dave crowned them all when he said, "Good heavens, look over there, Meg. That's a piano on the back!"

Dave and Meghan's room had a king-size bed. Meghan said nothing.

After a shower and a change, they took the elevator to the coffee shop to wait for Ylang. Meghan thought the young woman who approached them as they finished their coffee was beautiful; she switched her gaze to watch Dave as he stood up to welcome Ylang.

"Good afternoon. It's a pleasure to meet you, Ylang. Let's be informal; I'm Dave, and this is Meg."

Ylang put her conical hat down before shaking hands with Dave and Meghan. "I'm pleased to meet you both. Danh lives far from the airport, so he couldn't meet you. I'm sure you realise why, having seen the traffic. I know that it's morning for you. The six-hour time difference is a problem."

"We did manage to sleep in the plane—at least on the last leg—so it's not too bad."

"Danh will join us for a late dinner tonight, as you won't sleep until early tomorrow, but we'll go to the old market this afternoon; that's an entire tourism experience. I've organised a tourist trip for us tomorrow, as there are places you must see when you come here, but please wear walking shoes. We will leave at eleven. We can buy shoes in the old market if you haven't brought any."

Ylang bought traditional conical hats for Dave and Meghan as they entered the old market that afternoon. She said, "These are the best things to wear in the sun."

Dave and Meghan put the hats on, and they all continued browsing. Dave was happy at Meghan's delight when Ylang showed her a stall with local clothing and persuaded her to buy a colourful dress, but Ylang's insistence that he buy a similarly garish shirt puzzled him.

They met Danh outside a restaurant a short walk from the hotel. Meghan was not surprised when Danh embraced Ylang enthusiastically, but Dave was, for he had read a tourist website that said it was bad manners to show affection in public.

Danh had noticed his surprise, and once seated, he turned to

Dave and said, "I must apologise for my behaviour, but anyone watching must believe I'm here for love, not business."

"Danh, in London, it's considered normal; we're not offended."

"Thank you. Now let's order."

"I'm afraid you must do so for us, as I've no idea what these dishes are. Meg and I are not vegetarians. We will rely on you."

Danh and Ylang conferred and ordered sixteen small dishes with various things to taste, then Danh said, "Dave, after Ylang told me you were coming, I spoke to the man who was my mentor in Pathology. He read your articles and called me back on my satphone later. He wants to meet you on Monday.

"He is Research Director at a lab in the country that does research using macaque monkeys. You will, I hope, not be upset at the strict security. I'm sure he will explain the reason for the precautions, but tomorrow, when Ylang takes you on another tourist tour, please wear the clothes and the hats you bought today. Ylang will take photos of you for your identity badges. Please wear the clothes again on Monday."

"Is all of this necessary?" Dave asked.

"Perhaps not, but some unknown agents have followed you since you left the airport."

"Possibly the same guys that followed us in Africa."

"Please tell me about them, Dave."

Dave did.

"The guy who followed you is Asian; he fits in better here than in Africa. But don't worry about it; our escort will lose him on Monday."

Due to the time difference between Hanoi and London, Dave and Meghan struggled to fall asleep that night, with a heightened awareness that they were almost touching in the same bed.

"Good night, Dave."

"Good night, Meg."

Five minutes passed in silence, and then Dave murmured, "Meg, can I kiss you?"

"No."

"Why?"

"Because if you do, my resistance will go."

"It's hard not to want to."

"It's hard for me too. Do you love me?"

"I think so, Meg. Do you love me?"

"I think so too. But it would be better for us both to be sure. Sex is not the most important thing. Although it's hard refusing what a part of me desperately wants."

"Desperately, Meg?"

"Yes, now good night."

Minutes passed.

"Dave?"

"Yes, Meg?"

"When you slept with me in the hotel after the episode with the imposter, did I snuggle up to you?"

"Yes, Meg."

"I know now what Valerie meant when she said 'comfort'."

"So do I."

"Comfort me, nothing more."

They didn't sleep well.

"Good morning, Ylang. Where are you taking us?"

"Where all the tourists go. Although Hanoi is a relatively new city, it was a village two thousand years ago. It has oscillated over the centuries between the seat of an empire and nothing at all. We'll go to Vietnam's historical centres around Hoa Lư, in Ninh Bình Province, an hour's drive from here. First, we'll visit temples that were built a thousand years ago—I think you will be interested in comparing them to equivalent historical places in Europe. We'll take a boat ride through a famous cave complex, and then finally, I can offer you some exercise: a climb up five hundred steps to a pagoda on the top of Lying Dragon Mountain; the view is worth the effort."

After visiting the temples, which were without impressive buildings or decoration but had extensive tropical gardens, Dave remarked, "Ylang, the temples display a culture far different from that of the West. I feel the architects laid out these gardens as havens of peace, whereas in Europe, from Ancient Greece onwards, public buildings must show power and strength."

"I'm glad you sense it. People come here to absorb the peaceful atmosphere and relieve the stresses of daily life. Now, let's go for a boat ride."

In a bamboo sampan, they floated down the river and through a series of caves. When Meghan moved from the side of the boat to cling to Dave to avoid the cave walls, Dave put his arm around her and thought it was an ideal place for loving couples to hug and kiss in the gloom.

The steps looked formidable, worn, and uneven, and most were taller than a standard Western step.

Ylang said, "There's our ancient gym. Lots of people take one look and don't climb, but there are a couple of places you can stop at and admire the view, and from which you can return to the bottom."

Meghan didn't hesitate: "We're fit, Ylang, and I'm sure we can make it. Let's go, Dave."

Meghan needed two stops to catch her breath, but they reached the top. "Wow, that was hard, but the view is worth it," she said. "At least going down will be easier."

Fifteen minutes later, Dave said, "Meg, we can go down slowly if you've had enough rest."

"Ok, let's go."

She had gone down four steps when Dave called, "Meg, stop."

"Why?"

"Listen to what I'm going to say, but remember, I'm not Rory."

"Are you going to give me advice again?"

"No, I'm going to teach you something. Coming up the steps, you moved naturally, leaning forward, getting your weight over your front foot, and lifting yourself with that leg. Going down, you are making the classic mistake.

"Have you ever heard people going up and down a metal staircase?"

Meghan thought. "Yes, in a lighthouse."

"Is the noise louder going up or down?"

"Down."

"That's wasted energy; you're doing the same—leaning forward and falling to the next step, catching yourself on one foot. The impact is damaging to your knees and ankles, tiring, and if you lose your balance going forward when a step is lower than you thought, you might end up at the bottom with many broken bones."

"So, what do I do?"

"Watch me." Dave demonstrated. "I stay upright, my weight and balance on one leg, then bend it as if I'm doing a one-leg squat. The other leg feels for the lower step, toes pointed down, and as soon as I can feel it, I can transfer my weight to it. Hold my arm, move to the edge of the step, and close your eyes. Now go down one step.

"That's it; you'll be going down like a shadow in no time."

Tired, they slept well that night.

On Monday, dressed as ordered, Dave and Meghan climbed into the back seat of a dark-green 4×4. Danh sat in the front passenger's seat. They drove through the city, but then Dave had no idea where they were as they went down a narrow road in the country.

The driver had an earphone, and Dave heard him speak into a microphone. Shortly afterwards, Dave glimpsed an identical car ahead before their vehicle swung off the road into a hidden entrance, turned sharply left, and stopped behind a thick bamboo hedge.

Danh said, "This will only take a minute."

They heard another car accelerate past the hidden entrance, then a minute more passed, and they reversed and went back the way they had come until they took another road.

"That was neatly done, Danh."

"Yes, your tail will have a jolly afternoon touring and will see you, wearing those colourful clothes, take a boat ride together around the bay."

Dave now realised why Ylang had insisted he buy a garish shirt. They had hired doubles to pose as him and Meghan. The imposters would wear the same clothes as them and go about as tourists.

They drove through splendid scenery until they turned onto a private road that passed between two hills into a valley. They came to a large complex surrounded by an intimidating fence. Although Dave and Meghan couldn't read the language, the signs everywhere seemed to convey the same message as that found at any military installation in England: KEEP OUT.

At the security gate, a guard had to ask permission to let them through, and another got into the vehicle with them for the short drive to an office building. After they underwent a rigorous security check, a secretary showed them to an office where their host stood beside a desk. Another man sat in a corner. There was a recorder on a small table beside him. The man never spoke.

Danh introduced them. "Dave, Meg, this is an old college friend, Tôn Thất Loi, who is Research Director here."

Tôn Thất Loi bowed and greeted them, and then they all shook hands.

"Welcome to all of you, especially Dave and Meg, who have come so far. To begin with, I want to reassure you that this is not a military installation. There are no soldiers here; the guards are police officers. However, we operate under strict terms set by the government, and the police have a mandate to ensure we obey the rules. These also cover the dissemination of information. I cannot provide you with anything in writing, and I'll deny I ever said anything to you if this meeting becomes public. As you can see—" he nodded towards the man in the corner, "—he will record our discussion."

Dave said, "Sir, we know the scientific world well and never divulge anything without approval from everyone involved. Unfortunately, our world of fact is incompatible with the public world of fiction."

"Well said; I must remember that phrase. The security is in place because this lab does research that requires mammals, fish, and amphibians. Years ago, the practice drew a lot of negative publicity, and internationally agreed-upon rules were established for using animals in research. We follow those set by the British Government—the strictest of any country's rules—and a UK organisation does annual inspections and certification. But I'm sure you understand that the lunatic fringe ignores such things."

"I do, sir. Am I correct in assuming you breed all species for tests in captivity? And if you have rhesus macaques, are they hepatitis-free?"

"Yes, they are all bred here, and we have eliminated the hepatitis virus for its danger to lab staff. We test the animals according to a programme. Most of the buildings you'll see here are for animal welfare. We have no apes, but we have macaque and marmoset monkeys. Given a chance, a bunch of lunatics would free the monkeys—which have no survival skills—only for them to die in the wild. The security is principally for the safety of the animals."

"Sir, I didn't come here to question your ethics or business. I know of the necessity, and your security explanation is reassuring. But what can you tell us? As you have no human cases, it seems unusual that Danh's request is the cause of our visit."

"When Danh's request arrived, I at first ignored it; then, two days later, I asked one of our scientists if he had ever seen a bacterium with a corkscrew tail. He said no, but as no one had looked for such a bacterium, they might exist. He asked our other scientists, and one of them said they were common in the monkeys.

"We have an extensive store of slides produced over the years of our research. I set up a programme to draw all spinal-fluid slides and count the incidence of such bacteria. As Danh requested, I included the sex and age of the host.

"I want to show you around our labs, but I'll give you a summary of the results and our conclusions. First, all the bacteria seen have a left-hand helix. We haven't yet extended the search beyond the monkeys. Second, the bacterial count is zero before puberty, then rises, reaching a peak and plateau in the mature years, and then tails off to zero as the animal ages. We've studied the historical slides of the monkeys because they are our genetic companions. I can add that all the adults in the population have the bacteria."

"That's fantastic news, sir. Have you reached any conclusions?"

"Speculation only; we must experiment. Before puberty, our monkeys don't have bacteria. From childhood, they share masticated food, breastfeed, and spend hours grooming others, yet the bacteria only shows in them later. We can only assume that simple bodily contact and food cannot be agents of infection. Nor can it be airborne, as they share the same space. However, monkeys are sex-mad. Like humans, the females have a monthly cycle, and the monkeys' sexual activity is frequent and indiscriminate. Several males can attempt to impregnate a female within hours, and a male can have intercourse with many females in short succession. Like in humans, the sex drive dies down with age, so we conclude that sexual congress transmits the bacteria, male to female, and female to male. Therefore, in our captive population, one hundred per cent infection is inevitable."

"So you suggest the bacteria count in the older animals drops as the bacteria die?"

"That seems to be the case."

"But that leaves a question: How do the bacteria reproduce? Unless they multiply, the entire population of monkeys would be bacteria-free after a fixed time."

"That's the crucial question right now. Publishing what I've told you would bring ridicule unless we can answer that.

"We must first verify the population to ensure that the historical slides represent the current situation."

Meghan then asked, "Sir, another question of importance is: What effect do the bacteria have on the monkeys? From what you have said, the bacterium would seem to survive the immune system's effects, yet it brings no illness."

"That, I'm afraid, will be a prolonged test; we can only watch, hoping to catch an event."

"Every bit of information is important," Dave said, "and what you've told us is invaluable. Is it possible to look for the bacteria in the males' semen? It might provide further proof of transmission." He hesitated. "But let's leave that one for now. I have another question: A cholera mutation infects the monkeys and some people, too. Our human case in England has this cholera bacterium. I would like to know if this cholera mutation plays a role in the lifecycle of the corkscrew bacteria. Are the macaques similarly infected?"

"I don't know; we must find out."

"Thank you. I can assure you there will be no publication of what you have done or are doing without your specific permission."

"Thank you. I'll now show you around our labs; you'll find we have capabilities exceeding that of most labs. And I will make you an offer." He glanced over at the man in the corner. "I cannot release any information about experiments done here, but I can, with permission, report on analyses done on human samples sent from outside. If Danh finds a human subject with the bacteria, and you want analysis or an experiment done, please don't hesitate to ask if we can do it."

"Thank you, that's a generous offer."

"No, we're both trying to save human lives, so if there's something I can do to further cancer research, we're in the same boat."

They toured the labs, returned with Danh to the city, packed, and then left on a London flight at midnight.

In the departure lounge at the airport, Meghan said, "I like the people, the temples are magnificent, and the countryside we saw is fascinating. I looked up pictures of Hạ Long Bay, and they are inspiring—I'd love to take a boat ride there. But if you ask if I prefer this place to the desert, I shall say no."

"I won't ask because I agree, but Hạ Long would be a good place for a honeymoon."

Meghan didn't answer; she couldn't.

They had time on the flight to discuss what they had learned.

Dave asked, "What do you think we discovered, Meg?"

She replied, "That the virus may be harmless to monkeys and quite common, but it can jump across to human hosts."

"Cart before the horse; they have a captive population—one

hundred per cent infection may be a consequence. It might be limited to a single troop in the wild, so 'quite common' is speculation."

"And we know that people eat monkeys in various parts of the world."

"Yes, but Loi said he ruled out transmission in masticated food, so that's unlikely."

Meghan was stubborn: "Unlikely is not impossible."

"True, but in those parts of the world where people eat monkeys, I doubt many medical cases require a lumbar puncture. Finding a case of monkey-to-human transmission is less likely than winning the lottery."

"When Moussa finds a person who has the cholera or Corkys, we can ask him to check if monkeys are common in the same area. It might give us an indication that monkey-to-human transmission is occurring."

"We can do that."

"What will Loi do?"

"I don't know. There are many ways to proceed. Loi might create a bacteria-free control population by shifting pre-pubescent monkeys to a new cage. He could prove sexual transmission by adding an infected male to a small number of control females and vice versa."

"Don't you have one of your non-scientific leaps of imagination to offer?"

"Not one you'll believe."

"Tell me anyway."

"I think what I told Moussa may be true, although I only suggested using it as a lever. I think Kravitz catching both the left- and right-helix bacteria is a unique event, but in Africa and the East, Corkys play a role in protecting the monkeys, and a few people, from cholera. I don't know how this happens; it must be an ancient evolution." After a pause, Dave added, "Ok. We have lots to do. Now, let's catch some sleep before we land. You can put your head on my shoulder; I promise I won't kiss you."

"In these seats, you won't get closer than the top of my head. You can kiss that."

26

When Dave got back to the office in the afternoon, he found a short message waiting from Doctor Sankewicz: "Call Doctor Jack Mulligan, Director of a lab in a remote location in the Scottish Southern Uplands. He might be able to help."

A secretary routed Dave's call.

"Good afternoon, Mr Tennant. I've been expecting your call. How can I help?"

"I'm sorry I couldn't call sooner, Doctor; I've been overseas. First, do you have Green Monkeys as patients?"

"We do, Mr Tennant."

"Well, I would like to know if your patients have the same cholera bacteria and the same corkscrew-tailed bacteria as the human case we're investigating does."

"That's easy enough; we can certainly check. How can we tell what we're seeking?"

"I will send you electron micrographs."

"That's fine. I'll SMS you my email address. When we have a result, I'll call you."

Dave was trying to catch up with his delayed Monday paperwork when Meghan came in from the DNA lab.

"Dave, I've some interesting results from my DNA tests."

"What?"

"The cholera bacterium has a gene that differs from standard cholera."

"Well, it survives, so it must have."

"But the gene matches with one from Kravitz's DNA."

"That's impossible, Meg. How can the same strain of cholera be different in every animal body it infects?"

"I don't know, but that might be its disguise to avoid the immune system."

"How about the Corky? Is it also taking on a gene of the host to evade the immune system?"

"I'm going to research that tomorrow."

"Then I'll see you in the lab."

"Are you staring at my bum again, Dave?" Meghan was at a workbench, preparing a DNA sample.

"No, I was remembering you in Vietnam, in your colourful dress."

"Another excuse?"

"Not really. I was just trying to decide whether I'm a bum- or a boob-admirer, and I can't see the front of you, so I had to remember it."

Meghan laughed. "You continue to surprise me with inane statements. What have you decided?"

"Nothing; I like both."

"Better stay with bums; boobs tend to sag sooner. There, I'm going to run the sequencer. Two minutes to go." Then two minutes later: "The Corkys have the same gene as the cholera bacteria—the one adopted from the host."

"How does it happen?"

"I've no idea. There's only one way we can find out."

"How?"

"I must work in a lab where I can do DNA tests on bacteria cultures at set intervals."

"Then next week, we must go to that lab in Scotland run by Doctor Jack Mulligan and see what they can do to help. We should hear from them on Monday or Tuesday."

Doctor Jack Mulligan called and said their captive population of monkeys carried both bacteria, as Dave had suggested.

Dave arranged a visit; they were to fly to Prestwick, the airport serving the Glasgow area, on Wednesday afternoon, and return on Friday.

A minibus was waiting for them at Prestwick, the drive into the country was spectacular, and the lab, Dave couldn't help thinking, looked like the one in Vietnam, hidden in a valley remote from everything.

Doctor Jack Mulligan, accompanied by three others, welcomed Dave and Meghan and introduced them to his colleagues. "Malcolm Jennings, who does all our admin; Anna Broomhall, our animal psychologist researching behaviour; and Derek Mansfield, who oversees the menagerie. I expect you will meet our other researchers."

Meghan replied, "I'm sure that will be interesting, although Dave and I may not be here full time."

"None of us is, Miss MacDougal; this lab is so far from anywhere that only the security staff and a reduced animal-care crew are here at the weekend. We run buses to civilisation every Friday afternoon and Monday morning for those who want to take them. You are welcome to do so if you need to. Before we start discussing research, I must tell you about security. It's there to protect the menagerie, not the people. Malcolm will show you your rooms, and Derek will show you around."

The speech about security was almost identical to the one by Tôn Thất Loi in Vietnam. While Doctor Mulligan gave it, Meghan surreptitiously studied the other three. Derek seemed young, shy, and gangly. She thought him a likeable person who would be enthusiastic about animals. Malcolm gave her a look she had long ago classified as *"he's undressing me in his mind"*, and she instantly thought he was a man who believed himself irresistible and that all women were dying to jump into his bed. She glanced at Anna to find her looking at Malcolm; then Anna switched to look at her, smiled, and winked. It appeared Anna thought much the same about Malcolm. About the same height, weight, and body shape as Meghan, she could have been a sister except for her skin tone, deep-brown and almost-black hair cut in a short, 1920s style, and large, nut-brown eyes with golden glints; Meghan thought she was beautiful.

Doctor Mulligan finished and said, "I'll leave you to my colleagues, and we can meet again at two-thirty."

Malcolm said firmly, "Come; I'll show you to your rooms."

Anna spoke up, looking directly at Meghan: "Meg, I have a two-bedroom unit. Would you like to use the second bedroom?" Her eyes flickered towards Malcolm, then returned to her. "It would be nice to have some company in this male world."

Malcolm interjected, "I've got it all arranged, Anna."

"I'll bet you have," Anna remarked. "What do you say, Meg?"

Meghan hadn't missed the body language and Anna's innuendo; she could tell Malcolm was annoyed. "Thanks, Anna, it would be a pleasure to use your spare room. Then if I must go away for a few days, I can leave some things with you."

Trying to hide his dismay, Malcolm said, "Ok, I'll show Dave his room and meet you back here."

Anna took Meghan to the room. Meghan put her bag down, and

while Anna showed her around, she asked Anna, "You don't get along with Malcolm, do you?"

"If you haven't guessed already, Meg, I'm lesbian. Malcolm thinks I'm an insult to his idea of womanhood. He believes he's irresistible to women and continually tries to prove it. I felt I should do something to protect you from his advances. I expect he had planned to put you in a room next to his."

"Well, thanks, Anna. I feel better about coming to do some work here than when I arrived."

Derek took them on a tour. It was a much smaller lab than the one in Vietnam, but Dave thought it would provide sufficient facilities for Meghan and himself to make progress.

Dave asked, "With this number of animals, it must be a problem ensuring all get sufficient food. What do you feed the monkeys?"

"They need a balanced monkey diet to stay healthy. The bulk of their food is tropical fruits brought from Ghana and Nigeria in refrigerated containers. The suppliers refer to most of it as 'seconds'—not for human consumption as whole fruit but rather as fruit juice.

"We mix the fruits, but the monkeys need other things with trace elements: a few roots, some nectar from tropical flowers, and a choice of insects. They are natural foragers; when their bodies need something, that's what they look for. So we put everything, like mangoes and papayas, in separate bowls, vary the fruits, and have dishes with the other things their bodies need if they decide to eat some."

Dave and Meghan had lunch with Doctor Mulligan, Anna, and Derek. Then they described their quest to find out about Boris's infection. They didn't mention their visit to the East or Boris's escapades.

Then, they all mapped out a programme together.

Derek would conduct experiments harmless to the monkeys. He

would isolate a monkey, and they would then see if its Corky levels decreased. Then, when he returned the monkey to the group, they would assess whether these levels increased.

Dave asked, "We suspect there may be a link to sexual intercourse. Can you do the same for each sex?"

They agreed on testing procedures.

Then Dave asked, "We must learn how to culture the cholera bacteria. It's notoriously tricky to do, so we would like to try several different protocols simultaneously. Meg will come and do them, but she needs lab facilities and samples for each protocol."

"I'm sorry, but I'm against taking multiple samples from one animal," Derek said. "Can we take one from each of several monkeys?"

This didn't surprise Meghan. "Of course."

Dave asked, "Meg, when can you come?"

"How about Tuesday? Is there a bus from Prestwick?"

Doctor Mulligan replied, "Send me your flight number, and the driver can meet you if it's late afternoon or mid-morning when he has nothing to do. Anna can organise a lab bench for you, Meghan."

After the canteen dinner, they joined the other scientists in a lounge with a bar. Anna stuck close to Meghan, preventing Malcolm from launching an attempt at seduction. Both women were amused, for they sensed Malcolm's disgust.

Meghan decided that she should profit from the lab's proximity to Edinburgh by visiting her family. When she looked up alternative ways to get there, she decided to hire a car at Prestwick Airport and keep it until she returned to London. The lab was an hour and a half's drive from Edinburgh and forty-five minutes from Prestwick Airport.

She told Dave and added, "Did you pick up the vibes from Anna and Malcolm?"

"Yes, Meg, he's a sexual predator; you must watch out for him. Anna, I guess, is lesbian, so the two extremes clash. I'm glad she's looking after you—I didn't miss that either."

"You always surprise me. You don't feel I shall fall into bed with one or both of them?"

"Not with Malcolm; he's too blatant and egotistical to attract you. I'm not sure about Anna, but you aren't lesbian, and I don't think she will seduce you."

They took the early flight back to London.

27

Meghan arrived at the lab as planned to find an array of samples ready for her. Each was marked with the donor monkey's number, sex, and age. She labelled twenty Petri dishes, spread a different nutrient mix in each, then had a thought and asked a scientist at a neighbouring bench: "What is the normal body temperature of a Green Monkey?"

"It has a circadian cycle like humans do; a half to one degree higher than humans."

Meghan warmed the Petri dishes, dosed them from the samples, and then put them in the culture oven. Then she made slides for the microscope, one for each instance.

For the next two days, she regularly peeked at the Petri dishes while looking at the slides. Only two showed signs of multiplying cholera.

She used the time to isolate the cholera bacteria from two samples and do a DNA sequence on them and the monkey itself. The results were different, so she did the same for a third sample and got another result.

In the evening, she was in her room when she decided to call Dave from the satphone.

Dave answered: "Meg, I was about to commit suicide."

Meghan decided this was a nice exaggeration. "Dave, it's not worth killing yourself for love; what's her name?"

"Honey."

She was delighted by his response. "I suppose she walked out of the sea wearing a minute, skin-coloured bikini and a belt with a knife."

"Absolutely. One look at that blonde hair, and I was a goner."

"You didn't look at the boobs bursting from the bikini top? Or at the curved hips and tanned legs?"

"I didn't need to; I remembered yours."

Meghan felt a shiver. "I've confirmed that the cholera bacteria in each monkey carries a gene from its host, so each monkey's cholera is different."

"That's incredible; we can only assume that taking on the host gene is the protection mechanism it uses against the immune system, but how it's done, I have no idea."

"I don't know either. You must watch some more Bond films. I've got two growth mediums that are working, and I will expand the test with variations of each, so I must return next week. And this weekend, I'll visit my parents."

"Ok, Meg, I'll get the whole series of Bond films; just think of me drooling."

It rained heavily on Friday evening. The forecast said it would clear up by the morning. Meghan decided to stay for the night.

Malcolm saw her in the lounge as he was going out. "Haven't you gone yet, Meg?"

Meghan knew he would offer her a lift if she said she was waiting for the rain to stop, and an hour with the self-opinionated loudmouth was more than she could stand. "I'm waiting for a call. Then I'm leaving."

Half an hour later, she was alone.

Then Anna came into the lounge, surprised to see Meghan still there. "Meg, why haven't you gone yet?"

"Waiting for the rain. I'll go tomorrow. I'm too tired to peer through a wet windscreen at night. But why are you here?"

"Morag, my partner, is visiting her parents in Glasgow, so it's choosing between an empty flat in Kilmarnock and an empty room here. I'm glad to have some company."

The two women made a light supper in the kitchen, returned to the lounge, and switched on the TV. They sat side by side on the couch, watching a comedy show. When the adverts began, Anna turned to Meghan and said, "Meg, can I kiss you?"

From fourteen to sixteen, Meghan had shared a room at boarding school with Kim, and she remembered their experiments with their budding bodies. Kissing was part of it—done, as they both agreed, for practice. Meghan looked at Anna's earnest expression and thought, "*She wants to, and it might be nice, like years ago.*"

"Yes."

Anna leaned forward. It wasn't like it had been with Kim; Anna brushed her lips across Meghan's forehead, then ran the tip of her tongue across her eyelids, down her cheek, behind her ear, and under her chin. Eventually, her lips brushed across Meghan's, and Meghan felt a sensation building that she had never felt with Kim. Anna continued the feather-light caress, accentuated by a hand behind Meghan's head that caressed the back of her neck. The experience was so new that Meghan didn't object when Anna cupped a breast in one hand, slipped her hand between the blouse buttons, and caressed her breast and the hardening nipple under her bra.

"Meg, let's go to your room."

For a moment, Meghan struggled with a decision. If she were

to say no, she should do so now. But she wanted the feeling to continue. "Ok," she breathed.

Half an hour later, Anna said, "Meg, do what I do." Then she began to undress Meghan. Slowly, she removed one piece of clothing, pausing to let Meghan do the same to her until both women were naked on the bed.

Meghan was learning that many body parts could caress or be caressed. Her excitement had built slowly but steadily and reached a pitch as Anna's tongue ran across her most sensitive spot. She shuddered, then relaxed.

Anna said urgently, "Don't stop caressing me." Ten minutes later, Anna orgasmed.

They lay quietly together for a while, and then Meghan asked, "Is that how it is with Morag?"

"Morag's far more experienced than you, though you did very well. We can make it last for three or four hours. Sometimes though, it's fast. Our periods have synchronised, so we ovulate simultaneously, and the peak comes quicker. Did you enjoy it?"

"Yes, Anna, I enjoyed the physical part of it, but something was missing. I don't think I'll do it again."

"That's ok. I can't have two lovers simultaneously; it doesn't work, even for lesbians. Do you miss Dave?"

"Did you notice, Anna? Even though Dave's not my lover."

"I couldn't miss it. Why isn't he?"

"We agreed to hold off until we're both sure it will last. You know that when work romances break up, one of the pair always has to leave the company, and our project is not worth risking."

"Poor you. It must be hell."

"Yes, sometimes."

"Meg, I'll leave you to get some sleep; you must drive tomorrow. I'll sleep late."

Meghan had visited her parents on the weekend. She had constantly been wondering if Dave was watching Bond films.

On Tuesday, she decided to call Dave. "I'll finish here by Friday," she told him. "I can take the late flight home. I'll bring all my slides and some cultures."

"I may have a better plan. The manager of the BaVir lab in Glasgow called this morning; he has a blood sample from an immigrant African woman he was testing for sickle-cell anaemia. He says she has cholera bacteria in the blood. He's agreed to a visit on Saturday morning to look at his slides.

"I propose I fly to Prestwick on the late flight, and you meet me at the airport. Then we can visit him on Saturday, tour Loch Lomond Park, and return to London on Sunday."

"That's a great idea. When you make the booking, let me know where we'll be staying on Friday night. If I leave early, I'll check in to the place and fetch you when you arrive."

"Will do. Can you get hold of a cardboard box and put all the work stuff, including the slides, into it? I'll have a medical courier pick it up on Friday, and he can bring a warm box for the cultures."

"Why?"

"I don't want to lug it around Loch Lomond, and I think you will be safer that way in case someone is planning to steal the research. The cultures would have to come with a medical courier, so he can bring everything. Besides, the baggage handlers at the airport might break something. If Malcolm wants to know what you are doing, tell him; you can even say you're sending it using DHL Medical Express and that it's going on a flight from Prestwick, although it will go by train via Carlisle."

Meghan received a call from the courier to agree on a collection time. She was waiting with Anna in reception when he arrived. He took the box and left.

Malcolm came into reception and asked, "Who was that?"

Anna replied, "A courier; he came to pick up a parcel from Meghan."

"You should've asked me, Meghan; we have an account, and I would've shipped it for you free."

"It was free, Malcolm, prepaid; DHL Medical Express is taking it on a flight from Prestwick." Meghan watched Malcolm leave. "*Why does he look annoyed?*"

"Anna, did you feel Malcolm was angry that I shipped that box?"

"Yes, I have no idea why. I've always suspected Malcolm has a violent side, so be careful. You're okay with the security staff around, but watch out if you leave."

Meghan was working on her report of her week's work when Anna came into the room.

"Is this goodbye, Meg, or will you be back?"

"I've done what Dave and I planned, so it's goodbye unless there's a new reason for me to come back here. But if you visit London, please call me."

"Are you leaving now?"

"In half an hour or so; I want to finish and file this report and leave with a clean notebook."

"Ok, I'm going now. The best of luck with your research." Anna kissed Meghan. "It was fun, Meg; I'll remember your visit."

"Me too."

Meghan finished her work, looked out the window, and saw the light was fading, so she decided to get ready to leave.

Half an hour later, after a shower and a change, Meghan put her case of clothes on the back seat of the hired car.

The security guard said, "Have a good weekend, Miss MacDougal. You're the last to go, so I will lock up now. If you come back for any reason, hoot."

Meghan drove out, but ten minutes and ten kilometres later, she felt the rear right wheel wobbling. She had a flat tyre.

After stopping and switching on the hazard lights, she opened the boot, found the spare was fully inflated, removed the jack, but couldn't find the wheel spanner. It wasn't in the foam-block recess that held the jack—or anywhere else.

She tried her phone, but she was in a valley, so there was no signal. She could see the ground sloped uphill from the other side of the road, so she walked across and pushed her way through the bordering gorse. Then, stepping carefully on the uneven ground, she headed up the hill in fading light, trying to avoid the gorse and hoping to get a signal.

She had gone only fifty metres when she heard a car coming and saw headlamps from the direction of the lab. She paused and listened, wondering who it might be. The vehicle stopped, and then the driver was highlighted in the headlamps as he came to inspect her car. Meghan was sure it was Malcolm, yet he had left the lab before her.

She crouched down behind a gorse bush as she heard him shout.

"Meghan, where are you? Don't be stupid; you'll get lost on the moors, so come back now."

Fear made her move slowly and quietly further up the hillslope; she had to grit her teeth to keep herself from trembling, repeating to herself, "*Dave would tell me not to panic, and he will come.*" She heard Malcolm crashing around in the foliage, cursing. After a hundred metres more, suddenly, with no warning, a cold mist swirled around her, making it far harder to move. She felt panic again, but fought it down, held her breath, and thought, "*Dave wouldn't panic; I must be quiet,*" so she struggled onwards, feeling for the ground with her feet every step until she found what seemed like a track going uphill. She followed it, primarily by touch and sense, as night took hold. It led to a shepherd's hut built of stone

JEREMYHODGSON

and hardly big enough to crawl into to shelter from the mist's insidious, enveloping dampness.

Her phone still had no signal. Huddled in the shelter, she thought of what she could do. Then she remembered the cross that Tansy had asked her to wear. She pressed the centre to start the GPS alarm. A stray thought told her to put it in the open, so she removed it and placed it outside the entrance. She knew going out would lead to hypothermia; she was cold enough already, so she scraped together all the leaves and straw on the floor and lay on it, curled into a ball, as the cold began to take its toll. Soon, she felt she was in a dream world, but Dave was there. "*He loves me, he loves me, he loves ...*"

Dave arrived at Prestwick Airport to find that Meghan wasn't there. He tried to call her, but her phone was offline. He called the hotel; they said she had not checked in. He called the lab; after three tries, the security man answered and said she had left forty minutes ago. He was beginning to panic, but when he saw the missed calls from Tansy on his other, secret phone, he called her. "Tansy, Meghan has disappeared. There's no answer when I try to call her. I'm in Prestwick, and she left a lab east of here nearly an hour ago."

"I've been trying to call you. I think Meghan's phone is out of signal range, but she activated the alarm on the GPS cross I gave her. She's not moving. I'll SMS her position to you. It's a few hundred metres north of a road. I'll also give you a GPS position on the road nearest to her."

"If I go to the position you send, how do I get to her?"

"When you get there, open the app I installed on your phone with the icon that has the letters 'TFM'. When it asks you for a code, enter '6940'. I'll SMS you everything you need. Turn the

256

phone until the red dot is on the arrow, then walk in that direction."

"Ok, Tansy, and thanks."

"Dave, according to the weather forecast, it's misty and cold at Meghan's location. Get an electric car and make sure it has fog lights, speed control, and collision avoidance. Drive with the window open to listen out for shouting."

Fifteen minutes later, Dave left the airport. After half an hour of furious driving, he had to slow down and use the fog lights and speed control to help him go as quickly as he could.

Twenty minutes later, as the mist seemed to have a weird silver glow, Dave switched off the fog lights and found he could see slightly better. He followed the white line in the middle of the road. The moon had risen, and it cast a spooky light over everything. The car whispered on.

Ten minutes later, Dave felt the car slowing as it sensed an obstruction, and then it stopped. He got out, walked silently, and found Meghan's car with the flat tyre and open boot. He took her suitcase off the back seat, her handbag off the front seat, and put them into his car.

The car behind hers wasn't locked. The electronic key was lying on the passenger seat, so Dave took it. He turned his car around and parked by the roadside.

Dave opened the app Tansy had told him about and entered the code. It showed Meghan's beacon about two hundred metres to the north. Dave hung his cross—the one with a GPS tracker, that Tansy had given him—on the car's side-view mirror, triggered the alarm, and walked slowly and quietly up the hill. He heard someone cursing up ahead. The mist muffled the sound, so the direction was hard to establish.

Ten minutes later, sensing the different texture of the ground, his feet found the path, so he followed the trail, and soon found the shepherd's hut. Meghan's cross glinted in the faint light; he picked it up and looked inside at her huddled figure.

Dave had to get her attention, but he didn't want to alarm her and cause her to scream, so he repeated "I love you" in a whisper until she stirred. He said, "It's Dave, I love you," until she replied, "Dave?"

"Yes, come here, don't talk."

She crawled towards him with a colossal effort. The movement triggered more trembling.

Dave wrapped his coat around her, lifted her, and hugged her tightly to warm her. He breathed a sigh of relief when the trembling died away.

With Meghan stuck to him like a limpet, they followed the path to the road, and then the app told Dave which way to go to find the car.

Five minutes later, with the heater on full blast, they were driving back to Prestwick.

"Who was it, Meg?"

Meghan remained drowsy from the hypothermia, but she managed to answer: "I think it was Malcolm. I was scared. I don't know what he intended, but I knew you would come ..."

"I'll see what I can do about him."

Exhausted by her experience, Meghan slept the night in his arms in the hotel room Dave had booked. Dave thought it was a just reward.

Before breakfast, Dave made two phone calls. The first was to the Scottish lab's security. "Good morning, it's Dave Tennant here. I want to report that two cars are at the side of the road, about ten minutes' drive from you towards Prestwick. There may be someone in trouble there. One of the cars has a flat tyre and a missing wheel spanner."

The second call was to the hire-car company, telling them they had a car to collect.

Glasgow was a disappointment. Dave and Meghan learned only that the female patient was from northern Ghana, and when they looked at the blood slides, they found no sign of Corkys. They left after telling the lab manager to recommend she and her family all have cholera vaccinations immediately, although the bacteria were of the endemic type.

Their tour around Loch Lomond took their minds off everything, and the lovely old inn Dave had booked had a magnificent view of the loch.

That night, just as they were preparing to get into bed, Meghan said, "Dave, kiss me."

"Why, Meg?"

"Because I want to sleep in your arms like last night, and if you kiss me when in bed, I will break down. I must keep you thinking of your mother."

"Can't I do both, Meg?"

"I'm sure you can, but then your mother only gets a half, and that's not good enough."

"Meg, the medical courier delivered Boris's sample to the lab today. I will do the analysis tomorrow."

"You don't look happy."

"Is it that obvious?"

"Yes, I know you too well; what's worrying you?"

"Meg, I'm afraid of finding his cancer remission has reversed."

"Why?"

"Because Corkys die. There will be a cancer resurgence if there aren't enough of them."

"We are not responsible for Boris's condition. We are trying to help him, and worrying about what we might find is silly. Let's analyse the sample tomorrow and find out, then consider what we can do if necessary."

28

Ylang called Meghan on her satphone before they started the analysis of Boris's sample. Ylang was ultra-cautious, so Meghan encouraged her to discuss mundane matters, beginning with the dress Meghan had bought that week.

After they had exhausted that topic, Ylang asked a startling question: "Meg, can you tell me of a mix that would raise my average hormone balance to the level at ovulation?"

"Ylang, are you trying to become pregnant? Can't you wait for the normal cycle?"

"Yes, Meg, I want what the English call a 'corking little kid', and every time I ovulate, Danh is away."

"It will be difficult to calculate, Ylang. Can you send me data on your normal and ovulating hormone levels?"

"I can. I've only got three samples: before, during, and after."

"That will do, Ylang."

"Thank you. I'll send you a link. If it's a girl, I'll name her Meg."

"That will be an honour!"

Shortly after Meghan ended the call, she received a link from Ylang with data on the Vietnamese lab's findings regarding cholera and Corkys. It gave six numbers in two columns with headers in

Chinese pictograms. One symbol depicted a squiggly line, and the other a volcano.

"Dave, what do you think of those numbers?"

"It's straightforward. The squiggly-line column contains numbers for Corky counts before and during ovulation in monkeys. Over that period—although it doesn't say how long it is—the Corky count doubled. The other column contains the cholera count. Over the same period, it dropped."

"Why does the volcano indicate cholera?"

"Vietnam was under French rule for a long time, and the French word for 'anger' is 'colère'; a volcano illustrates an angry Earth."

"But we know the Corkys don't multiply by fission, so how do you explain this? Dave, jump to one of your ridiculous conclusions."

"Meg, we haven't been thinking analytically. We have not two but three Corky populations: East, West, and Boris. Ignore Boris. He's an unnatural occurrence.

"The two other populations include both male and female cases, and we know now that the Corkys in the females must eject phages when the female ovulates. The phages must attack cholera bacteria and transform them into Corkys.

"Corky is a symbiotic bacterium; its multiplication only happens in women when ovulation occurs, preventing massive cholera infection. The phages might attack various other bacteria to help the immune system."

"And copulation?"

"That's the physical transmission of phages to other monkeys. If they have cholera bacteria, the phages transform them into Corkys. Otherwise, the phages die, as they have nothing to do."

"But what happens if a male doesn't copulate with a female?"

"Then I would guess the bacteria multiply until the male dies, but look at the numbers Ylang sent. If the cholera bacteria multiply from the lowest number to the highest between monthly cycles, it's a low growth rate. I suspect the hormones also stimulate cholera multiplication. Males don't have hormones that stimulate cholera growth, and as the levels rise slowly, the immune system gets to work without phages from copulation.

"There's only one conclusion that fits what we know. We are certain the Corkys can produce phages when the left- and right-helix ones work together, but Boris is the only case we've seen. This shows that the left- or right-hand Corkys alone can do so when stimulated by hormones. It makes sense because we only have one variant of the Corky in the monkeys.

"The phages must attack cholera and convert it into Corkys. The sexual transmission is not of Corkys or cholera but phages. It's how the males get Corkys; the phages create them there, and as the male monkeys get older and their sex life wanes, the Corkys and bacteria die out. I remember suggesting a symbiotic relationship to Moussa to justify his research, but it might be true."

"But how do they end up with the genes of the parent monkey?"

"You said the cholera bacteria had a gene the same as the host, Meg."

"Yes, they do."

"Then I'll jump to another conclusion. The Corkys have a gene of the host because the cholera bacteria do. The cholera bacteria have the patient's genes because a mutation allowed them to mimic the parent body to avoid the immune system. That mutation might have reduced their virulence, but it gave them the time to infect others."

"A good theory, but cholera bacteria are short-lived; they might last six months to two years, but they would die out, and the phages have nothing to attack."

"But that wouldn't matter, Meg. It's a balance; if there is no cholera, the monkey doesn't need the Corkys."

"Ok, so to summarise, we think the cancer cells are eaten by two Corkys—one left- and one right-helix bacterium—so both must be present. The Corkys release phages when they eat a cancer cell but can also do so when female ovulation hormones stimulate them. The phages, we believe, merge with cholera bacteria and create new Corkys, and they combat cancer. We can force cancer into remission if we can learn how to dose a patient with the right proportions of Corkys and cholera."

"That's correct, but we could kill the patient if we get the dosage wrong."

"There's much to prove. Let's work on it and ignore the speculation. But first, let's do Boris's analysis."

The results were, as Dave feared, discouraging, but they were not as bad as he had imagined.

"Meg, it looks like it is ending."

"Let's get the graphs and add the latest data ... I agree it's ending; the new value is higher than expected if the remission had continued at the same rate."

Dave sounded angry. "What's the reason?" Then he repeated his question. "For God's sake, what's the reason?"

Meghan heard a desperate plea to Asclepius, the Greek god of medicine, whose serpent-entwined rod, over 2 500 years later, is still used as a symbol for medicine and healthcare.

"Dave, look at the graphs and listen to me. I'll make one of your ridiculous jumps to a conclusion. We can't expect a cure unless the immune system takes over; remember what Doctor Morrison said about medical arrogance?

"All we can hope for is to achieve a stable level, whatever that is, where the ongoing maintenance treatment keeps cancer at a low level; it's what doctors do today once they've achieved a low level of cancer.

"Think of the maintenance treatment we might need: Would it be hormone injections? Or injecting cholera bacteria?

"We need to know, and to know how much. The curves of regularly collected data help, as I said they would months ago.

"Think about the trick question: How many people must be in a room before you can *expect to find two with the same birthday?*"

"You think Boris's Corkys can't find cancer cells?"

"Right, or the phages can't find bacteria."

"Meg, we need to find an acceptable cholera bacteria count; perhaps Moussa can do a quick survey with hospital patients. But what do we tell Boris?"

"I would guess Moussa can get us a number, and we can do the calculation in a month. Let's tell Boris to give us another sample in a month."

"Ok, I'll call Morrison on Monday."

"You can't; it's a bank holiday."

"Damn, I forgot. Tuesday then. But what are you doing on Monday?"

"I have nothing planned at the moment. Just the usual housework and the laundry."

"Then how about coming skating on Monday afternoon?"

"Ice-skating?"

"Yes, do you know how?"

"I haven't skated since I was ten, but I think I'll manage to stay upright.

"But where did you learn, Dave?"

"In Medway, there was a rink that had open days for kids; we could go if we could get a pair of skates. Then after I started working, I went skating regularly; it's good exercise for balance and leg strength.

"We can hire skates for you. I have a pair that has served me for years, although they aren't fashionable.

"I'll come to your apartment at three-thirty."

Dave helped Meghan tighten her skates and then stepped onto the ice. Meghan didn't see him move his legs. He seemed not to move, except he began to glide away, going increasingly faster until he disappeared. Before she expected him to complete the rink circuit, he was back, gliding silently to a stop.

"Dave. You've got me doing it now."

"Doing what?"

"Thinking ridiculous things. What's the past tense of glide?"

"Glided."

"Well, it's wrong. It should be 'glid'."

He laughed and reached out a hand. "Come, don't try to skate; just step toward me."

Meghan took tentative, small steps forward until she got to him.

He slid behind, put his arms around her, and locked his hands together. "Press down on my arms. Take some of your weight off the ice.

"That's it, don't move your feet. Just feel me and my movement." He didn't move much, but they began to slide forward. "Now I'm going to sway a little; feel it and bend with me."

Meghan gasped as they swung right and left the next moment, weaving between skaters at an ever-increasing speed. As her arms tired, she didn't realise more of her weight fell on her skates. After five complete circuits, Dave brought her to a stop, lifting her into a half turn.

"Dave, that was marvellous."

"Yes, Meg, you're doing well. Now stand still; I'm coming round.

"We dance now—Latin American." He put an arm around her and, taking the other hand, said, "Now tight against me; you must feel my body."

"I am, including a bit I've never felt before."

"Don't think about that. Feel my legs with yours and keep yours stuck to mine. If I move a leg, yours must move with mine. Now close your eyes."

She could feel the air and the ice. She knew they were moving, their bodies moving together in rhythm. Buried memories were waking muscles that had almost forgotten how to work together to skate. Muscles remembered again. While her conscious mind thought of Dave's arms and the warmth of his body, no conflicting signals confused her feet.

"Meg, I'm going to weave a bit."

"Ok."

The breeze became fresher—she knew they were going fast—and the swaying, weaving movement grew. She didn't realise it, but she was skating on her own—backwards.

"You can open your eyes a little, slowly."

"Don't want to ..." came from her mouth muffled against his shoulder.

"Just a little."

It took some time to comprehend. Meghan found she was weaving through the circling crowd, in his arms, at twice the throng's speed. "Wow!"

"I'm going to slow down and spin, so I'm going backwards. I can't see where I'm going. You must guide me; lean the way I should go. Don't think of your feet. You sway, then I do, and your feet will follow."

Five circuits later, they were back to double the crowd's speed. Dave slowed and slid to the wall. "There, you can let go now."

"That was fantastic: *thrilling, marvellous*; all those words."

"Have a rest. Your muscles aren't used to it, so you mustn't overwork them. I'll do a couple of exercise circuits while you catch your breath."

Meghan watched while Dave glided around with his hands behind his back at what seemed a dangerous speed.

"Ok, Meg. Now come here. Put your hands behind you. I'll be behind, so you won't fall. Don't think; let your feet remember."

It was easy. After one circuit, Meghan was part of the crowd. Although she didn't dare turn her head to look at Dave.

After three circuits, she felt her legs tiring, and she *glid* to a stop at the wall. Then holding on, she turned and looked. Dave wasn't there! He arrived half a minute later.

"Well, Meg?"

"That was wonderful. When did you leave me, and why?"

He grinned at her. "Well, you seemed to be doing too well. I had hoped you'd fall on your bum and bruise it. So I looked for a girl who was falling."

Another fib?

"Why?"

"It's one of the rewards for taking a girl to the rink. You get to rub arnica on her posterior afterwards."

"You're degenerate. I'll let you massage my feet. I think I've had enough for today; I probably won't run for a month."

A voice from behind Meghan said, "Hi Dave."

Dave turned. "Hi, Marcello. Meg, this is Marcello; he runs the place. Marcello, this is Meghan."

"Dave, will you do your demo routine? Please. I have twenty free entries right here."

"Twice the usual, Marcello?"

"That's so you can bring Meg and teach her to dance. I watched; she'll be good, and I'm banking on your doing a dance demo."

"Ok, Marcello."

Dave slid away, and Meghan watched, astounded. It was announced on the loudspeakers that a demonstration would take place. Everyone made way, skating to the sides of the rink.

It was a virtuoso performance for Meghan, but Marcello said to her, "I've seen him do better. Bring him for practice. Barring the professionals, he's the most powerful skater we have."

"I'll try, Marcello, but we are busy with research."

"Skating relaxes the mind. After hours of study, it provides a necessary break. You can't think and fly simultaneously."

On the bus home, Meghan said, "Dave, I see the link. You walk and skate with the same silent effortless glide. Did you ever take your mother skating before she got sick?"

"I did. She managed to learn enough to go sedately round with the crowd. It was one of a few things we did together; most of the time, she worked, especially on weekends when the pay was better. I practised to impress her; she always said she enjoyed watching me."

"Then we must practise dancing together on the ice until I'm good enough for us to put on a great show for her. I'll look forward to that day."

"Meg—" Dave stopped before completing the sentence.

Meghan could tell that he was struggling to contain his emotions. "Yes, Dave?"

"Thanks."

She thought, "*I love this man, and he needs me.*" With a bright smile, she said, "It won't be long before we can demonstrate our skill."

Boris Kravitz returned three days late from a repair job in Bogotá, and Dave and Meghan met him the next day.

Boris looked worried. "Dave, let me have it straight if it's bad news."

"How do you feel now, Boris?"

"I've been getting better every month. I feel normal now. I'm doing everything like I did before I got cancer. I don't become tired either. The thought of going backwards is terrifying."

"We can appreciate that, but we must be careful not to make things worse when trying to improve them.

"You picked up a cholera bacterium that's endemic in West Africa, and then you had sex with a woman who, we suspect, was ovulating, as you said she was unclean two weeks later. The Corky bacteria produce mini viruses called phages when a female carrier of the Corky ovulates. The phages attack the cholera bacteria, merge with them, and create more Corkys, reducing the cholera count. We think the Corkys evolved for that purpose, but they did so on two different continents, in two different variants.

"It's a miracle that you were infected by both variants, and that when a pair of the left- and right-helix bacteria find a cancer cell, they eat it and produce phages.

"It's what caused your remission, but now your cholera count is nearing zero, and the Corkys are dying of old age; there are no replacements.

"We have the figures for the average in the last three months, which still shows a slight remission. Do you know what a negative exponential curve is?"

"I'm an engineer, so I know all about them. You mean that the less you have of something, the more difficult it gets to reduce it further and that it can take forever to clear out completely."

"That's right. Here's a graph of your cancer count over the months since you left the hospital. The dotted line shows a perfect negative exponential curve. However, your curve, indicated by the solid line, is flattening out too soon, so Meg and I believe it will begin to rise."

"So, what should I do?"

"Meg and I have decided to wait another month to get a new sample from you. A three-month average does not confirm the current situation. Then, depending on the result, we will have a proposition to make."

"Dave, how confident are you of being able to help?"

"We are very confident, Boris, but I must insist we can't cure your cancer, but we can possibly control it. You know that a negative exponential curve never reaches zero; the remaining bit can flare up at any time if you don't follow an ongoing treatment."

"Like chemo?"

"No, not at all; we'll tell you the details after the next sample."

Meghan began a culture of the last Boris Kravitz sample. It would be slow, but she wanted bacteria with Boris's genes to work with. She used the culture medium she had developed in the Scottish Southern Uplands lab. She kept looking at the Petri dishes throughout the day, hoping to see the culture growing.

On Wednesday, she said, "Dave, the cholera bacteria are not multiplying."

Dave asked, "You used the same agar and temperatures as in the lab up north?"

"Yes, identical."

"Then Boris's cholera is not the same as that found in the monkeys, or the agar doesn't suit his cholera."

"It's the same except for one gene. Give me one of your fantastic theories."

"The agar is just a house where the monkey bacteria grow. You used the monkeys' blood plasma for the cholera bacteria to feed on while they multiplied?"

"Yes."

"And here you have used Boris's bacteria and Boris's plasma?"

"Yes."

"Then there must be a difference in the plasma."

"What is it, Dave?"

"I don't know, and it would take months to analyse the

components of their plasma. Could it be that the monkeys and Boris don't eat the same things?"

"Can you call Derek and ask for a list of what his monkeys eat? He told us they ate fruit and stuff, but he didn't mention all of the kinds."

"Sure, Meg."

Thirty minutes later, Dave handed Meghan a list of foods.

"Let me buy some of this fruit; I'll get as many types as possible," Meghan said. "You try to find the other items, or get Derek to courier a pack of monkey food to us."

"What will you do with it?"

"It's worth a stab; I'll put it in the lab liquidiser for an hour and make juice."

"Meg, it will be hot after an hour."

"I'll put it in the fridge for cooling periods if it gets to body temperature. Then I'll centrifuge it to extract the dissolved material only. Then I'll add some to the agar and see what happens. While we wait for the other items, I'm going to try with the fruits only first."

"Dave, it's working better with the fruit juice. It's not fast, but it's working. I don't know how to improve it. You must think about it over the weekend. I promised Hamish I would go horseracing with him tomorrow."

Dave did think about it, but his mind repeatedly branched off to imagine Meghan at the races, Hamish, and her family in Scotland. He wondered if he would like them. Most of the Scots he had met had a fine sense of humour, and Meghan's parents and brother were all pharmacists, part of the healing fraternity. They would be his family one day. Then a thought intruded. *There had been an email from Scotland ...*

He found it in the *Encouragements* file. He remembered glancing at it, but he hadn't read it through—this time, Dave did.

A man of eighty-five from an address in Inverness had sent it via his housekeeper.

Dear Mr Tennant,

Jock Macintyre has asked me to forward his note, included below, to you; he has cancer and read your article in *Oncology*. Call me if you are interested in a visit; he will be delighted.

Muriel Coombs, 0643261729

Dear Mr Tennant,

I lived for fifty-two years in The Gambia, with a large garden surrounded by tropical flora and fauna; my daily companions and friends were a troop of Green Monkeys. I now live alone near Inverness with my spaniel, Grace. It would be a pleasure if you visited me, and I'm sure I could tell you a lot about Africa and my monkey family.

Regards,
Jock Macintyre (Dr)

Dave's initial reaction was adverse; visiting this man from the past century would be a waste of time. He hadn't forgotten it fifteen minutes later, so he reached for his phone.

"Is that Muriel Coombs? Dave Tennant here."

"Mr Tennant, I'm so glad you called; Jock keeps asking me when you're coming."

"Could you please give me his address? Are you his family?"

Muriel gave him the address, adding, "He has no family, Mr Tennant; he's outlived them all. I'm a social worker and visit him every week to check he's all right, chat, and drink tea with him."

"Thanks, Muriel. Does he have a phone?"

"Of course." She gave him the number.

He considered visiting Jock, but it was a long way. He didn't *think* it was an attractive idea because he wanted a weekend with Meghan, but the feeling lurked inside.

He called Meghan: "Hello Meg, how's the racing?"

"Two more races before the big one. Why did you call?"

"Just to check if you'd come to Inverness next weekend."

"Why?"

"To go and see a pensioner who sent an email that is in your encouragements file."

"I've nothing planned; you can tell me about it on Monday. I must go; the next race is in the starting gate."

Dave thought about it—they could fly to Inverness early Saturday. He called Muriel and told her when they would visit Jock.

"I'll tell him, Mr Tennant; he will be thrilled."

29

Emma Thompson came to see Dave and Meghan. Her first impression on entering the lab was of a feeling of happiness among the staff, a vibe she had never sensed in a lab before. She paused at the entrance and watched them work—they were smiling and chatting quietly as they went about their tasks and helped each other with small favours. A woman using a pipette to transfer a liquid from a flask to a beaker paused—the flask was almost empty and needed to be held at an angle—and the younger girl next to her reached over, murmured something, and tipped the flask.

Emma was wearing lab slippers, and she used the silence these afforded her to creep closer to peek into Dave and Meghan's office. The door was open, and to one side of it was a noticeboard on which the last four monthly reports—showing the steady improvement in lab performance—were pinned for all to see.

Emma realised that Meghan had never asked for a partition between her and Dave's workspaces; the two scientists were sitting side by side arguing playfully about something, pointing at the computer screen, smiling, and joking.

She was impressed with all that she'd seen so far. She shuffled her feet and—when the absorbed pair didn't hear her—cleared her throat.

Meghan looked up. "Hi, Mrs Thompson."

Dave looked up and echoed Meghan's greeting.

There were no guilty looks, and there was no surreptitious movement to put space between them; they seemed totally at ease.

"Hello to both of you. I've come to ask you to make a presentation to a group of managers and QA specialists from the other BaVir labs."

Meghan stood up and said, "I'll get you a chair, Mrs Thompson."

Emma noted that Dave helped Meghan by pulling her chair back to make more room for her to move.

Dave looked surprised as he asked, "What about?"

"What you have done here to improve the lab's efficiency. Your reports haven't gone unnoticed. Your error rate and procedure costs are way down."

Meghan returned with a chair for Emma, who sat down and explained more about what was needed. Dave and Meghan agreed to do the presentation.

Emma thanked them, got up, and started walking back to her office. As she neared the lab's door, she stopped to talk to Marjorie, one of the few married women in the lab.

"Hello Marjorie. You look happy."

"I am, Mrs Thompson; this lab is the best I've ever known."

"Do you know why?"

"Yes, everyone does. Dave and Meghan love working here."

"Are they in love?"

"No one knows, Mrs Thompson; we've never seen them touching or anything, but we all hope they will be. They make a wonderful team."

Emma returned to her office, thinking ...

Meghan and Dave landed at Inverness, collected the hire car, and drove to a small cottage with an immaculately kept garden on the outskirts of Culloden. When Dave knocked at the door, a middle-aged woman answered. "Good morning, Dave Tennant, I assume?"

"Good morning. Yes, and this is Meghan MacDougal. You must be Muriel Coombs."

"I am. Please come in. Jock is impatient to meet you."

Jock Macintyre was in a wheelchair in the small lounge, a spaniel lying beside him.

Dave walked over to greet him. "Jock, it's a pleasure to meet you." He shook Jock's hand, which trembled a little. He looked at the spaniel. "Is this Grace?"

The spaniel looked up expectantly at the mention of her name.

Jock put his hand on her head and said, "Yes, she's the reason I'm still alive."

Muriel interrupted, "I've nearly got tea ready. I'll fill the teapot and fetch the tray. Will you help, Meghan?"

"Of course. Dave, here's your package."

"Jock, Meg said a MacDougal can't visit a Macintyre without a gift. She chose this for you." Dave opened the package and gave Jock a bottle of Tullamore Dew.

"That will certainly make peace between the clans. I shall enjoy a dram every night."

The ladies returned with the tea tray and a plate of Scots shortbread.

Once the tea was poured and they were all seated, Dave said, "I've got some photos of Africa if you want to see them, but not of The Gambia, I'm afraid. I've never been there. You can tell me all about it."

The photos excited Jock; his love of Africa was visible. "The river looks just like one in The Gambia. My house was near the riverbank, on a high spot. I can remember it well. It had a wide veranda all around the house."

"How did you get there, Jock?"

His rambling story took them four hours, through tea and a snack lunch, starting with his job as a ship's medic and proceeding through how he jumped ship in The Gambia to spend fifty years there as a country doctor with no official status or degree. The vivid descriptions—especially his stories about his monkey friends—interested Meghan and Dave.

"They are intelligent, you know. I had many mango trees in my garden and never got any to eat at first, for when the mangoes ripen, the monkeys eat them all and start having babies, although they have sex all year. I had to teach them that one of the trees was mine, but they could have the others."

Meghan asked, "How did you do that, Jock?"

He laughed a pleasant, elderly cackle. "I had lots of chemicals and medicines in the house. One was phenolphthalein, for testing water. Every ten years, I sacrificed the crop on a single tree; the monkeys left it alone."

Dave asked, "How?"

"I injected all the mangoes with phenolphthalein before they ripened."

Meghan explained, "It's a drastically powerful laxative; it lasts for three or four days. The monkeys must have had serious diarrhoea."

Muriel asked, "What are your plans? When do you go back to London?"

"We planned to tour around here tomorrow, we're staying at the Culloden Hotel, and we fly back late Monday."

When Dave and Meghan arrived at the hotel, Dave suggested a drink in the pub.

When they were settled at a table and waiting for their orders, Meghan remarked, "That was a pleasant afternoon, and Jock is quite a character, but did it get us any further?"

"I don't know. I'll have to think about it. Would you like to have dinner here or go out to another restaurant?"

"I'm sure they have fresh salmon here, probably the day's catch, which would be nice."

Dinner over, Dave and Meghan went upstairs to their room.

When Meghan saw that there was only one bed, she remarked, "Dave, did you ask for a room with one big bed?"

"No, I didn't think about it; I just requested a double room, but in old hotels like this, I expect all double rooms have a big bed."

"You are making things difficult."

"It shouldn't be; many couples don't make love every time they go to bed."

"We aren't a couple yet."

"I think we are, although we haven't yet realised it. Emma Thompson has."

"How do you know?"

"Her attitude has changed; she means both of us when she says 'you'."

"Ok, we'll behave like a married couple too tired for sex. What are we doing tomorrow?"

"I'll never be too tired, Meg—not if it's you. We can change our return flight so that we depart from Edinburgh. That will allow us to drive through the Cairngorms and go to the Highland Games at Pitlochry."

Meghan was quiet for half a minute, then asked, "Dave, do you want us to be a couple?"

"Yes, and I'll ask you to marry me as soon as possible."

"You mustn't, not until we've saved your mother."

"And no sex until then?"

"No."

"Now *you* are making it difficult, but I accept."

Meghan laughed joyously. "Change the return flight; I'll call my mother—we can stay tomorrow night with them. And I'll show you Edinburgh."

Dave and Meghan arrived at the MacDougals' house just before six pm. Meghan had called to tell her parents they were coming, so Angus and Elspeth MacDougal were prepared to welcome them.

Meghan's father, Angus, hugged Meghan and then shook Dave's hand when she introduced him. Angus looked keenly at him and said, "You can call me 'Angus'; no 'sir' or 'mister'. You look like a man who can toss the caber, and it needs such a man to keep my girl safe from rapscallions. You're welcome here, Dave. Elspeth will ask, so I'll get in first: Are you going to marry Meg?"

Dave liked him at once. "I can't, Angus; Meg says I'm not allowed to ask until she tells me it's ok." He winked.

"Then I feel for you, Dave, and I'll let my wife do the persuadin'. Elspeth, come and meet Dave." Straight-faced, he added, "You should like him; he's a puir man like me, ruled by a woman."

Elspeth was grinning as she came forward and hugged Dave. "You're doubly welcome, and you had better learn to smack her on the bottom when she doesn't obey, as Angus does to me."

Meg was surprised at how relaxed her parents were with Dave; she had expected a brief period of stiff formality. She was about to protest against her mother's suggestion when Dave replied, cutting Meghan off: "Elspeth, I did once; now I know I must be careful."

"Why, what did she do?"

"She took her clothes off."

Meghan finally got a word in: "Don't believe a thing he said. An insect stung me on my back, and he was rubbing cream on the spot. I had already undressed when he slapped my bum."

Dave performed a mime of Meghan letting her bra drop. Meghan understood his meaning, and her face flushed.

Elspeth had seen Dave's mime from the corner of her eye and had also grasped it. She noticed Meghan's heightened colour and smiled. "*This is the man for Meghan, and I love him too,*" she thought.

Although Angus hadn't seen Dave's gesture, he roared with laughter. With tears in his eyes, he said, "I prefer Dave's version. Let's go in and open a bottle of whisky; the family is coming for dinner, and there's a lot to celebrate."

"All of them, Dad?"

"Yes, and Kenna as well."

Dave met them all: Rory and Kenna; and Hamish and Ella, with their two little girls, Bonni and Drew. He had never experienced an atmosphere like it; everyone talked at once, Bonni and Drew sat on his knees, and everyone "oohed" and "aahed" when Meghan told how they had ridden camels in the desert. Dave hadn't expected her to have the photo of him on the camel—the one in which he had Moussa's scimitar slung over his shoulder. As she passed it around, she added, "When I saw him like that, I said, 'Wow, you look dashing; no girl could resist you,' and then he asked, 'Can I carry you off to my tent?'

"And I said—" she clasped her hands in the pose she had used in the desert, "—'Yes, my hero.'"

The laughter was, Dave thought, that of a boisterous, happy family, *his family*.

Meghan didn't ask her mother why she had given them the spare room with the big bed.

When dinner was over, Ella gave Meg a piercing, sisterly look. Meg knew her expression from long years of sharing secrets. "Meg, I've got something to show you in my old room."

They went up the stairs to Ella's old bedroom. "What do you want to show me, Ella?"

"Not show you, Meg; tell you. Philippa mentioned you were going out with Colin and then said you'd broken up with him three months ago."

"That's right, Ella; we never got off the ground."

"Well, I only found out a week ago that Colin has a wife in Edinburgh; they have no children and haven't divorced, although he rarely comes to see her. She works for the same company as he does, so he must be scared she'll make a stink if he divorces her."

As Ella told her, Meghan felt disgusted; she had willingly gone to bed with a married man. Then she corrected herself: "*No, I hadn't been willing, just stupid, and it was less than an hour; a disaster.*"

"I'm glad it's over between you and Colin, Meg. Dave is a great guy. Dad has taken to him even though he's a Sassenach."

"You will never know, Ella, but you might learn that he's nothing like a Sassenach. He's like no man I've ever met. I shall marry him when he asks, but we have some research to finish first."

"Meg, I could get used to this."

"What, Dave?"

"Sleeping in a big bed with you beside me."

"Me too."

"But if we're not careful, we'll get bored."

"I'm sure we'll find a way to avoid boredom, but not yet. Now go to sleep."

"Meg, you snuggled."

"I thought you needed comforting. It was a fun but fruitless visit."

"I'm not sure, Meg. Would you like another jump to a ridiculous conclusion? It will be up to you to prove my theory."

"Go ahead."

"Jock explicitly said that when the mangoes ripened, the monkeys had babies, but they copulated all year."

"Yes, but we know there are seasons."

"Ok, so what if the mangoes somehow change the chemical balance in their bodies?"

"How?"

"I looked up mangoes last night while you were following the interminable process of preparing for bed."

"You mean for bed with a man?"

"Oh, I didn't know there was a difference. But while waiting, I figured out the reason married couples don't always have sex."

"What's the reason, Dave?"

"The husband is asleep by the time his wife comes out of the bathroom. I think I should let you go first."

"Not a bad idea, but what did you learn about mangoes?"

"They have stacks of mangiferin. Maybe if you add some to the agar, it will work."

"Ok, that's worth trying."

30

When Dave and Meghan were back at work, they had a chance to analyse Boris's latest blood sample.

"Meg, his cancer is increasing," Dave said. "We can't delay any longer. What do we do now?"

"We know that his cancer decreased when the cholera bacteria were present. The cholera is almost absent from this sample; Boris has very few remaining. The first step might be an injection to increase the cholera count."

"How much?"

"We can do it safely if we use small doses of his cultured bacteria; they won't stimulate his immune system. We should try to reach the levels Moussa sent from his survey."

"Ok, but that won't help if we don't have Corkys."

"Hormones, Dave—say just one dose. Let the hormones die away, see what increase in Corkys we get, and then repeat if necessary."

"Right, but I'm going to jump to another unjustified conclusion: the Corkys didn't evolve for cancer. That Corkys pair up and attack cancer is a miracle, but they might attack other cells, so we should keep the count high enough, but no higher, for the job we want them to do."

"How will we know, Dave?"

"We won't, but we can get a good idea from the curves. We need the Corkys to come down with the cancer count at the same or a slightly slower rate."

"Let's look at it differently: if we can do just enough to keep his cancer from growing, we will have time to get it right. Let's not go all out to reach remission. It will take time, but it's better to advance slowly. Can we do this in England?"

"I don't know."

"I think we should talk to Moussa again. I would like to go back there."

Dave made several satphone calls.

Boris Kravitz was already in the doctor's surgery when Dave and Meghan arrived. Doctor Morrison greeted them gravely, then said, "What you told me on the phone is worrying. Can you explain it to Boris?"

"I'll try," Dave said. "Boris, the most important thing is that your last analysis shows your cancer has started to increase, although the increment is small. Meg and I have a proposal to correct this and return to remission, but I must tell you what it is and why."

Boris was visibly shocked. "That's bad news. If you do nothing, how long will I have to live?"

"We don't know, but at best, we think the remission will have gained perhaps eighteen months on the prognosis you received when you left the hospital."

"Then explain what you propose."

"We told you at the last meeting what had caused your remission. But the cholera count is now almost zero, and the Corkys are few.

"What we propose is simple. We will do a blood test every day. We first want to give you an injection of your live cholera bacteria, which we have cultures of. Our hope is that the Corky count will rise and the cancer count drop.

"Suppose we don't see the Corkys increasing. In that case, we will give you a hormone injection. For a day, you'll have the same hormone levels women have during ovulation. This way, we'll stimulate the Corkys into multiplying. We might have to inject some Corkys—only very few—to get things going."

"Will I develop boobs?"

"No, Boris; the hormones are harmless unless we were to inject them over an extended period—this will be no more than one or two shots separated by several days."

"Is that all?"

"Essentially, yes."

"Then do it."

Doctor Morrison said, "This is illegal; I cannot be involved."

"Even self-administered, Doctor?"

"Dave, you and Meg will go to jail if anything goes wrong. For supplying the bacteria."

"Doctor, I wasn't going to suggest you be involved. A pathologist at the university in the city where Boris caught the cholera infection has offered to help. If Boris will fly there and see him, the pathologist will arrange the treatment, and the university lab will do the daily analyses."

The doctor was surprised: "Don't they have laws like in England?"

"They have fewer Western doctors than traditional herbalists using innumerable animal parts in the treatments they administer. Such laws are impossible to impose."

"Then it's out of my hands, and I don't want to know what happens. I have a house call to make, so you can talk to Boris here and then leave."

Doctor Morrison exited.

Boris agreed to fly to Ouagadougou in ten days. Dave would take two weeks' leave but depart two days before Boris, for he had things to organise. Meghan would join him the weekend after that.

Eight days later, when Dave arrived in Ouagadougou, Moussa took charge and told Dave they would only meet in Boris's room in the hospital and that Dave was to switch off his mobile phone and use only his satphone, even in town. "Those nosy buggers may come back."

"I expect they will, Moussa; I know one lot was getting desperate."

"When does Meghan arrive?"

"Next Friday."

"Dave, I think I'll ask for some help from my brothers."

Two days after Dave landed in Ouagadougou, Boris arrived and was admitted. Dave began treatment, which didn't show any results for two days. Boris had a plasma drip, so Dave could inject cholera bacteria into the bag.

Boris wanted to know what was happening, and Dave had to say, "The cholera count is not dropping, but an increase is not showing; be patient—it has to come."

On the third day, Dave said, "I promised it would increase, and it has. Tomorrow, if the cholera is up again, you get the hormones." The next day, Dave injected the hormone mix.

The first signs of success appeared on the fifth day, and Dave reported, "Boris, be happy. The Corky count is up. It may be several days before we see a cancer remission."

Boris knew the news was good on the seventh day when Dave came into his room with a broad smile.

"Boris, we aren't out of the woods yet. Many adjustments are still to come, but your cancer is in remission again."

"Dave, I've never kissed a man. Right now, I feel like kissing you."

"Meg's due on a flight this afternoon. Hold on a little. I'll give you permission to kiss her. Without her, we wouldn't be smiling today."

Dave collected Meghan from the airport and took her to the hotel. They were in the same room they had occupied during their first visit, when he had smacked her bottom.

She unpacked her things, and then they went to the rooftop lounge for tea. Dave recognised one of Moussa's brothers sitting near the entrance. They sat down to tea. Meghan had followed the daily progress when Dave had reported on the satphone, but he gave her the latest update and told her about Boris's good mood and that she was due for a kiss.

The next day, Moussa joined Dave and Meghan outside Boris's hospital room.

"Moussa, Boris wanted to kiss me yesterday, but I put him off by promising he could kiss Meg."

Moussa roared with laughter. "I can understand why he accepted that, Dave."

Meghan grinned. "He might be such a good kisser that I won't return to London with Dave!"

The hilarity was catching.

"When are you going back?"

"I've booked our flights for tomorrow," Dave replied. "I'm comfortable leaving Boris in your hands. I will tell him two weeks more, and then he can return, if that's ok with you."

"Fine, Dave; I'll send you the daily counts, and you can adjust the dosages."

Boris felt so good that he returned two days early with a prescription for a top-up regime—sent by his doctor in Ouagadougou.

Emma had asked the main reception desk at BaVir to tell her when Dave and Meghan were back. She was sure Dave would be in the lab until late, and she had two interviews to complete, so she only managed to go to the lab after the time when the staff left; she thought some privacy might be a good thing.

When she stepped into the lab, she stopped dead, amazed. It seemed most of the staff were still at work!

She stood there, bemused, until Marjorie noticed her. "Good evening, Mrs Thompson. Can I help you with anything?"

"Marjorie, perhaps you can explain why everyone is still here?"

"Not all—some had to leave—but everyone likes being here, so we don't rush off when the bell rings."

Distracted by an oddity, Emma asked, "You've changed your lipstick? And is that a tattoo on your cheek?"

"Oh, yes. Every day, all the women change their lipstick, hairstyles, makeup, and the stick-on tattoos that we've started wearing. It's a lot of fun. And Dave sports a different moustache daily; his Pedro Gonzales one is hilarious."

"Dave, with a moustache?"

"Yes, he takes it off when he goes out."

"I see. Please try to explain to me why everyone likes it here; it can't be just that Dave and Meghan love working here, as you said the last time we spoke."

"Well, it started like that, then we learned about Dave's mum and how he and Meghan are trying to find a cure for her, so one of the women suggested we try to take some of the load off them, to give them more time to research. Now it seems we all like it so much we can't stop. Look at Zoe and Janine standing at that bench.

289

Zoe's teaching her a procedure Janine doesn't know. And the three women over there are trying to determine why Marguerite's procedure didn't work. You know the dual-analyses checks that we do on random samples?"

"Yes."

"Well, we try to do them all on the same day now, instead of leaving them for the next day. Those two over there will finish theirs in a few minutes."

"Amazing. Do you all know how the research is going?"

"No, Mrs Thompson, we don't know anything; it's a secret. But we know when Dave and Meghan are happy, and they are *delighted* now, making our contribution worthwhile."

"Thanks, Marjorie." Emma decided she must bring Philip to the lab late tomorrow. She walked to Dave's office and saw Meghan was with him. "Good evening to you both."

"Hello, Emma; how can we help?"

She noted the "we", not "I", but didn't realise that the atmosphere in the lab had already raised her spirits. "Dave, I went to see your mother yesterday as you were away. And I spoke to the matron, who is an old friend. I came to say that if you need help, please come see me."

"That's very generous of you, Emma, but we have everything covered. We will let you know if there's anything."

"Ok, Dave. Just to let you know, I might bring Philip to the lab tomorrow evening."

"Why, Emma?"

"To see the variety of lipstick, makeup, and hairstyles here. Do you participate, Meghan?"

"Of course, Emma. It was Dave's idea; he said I looked the same every day, and he didn't know which day it was." Meghan grinned at Dave. "I think it makes him feel like a pasha with a harem."

"Then he should change the moustache. That one makes him look like a squadron leader."

Emma left, thinking she still had much to learn about HR.

31

"Dave, are you thinking about your mother?" Meghan asked.

"Yes, Meg; we succeeded with Boris, so, naturally, I do."

"We might need to keep in mind that the cases are very different. For a start, you should get a blood sample from your mother for us to analyse."

"Then I suppose I must see her oncologist. Since the last visit, when he said there was no hope, I've dreaded seeing him."

"I'll come with you."

Dave made an appointment.

Four days later, Dave and Meghan were sitting with the doctor in his office in Harley Street.

"I've brought my partner with me for mutual support," Dave told the doctor. "This is Meghan MacDougal."

"Wonderful. It's nice to meet you, Miss MacDougal. Dave, you called to ask for an update on your mother's condition. I am afraid I've no good news. She'll finish the last chemo programme in six weeks, and though we've kept her cancer at bay, it has weakened her further, as I told you it would."

"Yes, I remember, only too clearly. What are the next steps you propose to take, Doctor?"

"This meeting is fortuitous. Before you made the appointment, I was considering calling you, for I must make a judgement that I'm not allowed to make."

"What, Doctor?"

"Your mother will have no treatment for three months after the chemo. Her cancer will have flared up again by then, and we must put her on another chemo programme. However, I don't want to do that because she risks lapsing into a vegetative state."

"So what is the alternative, Doctor?"

"That I discharge her from the hospital, into your care. Depending on you, she will recover her faculties and strength enough to enjoy her last few months. I'll ensure a visiting nurse gives her morphine once the pain begins."

"Then how long has she got?"

"Six months at the most, with morphine when necessary for the last six weeks."

"Thank you, Doctor, I'll speak to her, but the choice is clear to me; a discharge will be best. As I told you, I am Lab Manager at BaVir in Cromwell Road, and when you release her into my care, I'll have samples taken for analysis at monthly intervals so I can follow her progress; I would like a benchmark sample now and on release."

"I wish more of my patients had sons like you. Your task will not be easy. I'll inform the hospital; you can call the matron, Mrs Murphy, tomorrow afternoon to arrange for the samples."

When Dave and Meghan left the oncologist's rooms, Dave said, "Meg, when my mother is discharged, we need to get her to Ouagadougou to begin her treatment. I'll call Boris—he might be able to help."

"Ok, Dave, let me know what he says. Once your mother's blood sample arrives, I have some things to do."

"What?"

"First, I need to keep it warm. Then, I need to get a DNA sample from it.

"I also want a blood and DNA sample from you, which I'll use for testing. I'll inject your blood with a packet of Boris's cholera and see what happens."

"Are you jumping to conclusions now?"

"It works for you; I think it's reasonable to allow me a jump. I want to see if Boris's cholera manages to adopt your genes. We know Boris's cholera bacteria have genes that match one of his. The cholera bacterium adopts a gene of its monkey host as well. We don't know how they do it, but that doesn't matter if they will adopt one of your genes."

"Ok, is that all?"

"No; half of your DNA is your mother's, and the other half is your father's, so if it works on you, half the cholera bacteria will adopt a gene from your mother.

"I want a cholera colony with your mother's DNA before doing what we did for Boris."

"Brilliant, and will you be able to collect phages from your Corky cultures?"

"Yes, with a dose of hormones. Then maybe I can make the right Corkys in vitro."

"I love you, Meg."

"Just keep that thought, Dave."

Dave called Boris. "Hello Boris, can we meet?"

"For you, Dave, anytime; just say where."

"How about the Rose and Crown at South Ealing?"

"Perfect, Dave, when?"

"Can you make it tonight? We can have a bite to eat. Say seven o'clock?"

"I'll be there."

Dave was already seated when Boris arrived, saw him, and walked over to join him.

"Boris, I'm thrilled you look so well."

"I am well, Dave; I've never felt better, thanks to you and Meg."

"You know about my mother and her cancer; Meg and I are ready to try the same thing on her as we did for you."

"Dave, just ask. You will never need to beg."

"She's bedridden, Boris; how do I get her to Ouagadougou?"

"I will organise a private plane and a pilot. Will Meg go with her?"

"Yes, and probably a physiotherapist as well."

"Can you get your mother to Biggin Hill?"

"Of course; I'll get an ambulance. What kind of plane, Boris?"

"I told you before: when one of the planes belonging to the airlines I work for has a breakdown, the company brings me in on a private flight. If it's only a small crew of mechanics and me, we fly in a small six-seater, but if we need to bring parts—sometimes engines weighing as much as ten tons—we use a cargo plane. I will ask the charter company what they have available for two people, and a patient on a stretcher, from Biggin Hill to Ouagadougou, and then I'll choose. We'll confirm the departure date and time, and then you can do the rest." After a pause, Boris added, "Dave, has your mother got a passport? She will get a three-month visa on arrival."

"Yes, luckily she does have one."

In the morning, Dave called Moussa on his satphone. "Moussa, can you do the same for my mother as you did for Boris?"

"Of course, Dave, I'll be thrilled to do so. Will you and Meg come too?"

"Meg and a physiotherapist will be with Emily during the first week, and I'll come in the second week. I'll confirm the date when I can, but it should be in about a month."

"Will your mother receive the same treatment as Boris?"

"No. Boris already had cholera and Corkys. First, we must introduce both to my mother. You can author the paper reporting on her treatment. If I do, someone will accuse me of breaking some law."

"That's generous, Dave. I'll get everything organised."

Fluffy was about to leave her flat for her first appointment when her phone rang. "Hello?" she answered without managing to check who was calling.

"Fluffy, it's Dave. I want to ask a favour."

"I should ask, 'Dave who?' because you haven't called for ages. What's the reason? Have you broken something?"

"Can you take two weeks' leave?"

"For you, anything. Yes, if I have two weeks' notice—I've bookings that need rescheduling. Are you taking me on holiday?"

"Not exactly, but you get an all-expenses-paid two weeks in West Africa, with trips around the country we're going to. You will travel in a private plane with a patient who is to be admitted to a hospital there. You'll be going with my fiancée, Meghan MacDougal."

"Oh dear, another man hung up and out of reach on a marriage hook. What's the catch? And who's the patient?"

"The patient is my mother, and the catch is that she will need massages while in the hospital."

"She's sick? What's she got?"

"Cancer, Fluffy, and we're going to cure her."

"Count me in. Just let me know in time. My passport is in order."

Meghan came into the office from the lab with a happy smile. "Dave, it's working. I've got cholera bacteria with your mother's DNA. Next week, I'll use some and add phages. It should be quick, as phages don't get much time after monkey intercourse to make Corkys."

Four days later, the happy smile became a delighted one when Meghan came from the lab. "Dave, I have the Corkys. I need eight days to build stocks. We're A-OK for lift-off."

Her smile took Dave to the moon. After more than two years of worry, he believed his mother would live. He didn't hesitate—he reached for his satphone and called Boris. "Boris, can you arrange a flight for around the sixth of next month?"

"Let me try. I'll call you back."

An hour later, Boris phoned. "Dave, you've got the sixth; take-off at thirteen hundred. It will be a Hawker-1000 set up for medivac."

"That's great, Boris, thank you."

"It's nothing; I'm the one who must say thanks. I'll be at the airport to ensure everything goes well."

Next, Dave called Fluffy. "Fluffy, can you dress as a nurse and meet us inside the hospital at ten-thirty on the morning of the sixth of next month? I'll send a courier to collect your suitcase and deliver it to the airport."

"I'll be there. Just ask the courier to come before nine-thirty in the morning; I need an hour to get to the hospital."

Meghan, who had hung around, asked, "If Fluffy can go as a nurse, why do I have to change in the hospital?"

Dave explained: "We don't want any interference from the spy crowd or anyone else; they could make it very difficult if they tried to block my mother's departure."

"How?"

"If anyone notified the police with an accusation that I was taking my mother out of the country to arrange a medically assisted suicide, it would delay our departure, perhaps for weeks. Those who have been following us know we visit my mother, and if they see you wearing a nurse's uniform, they will get suspicious. I'll arrange for a courier to collect your suitcase and Fluffy's. He'll deliver them to Biggin Hill."

Then Dave called the oncologist. "Doctor, I would like you to immediately stop my mother's chemo treatment and discharge her at eleven am on the sixth of next month. I've arranged accommodation and a nurse for my mother and will sign the release papers at the hospital."

"Thank you, Mr Tennant. She will be ready. I assume an ambulance will collect her?"

"Yes, Doctor, with two nurses and me."

"Good luck, Mr Tennant, and thank you."

Dave watched the executive jet taxi away with his mother, Meg, and Fluffy on board. Boris stood beside him in front of the charter company's hangar.

"Was it difficult to arrange the flight, Boris?"

"After four hundred and thirty flights, paid by airlines for me, I only had to ask once for a free one. When you want to bring your mother back, call me."

"*If* my mother comes back, Boris."

"No, Dave. I'm standing here, so I know she's coming back."

They watched until the jet took off and climbed away.

"Thanks, Boris. I'm now going to ride in the ambulance back to the hospital."

"Can't I take you?"

"The hospital has an entrance that ambulances use, and I went in through the visitor's one; I must come out the same way. I didn't want anyone asking questions about taking a cancer patient out of England to Africa, as it might have caused a delay we'd rather avoid."

Meghan and Fluffy, wearing nurses' uniforms, were sitting in the wide executive seats behind Emily Tennant, who was lying strapped to a stretcher in the space left by removed seats. As the aircraft levelled out and the seatbelt sign went off, Meghan unbuckled and checked on Emily. "Would you like me to loosen the straps?"

"Please, my dear, they are a bit tight."

"How do you feel? No nausea?"

"None at all. This is the first time I've flown. I would have liked to look out the window."

"Well, we have five hours of flying left, so we have lots of time. After all the excitement of leaving, this will be far more comfortable than the ambulance. Rest now, then Fluffy and I will see if we can get you up to have a look."

"Thank you, Meg. When are you and Dave getting married?"

"He hasn't asked me yet."

"I'll tell him not to waste a minute more."

Meghan returned to her seat. She hadn't had a moment to say anything more than hello to Fluffy, and with hours to spare, she had some questions to ask.

"Fluffy, Dave told me about you."

"Oh, what did he say?"

"Not much, only that he had met you at a club and that you were a physiotherapist with a teenager's passion for breakbeat music."

"That's about right. He didn't say any more?"

"I asked him if he had slept with you, and he said yes, but that you weren't having an affair."

"That's right too; only once—the second time we met—and it

was unintentional. Dave didn't call again until he asked me to go on this trip."

"What happened that time?"

"I live in north London, too far to go home from my club in the south, so I asked Dave if I could stay overnight at his flat. Dancing to breakbeat takes lots of energy, and when we returned to his flat after hours of dancing, I offered him a massage to relax his muscles. He said he had massaged his mum for months and would give me one after I'd finished. I had an orgasm from a massage for the first time ever. We didn't make love, but I couldn't resist the urge to have sex with him in the morning, so I asked.

"I'm sort of mixed up. I don't know what I want, only that it's not being a physiotherapist. I chose not to do nursing because I didn't want to have to empty bedpans, but no one told me that massaging stinking feet or bodies was worse."

"Why did you give up on Dave?"

"I didn't, Meg. He was nice to me, but I thought he was waiting for someone else to come. I know now it was you."

"Even in bed?"

"Yes, Meg; he's the most considerate man I've known, but I felt like his pet—he didn't give himself to me as I've always hoped some man would. I don't have a word for it; I use 'transcendental' to describe the feeling I believe exists but have never experienced."

"Fluffy, I've learned something important this year: when people talk about committing themselves to marriage with someone, they may be making a mistake. You must commit yourself to a way of life; if you decide you want to live on a farm, commit to doing that, and *then* marry a farmer. Marrying someone without committing to a way of life leads to a breakup. If you don't want to be a physiotherapist, give it up and choose something else, and when you find the life you want to lead, get a man who will share that life with you."

"Thanks, Meg, and thanks for understanding. Please invite me to your wedding.

"Now, tell me about where we're going."

"You didn't ask?"

"No. I said yes without asking anything more when Dave requested my help. Then didn't bother."

"We're going to Ouagadougou, Burkina Faso's capital city. I adore it; I'm sure you will too."

They got Emily up and sat her in a chair to look out the window for half an hour, then put her back on the stretcher and strapped her down for the landing.

Meghan was relieved when Moussa greeted them at the airport's executive terminal with an army of people who took over until they had Emily comfortably installed in a university hospital bed.

"Do we start now, Meg?" Moussa asked.

"Yes, as soon as possible."

"Right, let me fetch some equipment." He left the room, reappeared wearing a white lab coat, and installed a blood-sample tap and a plasma drip in Emily's arm. He watched the first drips, adjusted the rate, and said, "The bag will empty in four hours; we're ready for the first cholera dose."

Meghan handed him a syringe, and the contents went into the plasma bag. She told Emily, "You must sleep now. We'll be back tomorrow. If you need anything, a nurse is sitting right here."

After the first day, when no change was expected, Meghan visited Emily every eight hours, day and night, to take a blood sample that she would check for cholera bacteria.

Moussa made her miss every third visit; he could see she was tired, and the hotel was too far away. "Meg, you need to get some sleep," he told her. "You might make a mistake in your analyses. I will do one while you rest."

As the visits went by, Meghan became worried: "*Why are no cholera bacteria visible in the blood?*" She called Dave.

"Hi Meg, is there a problem?"

"No, but I'm not seeing any cholera yet; it's been thirty-six hours."

"Don't panic. How much blood are you drawing?"

"Five millilitres, enough for a few slides. Moussa said that's the sample size he took to establish the standard cholera level."

"Hang on.

"Meg, my mother should have five thousand millilitres of blood in her body. Before you can expect cholera in the sample, the cholera bacteria must spread everywhere. The quantity you inject should cause it to show in about fifty-five hours from the beginning."

"Thanks. I'll call again when I see them."

Meghan was in the university lab when she saw cholera in the seventh eight-hour sample. She called Dave and told him the news: "I can see the cholera bacteria!"

"Marvellous. Inject both left- and right-hand Corkys as planned, and then a hormone mix in two days."

Three days passed before Meghan had cause to phone Dave again. By now, she had a bed in a room next to the lab, since the hotel was too far away. Moussa was analysing alternate eight-hour samples to allow her enough time to sleep.

"Hi, Meg," Dave answered.

"Dave, despite the continuous cholera drip, the cholera level has stopped rising, but Corky numbers are increasing, as they produce phages with the aid of the hormones, and the phages gobble up the cholera bacteria."

"Then note the cholera count—maintain that level by reducing or increasing the cholera drip. The hormone effect should be ending; watch the cancer count."

Dave was surprised when Emma Thompson came to his office.

"Dave, I've a company policy change for display. But more importantly, I have a question."

"What is it, Emma?"

"I once said something like this to you months ago: 'The only thing we can do is grit our teeth and do our best to solve the problem.'"

"Yes, I remember the day Meg came to work here."

"I would be surprised if you didn't, Dave. Your mother is not at the hospital, Meghan is on leave, and you will be off next week. I don't know what you are doing, but I must ask: Do you know what you are doing, and is your mother ok?"

"Yes to both, Emma. She *is* in a hospital—in Africa. She's on an experimental treatment programme not legally available in England, administered by a doctor who qualified in Baltimore. She is doing well, and I hope she'll recover fully, although she must follow a maintenance programme for many years."

"That's splendid news. When you see her next week, tell her I wish her luck."

After she left, Dave looked at the notice:

Company Policy Change

BaVir believes in staying up to date in our changing world. Married couples are encouraged to remain employees of BaVir and may work together, providing the usual standard of decorum is maintained.

Dave landed in Ouagadougou on a scheduled flight, knowing his mother's cancer was in remission. He recognised one of Moussa's brothers, whom Moussa said would meet him and take him to the hotel. He was sure other brothers were watching.

Meghan was at the hotel. He hugged her when he saw her, and then they went to their room.

"Meg, how is she?"

"Looking happier every day. It's working, but it will be six months before she's clear."

"'Clear' is a much nicer word than 'dead'."

"Agreed. I've got lots to tell you. Let's go onto the rooftop terrace, get an iced drink, and I'll begin. Moussa will join us for dinner. We have only tonight because I must be at the airport tomorrow at midday."

Drink in hand, Dave asked, "Where's Fluffy?"

"I don't know; she comes daily to massage your mother, but the rest of the time, she's with Moussa's youngest brother—he's about my age and is her tour guide. She's been out in the desert with him, has ridden a camel, wears local clothes, and says it's transcendental."

Dave grinned. "At least I agree with her."

"She may be learning who she is. She told me she didn't want to be a physiotherapist."

Meghan and Dave stood beside Emily's bed. Dave was thrilled to see her looking so well.

"You are beautiful, my dear," Emily said to Meghan, who had dressed in the colourful local cotton. "Please give me your hand."

Meghan gave it to her.

"Dave, give me your hand as well."

"I don't know what my future will be—we all have our destiny—but I know what I want it to be." She smiled, and squeezed Meghan's hand. "I'm glad Dave has someone to look after him; you will, won't you, Meg?"

"Yes. Don't worry about Dave; I'll ensure he stays out of trouble."

"Thank you, Meg. I think I'll sleep now."

Dave didn't let go of his mother's hand; he raised it to his lips. "Ma, you'll be fine for many years." He smiled tenderly. "We'll make sure your destiny will be what you want."

Meghan let go of Emily's hand and turned to Dave. There were tears in her eyes. Dave didn't think; he just reached out and held her when she stepped into his arms, her head on his shoulder. After a minute or two, she leaned back, looked up at his face, then kissed him. It wasn't a passionate kiss, although Dave squeezed harder. The kiss was part of their joint comfort.

What seemed like a long time later, Meghan broke away. "Dave, take me to the hotel; I have a date with destiny."

Once they were in their room at the hotel, Dave reached out to take Meghan in his arms, but she pushed him back. "Dave, I'll tell you what I said to Fluffy on the plane. It's taken me nearly a year to learn that I want to live my life working and researching in a medical lab with you by my side. A successful commitment is not to a person but to a way of life and sharing that life with someone.

"I said it before—I love you; now more than ever—so I'm going to do what I promised your mother and look after you, which means keeping you from the clutches of women like Susan, Monica, or Ysabel.

"Now, kiss me again, and let's get into bed."

"Meg. Someone must look after *you*, and I've wanted to be the man who does so since we met, although I couldn't tell you then. I'll love you forever." Dave smiled at his memory of meeting her dad. "Can I ask you now?"

"What, Dave?"

"Will you marry me?"

"If you stop talking long enough and kiss me, you'll know my answer."

Later, much later, Meghan felt they were lying on a dune under a heavenly sky, and the stars reached down to gather Dave and her into one as they exploded like fireworks. She knew they were bound together as the display slowly died. "Dave, where are we?"

"In the desert, on top of a dune."

"So you felt it too?"

"Yes. I can't describe it, but 'transcendental' may be the best word."

"Do you remember I once warned you of involuntary sterilisation?"

"Yes, my darling, I'm glad you didn't cut my balls off."

"Me too. Do you know the expression, 'She's hung her robe on the same hook'?"

"Yes, it means a couple is living together."

"Well, I've an alternative meaning. Can you please hang me on your hook? Again."

Meghan thought Dave had learned a lot from Angela and Susan, and later, when Meghan told Dave about her experience with Anna, he knew she'd learned a thing or two herself.

The Final Diagnosis

Helisperia: A symbiotic bacterium discovered by researchers David Tennant and Meghan MacDougal that controls cholera infection in primates in Africa and Asia; see Cancer—biological treatments.

After five weeks in Burkina Faso, Emily came home in luxury, thanks to Boris. Dave and Meghan had found her a small country apartment in a retirement village.

The Christmas party was the happiest event Dave had ever experienced: even Uncle Paul was smiling, unlike at their previous meeting; Meghan's family was there; and Alice insisted that she and Devlin prepare the feast.

Marco held a New Year's Eve party a week later; everyone Dave knew who had played at Marco's attended. A smiling Italian woman he had never met was also there. Marco introduced her in a short speech: "Everyone, this restaurant now has a new boss, I'm retiring, and Maria is taking over."

Someone called out, "And what will you do, Marco?"

"Marry her."

The laughter and congratulations ensured no one would forget the party.

Meghan had noted Valerie's satisfied smile and swelling tummy. It seemed the bargepole had done its job.

Emily's remission continued until she needed no more than a small injection each month, as did Boris.

Fluffy never returned to London—she married Moussa's youngest brother—but there's a club in Ouagadougou that plays breakbeat.

Dave and Meghan submitted their paper to Cambridge four months after Emily left the London hospital. It did not include Emily's recovery, which was the subject of a similar paper presented by Moussa to his university on the same day.

Both documents went to Ylang with an added note: "There is a lot to learn, and no guarantee this will work on any other cancers."

Dave took his mother to see her oncologist unannounced. The oncologist first thought she was a ghost, then became an enthusiastic supporter of Dave and Meghan.

Cambridge awarded Dave and Meghan doctorates in Pathology. This was followed rapidly by honorary degrees awarded by Hanoi, where they met Danh, Ylang, and Tôn Thất Loi again. Ylang was showing signs of pregnancy. Meghan grinned at her and said, "Hormones worked, then?" The men didn't understand the joke.

The plane that Boris arranged was full on the flight to Ouagadougou for Meghan and Dave's wedding. Moussa's brother and Fluffy organised the event on a massive dune in the desert after sunset prayers. The party flew back without Meghan and Dave, who attended the ceremony in which Moussa accepted the appointment of Professor of Pathology and they received honorary degrees.

On their last night before returning to London, they sat on a dune watching the stars.

"Meg, everything we have discovered has been due to chance happenings. Starting with meeting the only person in the world infected by both Corkys. Do you know of the Greek goddess of chance, Tyche?"

"Yes, Dave, the capricious dispenser of good and ill fortune.

The Roman goddess, Fortuna, was later identified with Tyche. Her mother was Aphrodite; if Tyche has touched our lives, we have her blessing of love."

They named their daughter Florence, although they call her Fluffy. When asked, they say she loves her fluffy blanket.

Florence has a grandmother who goes skating with her son and daughter-in-law.

The child has two godmothers; one runs a London restaurant, and the other rides a camel in the Sahara.

Also by Jeremy Hodgson

Dance on the Terrace: A Novel (2021)
Secret in the Seas: A Novel (Forthcoming—2023)

www.ingramcontent.com/pod-product-compliance
Lightning Source LLC
Chambersburg PA
CBHW022137170626
46807CB00005B/1973